I0534276

ZED'S WORLD BOOK ONE & TWO

THE GATHERING HORDE | ROADS LESS TRAVELED

RICH BAKER

Edited by
SARA JONES

Illustrated by
ANGRY CHAIR DESIGNS

ZED'S WORLD BOOK ONE & TWO

THE GATHEFING HORDE | ROADS LESS TRAVELED

RICH BAKER

COPYRIGHT

This book is a work of fiction. The names, characters, places, and incidents are products of the author's imagination, or are used fictitiously and are not to be construed as real. Any resemblance to real events or people, living, dead, or undead, is purely coincidental.

Copyright © 2018 by Rich Baker

All rights reserved. No part of this book may be reproduced in any manner without written permission from the author or publisher.

ISBN: 978-0-9988282-1-3

DEDICATION

With thanks to the usual suspects—Mom, Dad, Wendy, Mike, Cookie, and Cosmo. Also, to the guys at Phalanx; Thanks for the support, advice and creative use of the English language. To be successful, it's said you must surround yourself with people who force you to do better. I've got that down.

DISCLAIMER

You're holding two separate books. Zed's World Book One: The Gathering Horde is the novella that started this universe. At 17,000 words I could not justify printing it separately, so I have included it in this print version. Consider it a little bonus for spending extra on the paperback. They're also combined in audio, but you you can still get them separately in ebook.

Enjoy!

R

ZED'S WORLD BOOK ONE

PROLOGUE | ALL GOOD THINGS

May 29, 2014 – Z-poc plus 377 days

The compression bandage has stopped the bleeding but twenty-eight-year-old Jason Bowling, forever called "D-Day" because he was born on June 6, knows he will not see twenty-nine. The blood vessels leading away from the wound have turned a dark gray even as the surrounding flesh loses its color. All around the bite, the skin is painful to the touch and getting worse as the minutes pass. He knows he needs to make a decision about what to do next; too much time has passed for amputation to be effective, so either he's going to have to ask one of the people he's been staying with, has trained and has bonded with, to kill him, or he's going to have to punch his own ticket.

Marc Wallace comes rushing in, out of breath from running. Marc is forty-four years old and is in the best shape of his life. It only took the end of the world—the end of human domination of the world—to get him out from behind his desk. He was a work-from-home web designer before the z-poc and still displays his nerdish leanings, but he's leaner and tougher now than he was in the spring. *Of course, everyone is,* D-Day thinks. He redirects his focus to Marc, still panting from his sprint into the room. He's holding his iPad out in front of him.

"The Parrot has more bad news!" he gasps, catching his breath.

On the ten-inch screen, they can see the familiar field, about a third of a mile south of them. Instead of out-of-control alfalfa grown by the former owner so he could claim the tax advantages of being a "farm," they watch about 2500 zeds loping toward their housing development. Some stagger and fall in the ruts left from the last time the field was plowed, more than a year ago, while some trip over the railroad tracks that run east to west at the edge of the field.

Some of the zeds that trip find themselves impaled on a length of rebar protruding from the ground ... several through the head, thanks to the statistical measurements Marc has provided. Even on this uneven topography for every one that has been auto-speared, there are fifteen more who flow like water, along the path of least resistance, following a single row until they reach the dirt road that borders the acreage. Some have already crossed the road and are stuck at the fence that separates the field from the green space that marks the southern end of their housing development.

Soon they'll find the opening where a gate used to

be, and once the first zeds make it through the opening, the rest will follow like molecules being dragged by invisible atomic bonds, following the sounds of the battle that just ended. Marc puts to words what everyone is thinking. "We've got about fifteen minutes to dig in or bug out."

They're all spellbound for a moment, watching the image being transmitted by the Parrot. The Parrot is Marc's four-bladed helo-drone, originally bought for having fun in the park ... or spying on his neighbor's property as a virtual neighborhood watch. Now it's their early warning system. At 150 feet in altitude, the Parrot can see for miles in any direction with the on-board HD camera. It has saved their skins several times, many of them on supply runs, and it gave them the upper hand in the battle that they just finished. Recharging the Parrot's batteries and the iPad, which controls it, always gets priority on their makeshift electric grid.

Kyle Puckett, the group's leader—though he does not like that title—takes about ten seconds to do the math in his head. "Kids, go-bags, now! We're bugging out!"

D-Day watches as the five younger members of their crew spring into action, their adrenaline from the battle they just escaped still coursing through their systems. They move with purpose, though; they've practiced this before and they each know what to do.

They've forgotten his condition for the moment as well, D-Day thinks. It's the combat mindset. Since

May 17, 2013, there has been little time for mourning the dead or weeping for the dying. In fact, in Zed's World, dead and dying are the same thing. D-Day knows they all wrote him off the minute he'd been bitten, knowing that when the time came, someone would do what was needed. Afterward, they'd bury him in the vacant lot down the street, next to the last member of the group they'd had to put down.

Marc goes back to the basement window and climbs into the tunnel that connects the houses. He has to get ready to move as well. At least now, with the images of that horde still fresh in his mind, D-Day knows what he needs to do about his own situation.

"Kyle, load me up. I'll need a popper too," D-Day says, using their colloquialism for a hand grenade, as he struggles to his feet.

"D-Day ..." Kyle starts to say, but D-Day holds up his good hand.

"I'm done, Kyle, and you know it. But before I go, I'm going to buy you all some time." He looks at his graying arm. "Time which neither of us have much of, by the way, so stop wasting it and help me get geared up."

Kyle looks at D-Day through tired eyes. Eyes that have seen more death, more horror over the last half year than anyone should see in a lifetime. They all have seen the same things, but Kyle bore the burden of leadership, whether he wanted it or not. He had made the hard decisions when other people had not had the desire to do so.

No one said it out loud, but it was easier to follow an order than to decide it was necessary. They have all been glad to have him make these choices since it absolved them of being the ones responsible, but that weight has taken a toll on Kyle these long five months. Here at the end of D-Day's time on this planet, someone other than Kyle is making the decision about how to end a life. D-Day has decided to go out on his terms, and Kyle respects his choice. He knows if the roles were reversed, he would do the same thing.

"Okay," he says as he reaches for the well-used rifle D-Day brought with him to their sanctuary. It was all he could say, but nothing more was needed.

1

DOUBT

K haleed Farouk is dying. It's more painful than he thought it would be. Maybe he thought it would be like going to sleep; he can't remember now, but if he did think that, he could not have been more wrong.

It feels like having razor blades drawn across his skin followed by gasoline being sprayed in the wounds. The brown flesh at the injection site where the pale green serum had been introduced to his body has faded to a pale gray, and the pain which began there radiates throughout his body. His heart, which beats WAY too fast, feels like it's pushing broken glass through his arteries. It wasn't until the virus reached his brain that he knew what the torment of Jahannum must feel like. For a moment, he feels pity for the kafir and their fate, then, as his heart goes through its final spasms and his synapses begin to shut down, he feels nothing. Khaleed Farouk is dead, martyred for the Jihad. He has died the honorable death of a true believer making the ultimate sacrifice for the cause.

In the raised antechamber, Almahdi Maloof and Najm al Din Abdul-Malik look through a large window of inch-thick polycarbonate ballistic glass at the prone figure of Khaleed on the stainless steel table. Both men have been in America for more than twenty years, waiting for the time when they would be called to support the Jihad. In the corner of the room below them, the man they simply call "The Scientist"—Asad Sajjad Bitar—packs up his gear. They've just watched him set up an IV drip into Farouk's arm and inject a pale green serum into the line. Farouk lies on the stainless steel table with his arms, legs, and waist restrained.

Even from this distance, they could see the effects of the serum when it hit his system. He started struggling against the restraints and screaming in pain. They could see the blood vessels closest to the skin turn grey as the drug worked its way into his system, followed by the skin draining of its color. The entire process, from injection to Farouk lying still, took about two minutes.

The Scientist checks Farouk for a pulse and looks up at the window where Maloof and Abdul-Malik stand watching. He shakes his head to indicate there is no pulse, takes the restraints off of the body, then grabs his bag and exits the room, taking care to turn the key in the deadbolt behind him.

Maloof and Abdul-Malik hear the clicking of The

Scientist's shoes on the tile in the hallway as he approaches the room, the steady spacing becoming more staccato as he climbs the ten stairs to the elevated level, from which they view the dead man on the table. The doorknob jingles, and The Scientist enters the observation room.

"He is dead," The Scientist says. "Now we wait and, Allah willing, he will rise and be a vector of death for America and the West."

"How long will it take?" Maloof asks him

"It depends," The Scientist says, going into lecture mode. Old habits die hard for the one-time professor. "The virus takes over the blood cells, using them as nourishment as it multiplies and moves to the brain. It reaches a critical mass and invades the nerves themselves, ultimately giving the illusion of life to the dead. They arise, not as their host reborn, but as something else. A predator. Their saliva has become an infectious venom; the viral waste that fills their circulatory system is a weapon of mass destruction. How long does the transition take? Many factors affect it. Age—younger people turn faster. Gender—men turn before women. Health. Those who are already ill succumb to the virus faster but take longer to reanimate. The longest we've recorded was eight minutes. The fastest was less than two. With regard to our hero below, I gave him a large bolus of pure serum straight into his venous system, so it should not be too long. Patience, patience," he replies as he starts typing into his iPhone, no doubt sending a coded status to

9

someone up the chain, someone Maloof would never meet.

While they are waiting, Maloof can't stop thinking about what they are doing. He knows he was sent here to be a sleeper agent for the Jihad; it's what he was trained for, but he has grown fond of his adopted country. And he never in his wildest dreams thought he would be unleashing a plague of this nature upon the world. They have been assured that all the faithful will receive a vaccine, but given their timetable, he doesn't see how they can immunize a billion people unless they started long ago.

He knows he can never give voice to his thoughts, but the fire and anger he felt toward America in the early 90s, after Osama's failed attempt to bring down the World Trade Center from below, has ebbed. After the Towers fell on 9/11, all of the stealth mujahedeen like himself and Abdul-Malik had been instructed to express outrage and grief like all other Americans were doing, and for Maloof, it had not been hard to do. Living here, in picturesque Fort Collins, Colorado, has been the most pleasant time of his life.

Virtually nothing he was told about America, or Americans for that matter, has proven true. They are not all selfish, intolerant crusaders who want to rule the world. They are giving, kind people for the most part. They value and protect their families and they keep close friendships with their neighbors. They had kept his cover business, a furniture outlet, swimming in cash and his adopted community had opened its arms to him and his family. His neighbors brought him gifts when his children were born and looked after them when he and his wife had been in an auto accident. In fact, were it not for his regular attendance at the local Islamic center where his handler met with him, he may have completely assimilated in to this lovely town and the American culture.

Yes, on the inside, he struggles with grave doubts about what they're about to do. He knows in his heart that the conflict between Islam and the West is not necessary, but he also feels like there's nothing he can do to stop the machine that is currently in motion, and there is no way he can bow out now, not after every-thing the heads of the program have invested in him. He knows they would never allow him to leave alive.

He's brought back to the present by movement in the room below. A pair of microphones hanging from the ceiling of the room below feeds a set of speakers in the observation room. Abdul-Malik flips a switch on the wall next to the window to turn on the speakers, and a low, guttural growl fills the room.

Less than two minutes after dying, the figure who used to be Khaleed Farouk tries to sit up on the table. Free from the restraints, the arms swing loosely. All at once, the figure rolls off of the table and lands on the floor with a loud thud, but if the body has been injured, the figure does not register it. He (IT?!) draws upright. The shaven head turns and pivots, the dilated pupils making the sunken eyes appear black and evil. It doesn't move, just sways where it stands.

"Success!" shouts Abdul-Malik. He grabs Maloof by the shoulders and shakes him. "And it happened so quickly! Do you know what this means? We are about to destroy America!" He is jubilant.

"Not so fast," says The Scientist. "Not all of the infections will be this clean." At this, he holds up his phone and displays a message neither of them are able to read. "There is another test that must be performed before we can celebrate."

"Well then, let's do it! No waiting!" Abdul-Malik exclaims, grinning like he just won the Lotto.

A smile—more of a sneer—spreads across The Scientist's face. "Your enthusiasm strengthens my heart, Najm." Here he pauses and looks at the figure swaying in place in the room below. "Please, come with me. As you say, let's do it!" he turns on his heel and leaves the room.

The grin fades from Najm al Din Abdul-Malik's face as it dawns on him what the next test is. He looks at the graying flesh that until a few minutes ago was Khaleed Farouk, and he swallows hard.

From the hallway, The Scientist calls out, "Come now, Najm! Time to play your role. Greatness awaits you!"

His shoulders slump and his jubilation is gone, but he knows he has no choice. If he refuses, he will be killed anyway. He thinks about the martyrs who blow themselves to pieces and take a few dozen kafir with them. *At least I will claim more than that*, he thinks. *Ten times, a hundred times more! Besides, I cannot let*

Khaleed Farouk do what I could not. I cannot bring that shame to my family. Resigned to his fate, he walks into the hall without looking at Maloof and follows The Scientist down the stairs.

Maloof watches in horror as the door to the room below opens. The Scientist shoves Najm al Din Abdul-Malik inside and shuts the door, again locking it. The thing that was Khaleed Farouk turns its focus to Abdul Malik, who has lost his nascent nerve and is trying in vain to open the door. The creature springs at Abdul-Malik and begins tearing at him furiously, biting and pulling flesh from his body.

Maloof reaches over and switches the speaker switch off, but the screams still echo in his mind.

Yes, Ahlmadi Maloof has massive doubts about what they are doing.

THE LAST HURRAH

focus

"Do you think he's okay?"

The question hangs in the air for a minute as Kyle Puckett and his wife, Naomi, watch their neighbor, Marc Wallace, messing around with his iPad in the alley behind his house. Up and down the alley, garage doors are open. Music plays from a number of different stereos, people laugh, and the entire area is hazed with smoke from a dozen different barbeques.

The Sunny Meadow neighborhood's annual First Barbeque of the Year features some people just offering basic hot dogs and hamburgers, others grilling ears of corn and turkey legs, or their family secret recipe ribs or shish-ke-babs. Each house has a cooler with sodas out for the kids, and while most have some bottled beer, at least three of them have their home brewed beer and wine out for the adults. All except for Marc's house.

Marc plays with his iPad, oblivious to the commotion around him. Everyone else is content to let him be. Other than the few dinners Naomi has demanded he come over for, he's been disconnected from people since his wife was killed in a car crash at the end of the previous summer. He's a web designer by trade and has always been somewhat socially awkward, but after the accident, people don't quite know how to approach him, so they mostly leave him alone.

Kyle turns to Naomi. "He's going to be fine, babe. He's just dealing with things his own way. At least he's outside while the rest of the neighborhood is. It's been a while since he's stayed out this long with people around. It's only been what, nine months? He just needs time."

"Baby steps, I guess," she replies.

A man walks up and hits the back of Kyle's knee, almost making him fall. The man laughs.

"Man, your situational awareness is for shit," he says.

Kyle smiles at Danny Harris, who lives two doors north of Kyle. The two men have differing styles. Where Kyle wears a golf shirt and a pair of pleated tan shorts, Danny wears camouflage cargo shorts and a black t-shirt with a white silhouette of an AR-15 on it; above the rifle, the shirt says "This is a tool" and below the rifle "I AM THE WEAPON."

"Danny, one of these days I'm going drop you on your ass," Kyle says with a grin.

"You're welcome to try. What are you gonna do, project manage me to the ground?" he asks, poking fun at Kyle's job. "Here," he says as he extends a red plastic cup full of beer to Kyle. "It's my latest IPA. Super hoppy with a citrus finish. You'll love it."

Kyle takes a drink and can't help making a Homer Simpson-esque "mmmm" noise. It's that fantastic. Danny nods and smiles at the compliment, then nods in Marc's direction.

"Why are you guys staring at Marc Dotcom?"

"Don't call him that; it's rude," Naomi says. "And we're not staring at him."

"Whatever," he says, throwing a look at Naomi. "He doesn't care. You know he's not an egg, right? He won't break if you treat him like a normal person. His wife died; he didn't. All I know is that dude has some freaky connections. I used to joke that he was part of Anonymous or something, but I don't know how much of a joke that is any more. Remember when I had that issue with my bank accounts a couple of months ago?"

Kyle remembers. Danny works as a gunsmith out of his basement and garage, building, repairing, and restoring all manner of guns. He also makes and sells holsters and other gun-related tactical gear, and with his ATF license he buys, reloads, and sells ammunition and a few other licensed firearm accessories. He some-times deals in a few things that aren't exactly on the up and up, but those he keeps off the books and reserved for special clientele.

During the fierce gun control debate in the winter and early spring of 2013, his bank accounts got hacked and his funds were drained. He had a hell of a time trying to get the bank to do anything about it. He told the group about it at one of the dinners Naomi had forced Marc to attend. Marc whipped out his iPad and started an online conversation with someone. Within fifteen minutes, everything had been restored to Danny's accounts. All Marc said was he "knew someone who knew someone who knew someone" who could get it fixed.

"Dude is a wizard on the web, man, and I still owe him big for fixing that deal," Danny continues. "All I'm saying is I'm staying on his good side. He's not in the best physical shape, but when the shit hits the fan, we're going to need people with his skills."

Danny always works the "shit hitting the fan" into a conversation. He's even convinced Kyle to put together a BOB or "bug out bag." Danny has a way of making people feel like society is one step from anarchy; and truth be told, it does make Kyle feel better knowing that he has enough food and supplies in the house for he and Naomi to weather a two to three week storm, be it an actual storm or an extended period of social unrest. His modest arsenal of weapons isn't like the hardware that Danny has access to, but it is sufficient for home protection.

"The kids coming down soon?" Danny asks, taking a drink of his beer.

Kyle's son, Ben, and Marc's boy, Keith, both go to Colorado State University in Fort Collins. Keith is a year and a half older than Ben and is a junior; Ben is a sophomore. They've been close friends for the better part of a decade, going back to elementary school. Until Keith left for CSU when Ben was a high school senior, it was unusual to see one without the other.

"They've got finals next week and then they're done. I think they're coming down for a few days starting Saturday," Kyle says.

"Too bad, we'll just miss 'em. We're heading up to the Preserve for a couple of weeks, leaving Saturday mid-morning, and I'm sure they won't be down until they recover from their hangovers." At this, Naomi throws Danny a disapproving look, but he ignores it. "Hey, by the way, would you mind watching the place, getting the ads off my lawn and shit like that? I'll help you finally get an AR put together!"

The Preserve is what Danny calls his land in the mountains. He's only taken a few people up there, and Kyle's never been invited. It's hard to get to, and according to Danny, he can be completely self-sufficient, off the grid, and completely secure for extended periods of time. Only a bunker buster "like they use in the 'Stan" can get them out once they're dug in, he says. Based on Danny's descriptions, Kyle imagines it to be a cave dug into the hillside somewhere near Estes Park.

They spend a couple of weeks at the Preserve every few months to refresh their supplies, do work on their living quarters, or just to get away for a short time. While his house in Longview is highly customized for added protection of his wares, and features a high-tech security system, that doesn't stop people from hanging flyers on his front door or throwing rolled up ads masquerading as newspapers on his lawn while he's out. Nothing says 'we're not home' like a yard full of ads and flyers.

"Sure, no problem," Kyle says. "And I don't need an AR."

"I hope you never NEED one, but when the shit hits the fan, you're going to want one. Your .22 ain't going to get the job done at a distance, man. Anyway, thanks for watching the place," Danny says, his eyes diverting to a shapely woman in tight khaki shorts and a sleeveless top walking up the driveway with two tall glasses of a dark red liquid.

"Naomi, I brought you some of my special sangria!" she exclaims. Elaine Harris is Danny's wife. She's equal parts athlete, tomboy, and suburban chic, and she and Naomi are good friends. Elaine dresses to flaunt her fitness level and, according to Danny, she shoots any of their guns with a high degree of accuracy. That's always his measure of someone's worth—how well they can handle a gun. Kyle figures he ranks low on the list, but since the two wives are close friends, he and Danny, by proxy, have to be as well. Though Danny can be rough around the edges, Kyle enjoys his antics to a point. It's a good thing, too, because his tolerance of Danny is higher than Naomi's.

Over the fence to the south, a whirring noise catches their attention, and a remote helicopter of some sort lifts off from Marc Wallace's backyard and soars to about fifty feet over the alley. As if acknowledging Kyle's thoughts, Danny says, "What the balls is that thing?"

He and Kyle leave the women talking to each other and mosey over to the fence where Marc stands with his iPad, beaming a big smile.

"What the hell is that, Marc?" Danny asks him.

"Fellas, meet the eye in the sky: the Parrot!" Marc says proudly, fiddling with the iPad. "It has a range of about 150 feet, on-board HD camera, and records directly on the 'Pad. It's going to take our neighborhood watch to a new level!" He turns the iPad around and Kyle and Danny see themselves on the screen, as viewed from 50 feet overhead. Danny waves an arm up and down and watches his on-screen self do the same.

"Bad ass, buddy," he says. "You come up with the coolest shit."

Marc is beaming a giant smile. *It's good to see him smiling*, Kyle thinks. Maybe he's turned a corner and is coming back out of his shell, like his world is back on its proper axis again.

As he thinks this last thought, he is completely unaware that by this time next week their world—everyone's world—will never be the same.

SATURDAY, May 11, 2013 – Fort Collins, CO

"I don't know, man. I'm telling you, she's acting weird." Keith Wallace is complaining to his roommate, Ben Puckett. "She graduates next week and she's going back to Cali to her folks' place. I don't think she's coming back here, and every time I bring it up, she changes the subject or says 'can we talk about this later?' Like I can't read the signs."

Ben considers his friend for a moment. "She's practically living here, man. And she goes home every year after school's out so that's not anything new. I get it, she's graduating, but it's not like she has a job lined up, right? I mean, she could end up going anywhere, so it's not like Cali is end of the world."

"I'm telling you, something's off," Keith says. "I should break up with her first, as a pre-emptive strike."

"*That's* why she's going to end it with you. You always jump to conclusions without knowing the facts. Remember Kim?"

"Kim cheated on me, dude. I knew it was happening and I called her on it."

"Yeah," Ben says. "She cheated on you *after* you accused her of it and slept with that blonde from Pi Beta Phi."

"Oh yeah, I forgot about the Pi Phi," Keith says. "But seriously, I would have been crazy to pass that one up! You have to give me that."

"Yeah, she was hot, but that's not the point," Ben

says. "After Kim broke up with you, you moped for a month. And the Pi Phi almost had you arrested for stalking when you broke into their house to see her. All I'm saying is you need to just have a talk with Danielle. If she says 'let's talk later' then you need to pin her to a time so you can focus on ending the semester before you end your relationship."

"I hear you, man. I think I'll wait until after finals," Keith says. "I don't need that distraction when my semester's on the line. Dad's gonna flip if I don't get at least a 2.5 this semester, and I need B's or better across the board to make that happen."

"And yet I haven't seen you crack a book this week," Ben says.

"Pacing myself, dude. If I cram too early, I'll forget it all on test day. I know my mind; I just have to outsmart myself."

"Sounds like a real clash of the mental titans." The voice makes them both jump. They look at the doorway and Toni Glass, Ben's girlfriend, is standing there, smiling about her jab at Keith's wits, or lack thereof.

"Jesus, Toni," Keith says. "Your damn Indian feet creep up all quiet like."

"I'll take that as a compliment to my ancestral people, Keith," she replies. "Now scoot, before I scalp you. You've taken enough of my man's time."

Keith gets up and sidesteps around her, putting his hands on his head to protect his scalp as he walks past. She shuts the door and dives onto Ben's bed.

"Danielle's breaking up with him, isn't she?" Ben asks.

"Yep. As soon as she graduates. She's sworn us to secrecy," Toni says. "She won't shut up about graduation, going back to San Diego, getting a real job, and saying goodbye to Colorado forever. Natalie and I are getting sick of it.'

"And you guys are supposed to be her friends," Ben says. "Nice way for her to bag on you guys."

Toni shrugs. "We're used to it. She's a real user. If she weren't dating Keith, I don't think we'd ever hang out with her."

"That sucks," Ben says.

"Enough about her and Keith. I'm more concerned about how overdressed you are," she says with a wicked smile spread across her face.

"Easy fix," Ben says, taking off his shirt.

3

BETRAYED

Thursday, May 16, 2013 – Z-poc minus 1

After Khaleed Farouk, or at least his undead corpse, attacked and killed Najm al Din Abdul-Malik, Almahdi Maloof knew they were not going down a righteous path. Unknown to Maloof, the terror group, which would be known as the Undying Jihad had cells like this one in every city of more than 150,000 people in the United States, Europe, Australia, and India. It was the most ambitious undertaking in the history of mankind, and somehow, miraculously, the great secret had been kept.

Some parts of their network had been taken out, but the organization was so loose that there was virtually nothing connecting one cell to another, at least as far as the various law enforcement agencies were concerned, and the government intelligence agencies hadn't put together what they were really up to. The distribution of the serum was the hardest part, but even that had been solved with some staged eBay transactions. They hadn't even decided on the name of the group until this last week, and really the name was unimportant as long as the message got out before the end came. For his part, Maloof was unaware of these things because he was not far enough up the chain of command to be privy to that level of detail.

Maloof's thoughts drift back to two weeks ago. On that day, May 3rd—specifically the five minutes that Maloof sees in his mind every time he closes his eyes—Maloof watched as Farouk attacked Abdul-Malik, his fingers tearing at Abdul-Malik's neck and chest, ripping his shirt and exposing the flesh of his neck and shoulder. Abdul-Malik had tried to open the door, to no avail, and when the revenant sank its teeth into his shoulder, he screamed so hard he tore his vocal chords. He pulled away from the creature that was Khaleed Farouk, leaving flesh and blood vessels dangling from its mouth as he did so. Blood was spurting from the massive wound, staining his tattered shirt a deep crimson. Abdul-Malik didn't know it, but he was already dead.

Still, he fought for every second he had left. The creature was surprisingly fast though, and it caught hold of Abdul-Malik's left arm, tearing open new wounds as it spun him around. It bit Abdul-Malik's hand, taking his pinky and ring fingers off at the base. More blood flowed from the new wounds. With his vocal chords damaged, Abdul-Malik's screams no longer sounded human. He tried in vain again to get away from the grasp of the creature, but it was no use. He died while the creature was chewing on his arm. Within seconds of Abdul-Malik's heart stopping, the re-animated Farouk dropped the arm it was feeding on and slowly stood erect, its head moving from side to side now and then, like it was scanning for something.

A couple of minutes later, Najm al Din Abdul-Malik's bloody corpse began to twitch and move, until it too stood up. Ragged wounds were leaking a blackish fluid that was no longer entirely blood, but it was gravity rather than a heartbeat that emptied the vessels. The left arm hung limp, the muscles rent to the bone in several places.

As he watched this, Maloof knew he was not going to be able to go through with the plan. He also knew that if he was not careful, his fate would be the same as that of Abdul-Malik; he would be turned into a ghoul with gray flesh, sunken, black eyes and a hunger for living tissue.

The Scientist speaks, startling Maloof.

"They are much faster than we had anticipated," he says, breaking Maloof out of his reverie. "We will have to put the rest of the martyrs in there in groups numbering at least as high as that of our soldiers or they will be torn apart to the point of being useless." He says this as though speaking of a lesson learned from a failed project at a software company.

That The Scientist referred to the undead as "soldiers" is not lost on Maloof. He decides he should ask a question so he can appear to be engaged in the process.

"Why don't you use the serum like you did with Khaleed? Wouldn't that be...cleaner?" he asks.

"Indeed, yes Almahdi, yes it would. The serum is valuable though, and there isn't an unlimited supply. We need it for contingency, in case things don't go as planned," The Scientist replies. "No, this is the way to go. It's more ... savage, but effective for building Allah's army."

What The Scientist doesn't tell Maloof is that he received that direction from someone else; the master cell in Bangalore, India, had perfected that technique a week ago in their warehouse off of MG Road. The superior speed and strength of the revenants only lasts as long as they don't sustain torn muscles in their all-out attacks or broken bones as they charge headlong in to objects while chasing their prey. The team in Bangalore has done a lot of work in that warehouse, so the field teams like The Scientist's have some idea of what to expect.

Even with this advanced knowledge, The Scientist was still surprised by Farouk's speed. The thought of a thousand, ten thousand of these creatures running through the streets and tearing Americans apart, creating hundreds of thousands just like them within minutes makes him smile.

Two days later, on May 5th, Maloof stood with The Scientist as they watched the two *soldiers* tear into the next round of martyrs. The Scientist had, moments before, ushered two men and a woman into the room and locked the door behind them. By the time he made it to the observation room the woman's carotid artery had been torn open, sending arterial spray in a red stripe eight feet up the wall. She dropped dead not long after that and the soldier—Abdul-Malik—moved to the second man, the first one having been dispatched by the corpse of Khaleed Farouk. Nine minutes later, there were five soldiers standing the in the room.

MALOOF SHAKES HIS HEAD, as if to drive those memories out of his mind, and brings his thoughts back to the present. The plans have moved forward over the ensuing two weeks and now there are two dozen reanimates in the room below. Maloof has been mentally torn in two for the last fortnight. He knows why he's been placed here, why he's been set up in such a cozy lifestyle. The destruction of western society is the ultimate goal of the jihad; but at the same time, he has become certain that what they are doing now is wrong. He's reached a decision that he has to take a stand. He actually feels guilty for taking so long to reach this decision, but he soothes that guilt by reminding himself he has a lifetime of programming to overcome.

He knows he can't do anything from the office. The Scientist lurks around every corner, it seems, and Maloof suspects that he has the phone lines bugged. The Scientist has become increasingly more paranoid and controlling as time has progressed. No, Maloof thinks, it will have to wait until I go home tonight. His family is supposed to prepare for their exodus in the morning, so as he makes ready to leave, nothing will seem out of place even if he's being watched.

He'll have to move quickly and he doubts the FBI will listen to something as seemingly outlandish as what the Undying Jihad is planning. Maloof winces as he thinks of the name they're going to release to the media. He decides that a call to Homeland Security will get better results. No matter what, he cannot let this plan go through, and there's not much time left so he has to act now. If he knew the full scope of the plan, he would not have had any illusions about his ability to stop it. But as it is, his choice of action has been made. He's not turning back now.

He picks up his keys as The Scientist looks up at him.

"I have final preparations to make," Maloof says.

"Of course, you should go. You've done well, Alhmahdi," The Scientist replies.

Maloof thanks him for the praise, takes his leave, and is almost running by the time he reaches the parking lot.

The Scientist looks at the folder on the desk in Maloof's office. In it are tickets for Maloof, his wife, and their two children to fly to Minneapolis in the morning. The Scientist would have found it curious that Maloof left them behind had he not been observing the way he'd behaved over the last two weeks. He needed Maloof's store for cover, or he would have addressed his commitment level before now. At this stage, however, Maloof is no longer needed and has become a liability to the plan.

He glances out the window and watches Maloof make the left turn out of the parking lot, aiming the blue van west, toward the mountains, toward his home. The Scientist picks up the phone and dials a local number.

"Hello?" says a female voice on the other end of the line.

"He is on his way. I fear he has lost his resolve," The Scientist says.

"I know. I've seen it in his eyes. I will take care of it."

"Excellent. I'll follow up in the morning. This does not change the plan. We must proceed as—"

"I said I will take care of it," she says in a more hostile tone, cutting him short.

"I know you will," he says, his voice kind. "You've never let me down. See you tomorrow," The Scientist says, and he hangs up.

On the other end of the call, Almahdi Maloof's wife A'ishah presses "end" on her burner phone and waits for her husband to arrive home.

4

...MUST COME TO AN END

Friday, May 17, 2013 – Z-poc minus 6 hours

A'ishah Maloof watches the van leave with her two daughters. They're going to an encampment in Minnesota before the larger group of young Muslim children will be travelling to Mecca, where a safe zone has been established for the faithful. She has no illusion about her fate and knows she'll never see the safe zone, but it comforts her to know she's helping to leave a better world for her children.

She turns and walks out to the two-car garage, where her husband is sedated and restrained in a wheelchair.

When she ended her call with The Scientist the evening before, she knew she had to act quickly to subdue her husband, so she loaded her CO_2-powered tranquilizer gun. The dart was loaded with fentanyl in a dose high enough to incapacitate Maloof within a few seconds. She was lucky that it was not enough to kill, as she had a use in mind for him.

He pulled the blue minivan into the garage and as he got out, A'ishah came out of the house. Maloof looked at her; she could tell he was struggling internally. He managed an attempt at a smile, and she smiled back.

As he took a step toward her, she drew the gun from under her tunic. Before Maloof could react, she pulled the trigger. The dart struck him in the chest and he stopped where he was for a moment. His eyes widened and she could see the recognition of her betrayal in them. He took a step toward her as his pupils began to dilate. Another step and he dropped his phone, which sent several plastic shards flying when it struck the concrete.

A'ishah took a couple of steps sideways to keep some distance between them. He took another stumbling step and dropped to one knee. He looked at her with pleading eyes. "Aye. Ish. Please. Don't," he managed to say before he collapsed unconscious to the garage floor.

She retrieved the wheelchair from the basement and lifted his dead weight into it. She got a nylon strap and secured his chest to the chair so he was in a quasi-sitting position, though his arms hung limply and his head lolled forward. She tied his legs to the metal supports and then lashed his arms to the armrests, one strap at the elbow and one at the wrist.

She wheeled him over to the wall and retrieved an

IV bag from the house, which she hung from a nail on the wall, and put the IV needle into the vein on the back of his right hand. She hoped her calculations were correct so the dosage wouldn't kill him.

Now, fifteen hours later, as she goes into the garage, Maloof is awake but groggy.

"A'ishah, why? Why are you doing this? It's madness!"

"Please be quiet, Almahdi. Your part in this is still coming. You're weak, and I've known that for a long time. This is something I had planned for," she says. She's completely calm.

"So you're part of this? Why would you hide it from me? How long have you known what was going to happen?"

"From the very beginning. The hydra has a thousand heads, Almahdi. I'm sorry it's turned out this way, but this is how it has to be."

"A'ishah, this is madness. The Scientist I've been working with, he is insane, this whole thing is insane! We have to stop him! This is not moral, it is not the righteous path!"

Her voice gains a hard edge. "The Scientist, the man you say is insane, is my father. He is a great man, and this plan will go forward as Allah intends."

Maloof is in a state of shock. She told him her parents had died in 1997, three years before their marriage. Now A'ishah is telling him she's the daughter of the man who is releasing the plague of living death upon the world? He struggles against the restraints (where did these come from anyway?) but can only watch as A'ishah replaces the IV bag and inserts a syringe into the injection port just below the bag.

"Good night, Almahdi," A'ishah says, her voice filled with pity. "May Allah forgive your weakness and grant you passage!"

He feels the heat of the drug, whatever it is, as it hits his veins, and very quickly everything goes dark. The last thing he sees, the last thing he will ever see, is A'ishah's stern face looking down at him. She looks evil, and his last conscious thought is that he unknowingly married a demon.

FRIDAY, May 17, 2013 – Z-poc minus 2 hours

Ben Puckett drops off a bowl of breadsticks at table five and heads back to the kitchen of Johnny Rissetti's Italian Restaurant. His phone rings for the fourth time in the last few minutes and he finally pulls it from his pocket. He sees his friend's picture on the screen and answers it.

"Keith, dude, I'm working. What's up?" he says as he answers.

"Are you coming to the party after your shift, or what?"

"Which one is that? Finals are over and some people are graduating tonight. There's about a thousand parties," Ben says.

"The one on Whitcomb," Keith replies. "That guy from my chem lab is throwing it, remember?"

"Um, yeah, I remember. I think I can make it, yeah," Ben says.

"Dude, that's about as pussified an answer as you can give me. You gonna be here or not?"

Ben waves at Toni Glass. She comes over to him and he covers the mic on his phone. "You wanna go to that party on Whitcomb after work?"

"Only if I can stay at your place tonight," she says and gives him her devilish smile.

Ben turns back to his phone. "Dude, we're in. See you after work," he says and presses end before Keith can give him any grief about responding with "we" then he grabs his order from the ready station and takes it out to table four.

FRIDAY, May 17, 2013 – Z-poc minus 30 minutes

The soldiers have been loaded into cages similar to shark cages, and forklifts are loading them into the back of the furniture shop's delivery vans. There are twenty-four soldiers in all, and they've divided them into groups of eight. One van is going to go through old town (the bar district) and release the "payload" among the partiers. Another one is going to the hospital and releasing them there. The final one is releasing them in random neighborhoods where there are large parties. The driver of this van watches his younger partner as he scrolls through a Facebook feed on his tablet and cross-references a map.

"Ok, Saji, where are we going?" he says to the young man.

"Um ... I say we go in a semi-circle. First, we go to the apartment complex at the corner of Horsetooth and Shields. There's a big party going on there ... next let's hit Valley Forge off of Taft Hill. Up in Ramblewood Apartments there is a HUGE party. They've already started posting pictures. We can probably drop two there. Then there is one on Whitcomb that looks like it's a good one. Then ..."

The driver interrupts him. "Enough, that's more than needed to heat things up. We'll have the police chasing their tails and the end will be on them before they know what's happening!"

The younger man agrees and puts his tablet on the passenger seat, then heads to the restroom.

A fourth van idles by the warehouse doors. A'ishah Maloof stands next to it talking to her father, The Scientist.

"You're ready?" he asks.

"Father, yes. I have this under control."

"I know. You do a great thing tonight. You honor our family's name." He smiles at her with a tenderness she has not seen since she was a child, before her brother was killed in Afghanistan by partisans originally armed by the CIA to fight the Soviets.

"WE are doing a great thing," she says. "This plan would not have happened without you guiding it."

"There are hundreds of people doing what I have done. Planning is easy. The execution is the crucial part. The people who have the resolve to see this through to the end are the people who do the great works. Allah be praised, A'ishah. You are living up to your name tonight." He kisses her on the cheek, turns, and walks away before she can see the tear running down his cheek.

A'ishah gets behind the wheel and presses the button on the remote that is attached to the visor. She knows she was named for the Prophet's wife but never has she felt that connection more strongly than she does right now. She drives through the doorway before the door rolls all the way up. She presses the button again and the door drops down behind her.

She heads west on Horsetooth to Shields, an intersection that very soon will be consumed by chaos, where she turns north for a half mile. She pulls into the parking lot at Colorado State University's Moby Gymnasium and parks in a handicap space. She checks that the tranquilizer gun and the black case with the syringes and darts are hidden under her tunic. She goes around to the passenger side of the van, opens the sliding door, and steps in to get Maloof out in his wheelchair. She's outfit him in a special salwar kameez that she's modified to hide his restraints.

She presses the button for the lift and the electronic shelf slides them sideways and lowers them to the ground. After rolling him off of the lift, she presses the button to retract it and closes the side door. She pushes him on the sidewalk and follows the signs to the graduation ceremony. The big ceremony for the larger schools and majors is in the morning, but there are enough people here at the early ceremony for the specialty majors to suit her purposes.

The security guards merely nod at her as she rolls her immobilized husband through the doors. College campuses are so consumed with multi-culturalism she knows the campus employees dare not look twice at her or her supposedly invalid companion. She finds the handicapped seating area in the rear of the first section, where folding stadium seats have been removed to accommodate wheelchairs and motorized scooters, and parks the wheelchair, taking care to set the brakes. She bends down and undoes the restraints on his legs, letting his feet sit on the folding footrests. People around her try not to look as she fusses with him. Another thing she knows will work to her advantage is that Americans consider it rude to stare at handi-capped people, so they consciously try to avoid watching what she's doing. She carefully loosens the restraints on his arms and unclips the plastic clasp on the strap holding his torso tight to the chair. His limp body lists to the left. Finally, she takes the black pouch from under her tunic and withdraws a syringe containing a green serum. She inserts the needle into Almahdi's neck and presses the plunger.

The effect is immediate. His body jerks in the chair, but the loose restraints on his arms keep him from tumbling forward. The vessels in his neck begin to turn black and every few seconds, he suffers a spasm. Even though he's unconscious, his body still registers the pain.

Now people are starting to look at them, so A'ishah turns and walks out. She can hear people murmuring as she leaves. "Is he having a seizure?" and "Is she leaving him? Where the hell is she going?" These comments register in her ears as she exits the area. After a few seconds' hesitation, one person gets up and follows her. She's trying to remain calm as the nosy Good Samaritan sees her heading toward the exit and flags down a security guard.

After a moment of discussion with the Samaritan, the guard calls out, "Ma'am!" as he quicksteps toward her.

She spins and shoots him with a dart from her CO_2 pistol. The green fluid it injects into him instantly makes his skin burn. He looks at the dart sticking from his chest, pulls it out, and a tremendous wave of pain almost brings him to his knees. A'ishah is now nearly outside. Behind her, the Samaritan dials 911; the security guard radios for help, and people have started screaming back in the section of the arena where she left Maloof. She smiles at the sound and exits the arena.

ACROSS TOWN, a van has just pulled into the emergency room entrance of Poudre Valley Hospital.

The passenger gets out, opens the back doors, and pulls a cable that releases the door to the cage housing the undead cargo. He runs back around to the front of the van and gets back in the passenger seat. Eight gray-fleshed, bloody bodies with varying degrees of injuries exit the rear of the van, falling out rather than jumping. As the van speeds away, ER staff rush out and are immediately attacked by the undead creatures.

SOUTH OF THE COLLEGE CAMPUS, a pair of similar undead creatures are released in the parking lot of an apartment complex. The spring-loaded door to the cage is pulled shut with another cable from the front of the van, and it speeds away while the pair of revenants rush into a crowd of partygoers and begin tearing and biting at whomever they can get their gray fingers on.

The final stop this van plans to make is on Whitcomb Street, where Ben Puckett and his girlfriend, Toni Glass, who just ended their shifts at Johnny Rissetti's, are meeting Keith Wallace and a few other friends eager to get their summer started.

NORTHWEST OF CAMPUS, the last van stops at the north end of Old Town Square. An open-air pedestrian mall, Old Town Square is home to a multitude of bars and restaurants, most with patio seating. The square is full of people celebrating the end of the school year. The passenger again gets out and opens the rear doors, springs the latch on the cage, and sprints to the cab. As soon as the door shuts, the driver hits the gas and jumps the curb, driving onto the pedestrian mall as the first creature falls from the back of the van. He hits the gas for a second, and a second creature falls out. Every surge of gas, another vessel of death hits the brick courtyard. The driver honks the horn as people look to see what is happening in the square. Moments later, screams fill the air.

BACK ON CAMPUS, A'ishah Maloof has left her van in its parking space to avoid the security guards who have gotten in her way and is running into the center of the campus. The guards have called the campus police to report her actions, and 911 calls are flooding from the arena where her husband has risen from his wheelchair and has begun attacking people. The security guard she shot with the dart has collapsed, and in moments, he too will wake and start attacking the people who are trying to help him.

A campus police car drives hops the curb and onto the grassy field where A'ishah is running. It gets in front of her, stops, and two officers, a man and a woman, get out with weapons drawn and call for her to stop where she is. A'ishah raises the CO_2 gun and keeps running. The police hesitate, and she pulls the trigger.

The female officer takes the dart in the abdomen and cries out in pain. The male officer fires his pistol, and A'ishah is knocked to the turf by the .40-caliber round, blood spilling from a chest wound. While the man checks on his female partner, A'ishah presses the CO_2 gun against her neck, pulls the trigger, and sends the last dart into her flesh, the serum burning in her carotid artery and hitting her brain within seconds. She feels pain, the worst pain she's ever felt, as if every nerve in her body has been set on fire, and then she's gone.

5

TOO LITTLE, TOO LATE

Friday, May 17, 2013 – Z-poc plus 20 minutes.

Outside Moby Gymnasium, the Ft. Collins police are struggling to maintain control. There were maybe two-thousand people in the gym for the graduation ceremony, and now dozens of them are wounded and bleeding both inside and outside the building. The police have only been on the scene for about ten minutes, but the situation has gotten much worse in that time. A massive triage area has been set up in the grass at the northwest corner of the arena, where the Colorado State Rams play their home basketball and volleyball games and where, tonight, a riot erupted in the middle of the early graduation ceremony.

Standing behind his cruiser parked outside the big arena, Sergeant Bob Foster adjusts his tactical vest for the hundredth time. All members of the Ft. Collins

Police Department were issued this gear in late 2009 when the government's stimulus money was being spent freely, but they have had rare occasions to use it, and Bob has added a few pounds since then. The vest is adjustable, but he's having a hard time getting comfortable, especially with the five 30-round magazines for his Windham short-barreled M4 stuffed in their pouches. The other officers are similarly equipped, except anyone under the rank of sergeant has a Windham semi-automatic AR-15 rather than the select fire rifle Foster has.

An EMT approaches him from the triage area. "Sergeant Foster?" he inquires.

"Yeah, that's me," he says, irritated at the interruption. He stops fidgeting for a moment and fixes his gaze on the EMT. "You are?"

"Ted Williams. My bus is affiliated with PVH," he says, using shorthand for Poudre Valley Hospital. "Look, Sergeant, this is out of control. People are still in there attacking each other. I can't send any of my guys in there, and the people we're treating out here are dropping like flies. I can't evac them fast enough."

Almost on cue, an ambulance turns on its sirens and crosses North Street, which runs, aptly enough, along the north side of the arena. It continues past Westfall Hall dormitory (which, thankfully is almost empty now that classes are over) before turning right onto Laurel Street, the main east-west thoroughfare that marks the northern boundary of the campus.

"Gotcha, Ted," Foster says. He's heard enough

whining from the EMTs over the years. They're all adrenaline junkies but don't want to be in any REAL danger. "We're about five minutes from going in there. I'm just waiting for a few more units to show up. I don't know what's going on tonight, Ted, but there's shit going down all over town. The last day of school is normally pretty crazy, but this is something else altogether. My lieutenant is going to give us the rundown in a minute so we can hopefully get in there and shut this thing down."

"Sarge?" Williams says. "Your LT went down about five minutes ago. Has no one told you?"

Foster checks his radio and finds that in his fussing, he's knocked the mic loose and hasn't been hearing any updates. *I thought things had just gone quiet*, he thinks, *but hell, someone should have grabbed me by now!* Embarrassed, he reconnects the cable and turns his attention back to the EMT.

"Went down? What the fuck happened?"

"One of the people we thought was dead jumped him, and he's en route to PVH right now. That was his bus that just left."

"Come again? A dead guy jumped him? I'm not following." Foster thinks the EMT may be suffering from shock.

"We were working on this guy, had a wicked neck wound like he'd been bitten. I mean, his neck was ripped wide open. We couldn't clamp the bleeders, and he bled out. No pulse, no pupil response, nothing, just these crazy black spider webs spreading through his blood vessels. I moved to the next triage. Couple of minutes later, there's this commotion, and Neck Wound is all over your LT, just ripping at him. One of your guys busted Neck Wound in the back of the head with his rifle stock, and it was like someone hit the off switch."

Foster is stunned. "So the dead guy is dead again?"

"Yep. I think the kid—Muesli or something like that, a young guy—snapped the guy's spine right at the base of the skull. He's pretty shook up about it. Anyway, the guys told me YOU'RE the one in charge now, Sarge, and they need you over there."

Fuck me, Foster thinks to himself. *This is a goddamn shitstorm, and I'm right in its fucking path. No way is any of this ending well.*

He's interrupted by a salvo of gunfire and yelling from multiple people. He grabs his Windham, slams the trunk on his cruiser, and starts running to the front of the gym.

He finds a grisly scene. The police are all training their guns on the people who have been bloodied in the melee inside the gym. Several bodies lay on the ground, and the remaining EMTs have fallen back behind the police line.

"STAY BACK!" one of cops yells at a woman who is staggering to her feet.

One of the EMTs is bleeding profusely from a wound on his arm, and a couple of other EMTs are tending to him. Ted leaves Foster to check on them.

The young cop Ted had referred to, Misselli, not

Muesli, comes running over to Foster while the other cops scream instructions at the wounded.

"Sarge, this is FUBAR. These people are just attacking us like wild fucking animals. You heard what happened to LT?"

"I heard."

"The medic over there just lost a huge chunk of his arm when one of these fuckers bit him. Sarge, it fucking ATE the hunk of flesh. I've never seen anything like this shit! We tried tasing him, and he wasn't even affected by it. He'd stop when we juiced him, but soon as we'd turn off the current, the fucker would come right at us like nothing had happened. Jennings had to drop him, and we dropped three others that were closing on Jennings."

Foster thumbs the mic on his radio as he scans the increasing number of dead bodies on the lawn.

"Two-fifteen to dispatch," he says into the mic.

"Two-fifteen," comes the reply acknowledging him, the "two" indicating his rank as sergeant and fifteen being his unit number.

"Situation at Moby is code Charles. Multiple subjects code Black, code 6. We need to lock the site down, request code 10 on North Street at Shields." Foster uses police shorthand to tell the dispatcher that they are encountering civil unrest (code Charles), that there are people dead (code Black), showing signs of mental instability or are under influence of drugs (code 6), and he needs covering units (code 10) to shut down traffic on Shields Street. Shields makes up the western border of the campus and, along with North Street, is the other main entry point into the arena's parking area.

"Copy 215. All units occupied; will code 10 ASAP ..." the dispatcher trails off, and a new voice comes on the radio.

"Foster, Hutton."

Shit, the chief! Foster thinks. *I'm in the crosshairs of this thing now.*

"Copy, Chief," he says to the mic.

"I'm calling in every off-duty officer on this, Foster. The sheriff's department is in the loop, and we're setting up a command center. All sheriff on-calls are being brought in as well; we're going to run joint juris-diction on this. We have shit like this all over town, Foster, at least twenty code Black so far outside your location. We have massive fights where parties have gotten completely out of control, Old Town is a fucking blood bath, and I don't know what the hell is happening at PVH, but it's not good. Now this shit at Moby. Put this riot down, Foster. If you have to drop everyone who resists, you put this down."

The pause after the last statement let Foster know the chief was done. "Copy Chief," he says as he clips the mic onto the bracket on his shoulder. He turns back to the situation the rest of the cops are facing, knowing they all heard what the chief had to say.

Foster looks hard at the woman who has now regained her feet. *She looks like she's dead,* he thinks. She's turned gray and has black lines tracing the paths of her blood vessels where they are near the surface of the skin. She is not responding to the commands shouted at her. Suddenly, she launches into a dead sprint, charging the line of policemen, snarling like a mad dog the whole time.

"WE WILL FIRE! STOP WHERE YOU ARE" the cop named Jennings yells at her. A second later, he shoots her in the chest. She barely notices, the impact from the bullet turning her on a slightly different course, but she's still coming.

Foster raises his M4 and fires a three-round burst. All three rounds hit her in the chest, and she falls forward, skidding on the concrete within five feet of the closest cop, who takes a few big steps back. To a man, they're all shocked when the woman pushes herself up from the concrete. Her face has some serious damage from the slide she just did. Her skull is gleaming through her forehead, a ragged flap of skin hanging down from the wound. There's no blood. Her nose is broken, and a couple of her teeth have gone missing. She launches forward from a crouch, straight at Foster.

A single shot rings out. Misselli has his AR aimed at her head. His aim is good, and her forehead collapses as the bullet penetrates her skull. The woman topples to the concrete face down, this time for good. Brain matter and an oily fluid seep onto the concrete under her face and start to drain toward the street.

"They're fucking zombies," Misselli says. "Holy

fucking Jesus, they're zombies. You have to shoot them in the head."

"Bullshit," Foster says. "It's some sort of aerosolized PCP some asshole pumped into the arena. They're all fucking whacked out. Has to be some explanation other than zombies."

Still, he thinks, *the head shot stopped her cold after three hits to the chest didn't seem to faze her ...*

A moan stops him in his tracks. The cops all look up from the dead woman to see another half dozen of the gray-fleshed ghouls looking at them from the triage area. One by one, they launch into sprint mode and the officers open fire. This time, they all aim for the head, even the dubious Foster, and they make quick work of the six reanimates.

Foster surveys the scene. There are another thirty or so people with various wounds still waiting for treatment. There were a lot more, but some of them fled when the shooting started.

That can't be good, Foster thinks. *We've done a piss-poor job of securing the area. If these sickos get into the neighborhoods, this will go from an ugly situation to a straight-up ass-fucking real quick. Where are those damn code 10s?* Then he looks up at the gym and blanches at what he sees.

The glass entryway is packed with people. Gray-faced people. Gray-faced people just staring at them hungrily. The double set of outer-and-inner doors at the entryway seems to have them confounded for the time being and the glass that lines the side of the building is holding, for now. The other policemen see Foster's gaping mouth and follow his gaze.

"Holy shit," says Misselli. "There must be two hundred of them."

"They said there were about two-thousand in attendance tonight," Jennings says. "What if they're all like this?"

"Then we're going to need more ammo," Foster says, pulling himself together. "Look, you guys heard the chief. He wants us to stop this here and now. Everyone gear up, load up, and let's get ready to go in." He points to the entry with the horde behind it. "But we ain't going in through that door, I'll tell you that for nothing. We need another entrance where we don't have such a large welcoming committee. Jennings—find me another entry point. Everyone else, get your gear!"

The men head to their cars to get more equipment—helmets, tactical gloves, shin guards, elbow pads, and more ammo and magazines for their rifles. In the triage area, more victims start moaning the horrible, raspy sound that Foster now knows means only one thing. He puts a full magazine in his M4 and heads for the moans.

It's going to be a long night.

THE KIDS AREN'T ALRIGHT

Friday, May 17, 2013 – Z-poc plus 30 minutes.

While Sergeant Foster is dealing with the situation at Moby Arena, Ben Puckett shifts his 1978 Toyota FJ Land Cruiser into second gear as traffic slows down, yet again. He lets out a sigh, which elicits a response from Toni.

"Ben, we'll get there. You know traffic on College sucks," she says. "But getting all pissed off isn't going to make it go faster."

The truth was that traffic on College Avenue sucked most of the time; it was just especially bad tonight. *School's over, and many of the students have already left,* he thinks, *so why is traffic so slow?*

"I know," he replies out loud. "I'm just ready to cut loose, and these people REFUSE TO GO THE SPEED LIMIT!" He yells this last part past the windshield at the cars in front of him. Toni just shakes her head.

They get closer to Laurel Street, where Ben wants to turn left, and he can see lights flashing as a police car pulls through the intersection and stops next to an unmarked police car that is already blocking the westbound lanes of Laurel. He sees the people in the double left turn lane trying to merge back into the northbound traffic, which is what has everything so jammed up. Laurel Street is closed.

"Well, what the hell is going on here?" he says. He cranes his head, but no matter what angle he tries, he sees no accident, no emergency vehicle other than the squad cars parked across the westbound side of the intersection.

"I don't know why the street's closed, but why does that cop have a machine gun?" Toni asks.

As they creep closer, Ben sees the short-barreled rifle slung from the officer's uniform, which is no normal patrolman's uniform. He's wearing black cargo-style pants, black boots, a black shirt covered with a tactical vest. The word 'POLICE" is emblazoned across the front and back of the vest. He has multiple magazines for both the rifle and his pistol in various pockets on the vest. He's preoccupied with something in the trunk of the car. As they get closer to the cross street, he can see a second officer in the middle of the intersection, directing traffic north. He's dressed in a similar fashion.

They crawl along as people still fight to merge back

into traffic. When they finally get near enough to be heard, Ben rolls his window down and asks, "What's going on?"

"There's been an incident at Moby," the officer says.

"What kind of incident?"

"It's a police matter. Please keep traffic moving." The officer waves him forward.

"What kind of incident? What does that mean?" Ben persists.

"Keep it moving! Let's GO!" the officer shouts, waving Ben forward, signaling that Q&A time is over.

Ben looks at Toni for a second without saying anything. She finally breaks the tension.

"That's messed up," she says. "'A police matter'? That's the best he can say? He's dressed for a bad day in Afghanistan and all he can say is 'it's a police matter'?!"

"I'll bet there was a bomb," Ben says. It's only been a month since the Boston Marathon bombing and the shootout that followed a few days later, where hundreds of black-booted police and federal agents of different stripes swarmed Boston neighborhoods in search of the suspects. Out loud, he says, "That's exactly how the cops dressed in Boston after the marathon bombing. They were ready for all-out combat."

"No way. Here? What would they blow up?" Toni says dubiously.

"There's a graduation thing tonight in the gym.

Maybe someone screwed up and didn't graduate, and they figure if they can't, no one can."

"That's stupid even for a terrorist."

"Well, he's clearly stupid if he didn't graduate," Ben replies, and they both chuckle.

Ben turns the corner onto Mulberry Street and heads toward Whitcomb and his date with a keg of beer. He drives the few blocks to Whitcomb and turns left, back toward the campus.

He's always amazed when they go to a party in one of these houses right by campus. The houses are always trashed, even in their normal, non-party state, but the rent is so damn expensive! The apartment that Ben shares with Keith and their friend Andy is not that much farther from campus—maybe a half mile—but it's a lot nicer than most of these houses and nowhere near the rent.

Ben spots an open parking space a few houses up from the party so he pulls in before someone else can grab it. He and Toni exit the 4x4 and head toward the noise. Even from three houses away, they can hear people yelling, and the music blaring is overwhelming the neighborhood.

"The cops are going to be here in no time," Toni says.

"Nah, remember, there's an 'incident' at Moby. They have better things to do than harsh our buzz!" Ben replies with a smile.

There's a pause in the music and "Good Good Night" by Roscoe Dash begins playing from speakers on the front porch. Out in front of the house, and in the yards of the houses on either side of the party house, there's a game of football being played—if you can call the skills being displayed *playing*—which involves the team that gets scored on having to chug a beer. Based on the level of dexterity both teams are showcasing, the game is a shoot-out. Ben and Toni hustle through the yard and into the house.

Inside, the volume is even louder and there's a small mosh pit in what would be a living room if a family lived here rather than four or five, or who knows how many, college students. A red cup half full of beer barely misses Ben on its way to the wall by the entry-way. A kid with bloodshot eyes, a sleeve of plastic cups under his arm and the stench of marijuana on his clothes steps out of the mosh room and heads them off before they can get past him.

"Two bucks a cup. Keg's in the kitchen," he says, apparently assuming they already know where the kitchen is.

Ben gives him a five and the kid stares at it for a minute, trying to come to terms with the higher math of making change, so Ben says, "Keep it."

"Oh, right on. Here, let me mark you."

The stoner produces a felt marker and puts a black 'X' on each of their right hands. "So I don't charge you twice!" he says, and re-joins the moshers in the living room.

The kitchen isn't hard to find, and when they get there, Keith is running the keg, filling the cups for the people in line and filling his own whenever it needs it.

"We should have known!" Ben says. Keith's modus operandi at a party is to get control of the keg and fairly dispense the beverage. By fair, he means pouring beer for people while ensuring he and his friends get filled first when they're empty. Then, once he's reached his desired level of drunkenness, he leaves the keg to whoever is next in line.

"Benji!!!" he shouts once he catches sight of them. "Get over here! Fill up! You—step back a minute, let these guys get the night started!" He gestures for the person whose beer he was filling to step back. The kid protests, but only a little, and Keith fills Toni's cup first and then Ben's. He holds his own cup up while thrusting the spigot back at the kid in line who has to quickly get his cup under the valve to keep from getting splashed with beer.

With his cup held high, Keith shouts, "For those about to rock, we salute you!" He clacks cups with Ben and the two chug their beers, Keith finishing a few seconds ahead of Ben. He pauses the line to refill their beers and turns to Toni.

"Toni, you're driving tonight, right?" he asks.

"Sure. I love driving your drunk asses home in a forty-year-old SUV that doesn't have power steering," she says.

"You're the best," he says, either missing the sarcasm or ignoring it. It's hard to tell which. "I can see why Ben likes you. Plus, you've got a great rack."

Toni gives him the finger and asks where Danielle is. Keith makes a sour face. They all know Danielle is graduating tomorrow, and the future of their relationship is uncertain at best.

"She's out back with Andy and Natalie. No doubt boring them to death with all her plans for life after college." There's more than a hint of resentment in Keith's voice.

Ben raises his eyebrows a little as if to say "aaaawkward..." Toni returns the gesture and says to Ben, "I'm going to find them. You boys have fun. Come find me in a bit." Ben watches her rear end as she sashays out of the kitchen toward the back door.

"So I guess you never had that talk with Danielle?" Ben asks.

"Fuck that, man," Keith says. "She's leaving anyway. It'll resolve itself. I don't want to start a fight right before graduation and miss out on graduation sex, farewell sex, and so on. Maybe we can do it in Moby before the ceremony!" Keith coughs, spitting beer, and hands the tap to the next guy in line. "Dude," he says, "speaking of Moby, did you see Watts's live stream?"

Ben replies with no, but even if he said yes, Keith is already thrusting his phone at him with the video player buffering. On screen, their friend Tim Watts appears. Tim is an audiovisual technology major, and he does a lot of work at Moby Gym. Tonight he's running the show for the early graduation ceremony. The audio quality of the video is, ironically given his major, pretty terrible. He starts shouting at the camera on his phone.

"I don't know what started it, but the crowd here at early graduation is in full riot mode. I'm recording on the big cams here in the control booth, but we're not broadcasting tonight and I don't have access to activate the feeds, so this will have to do for now."

He holds the iPhone up and pans the crowd with it. From his vantage point in the control booth, you can see just about everywhere in the arena except immediately below the booth itself. The image shows hundreds of people fighting, screaming, and running. People can be seen trampling one another. Some people are covered in blood—and there's a LOT of blood—and the noise from the arena is oppressive. The camera returns to Tim.

"You can see it's total chaos out there. I just got off the phone with 911. The operator told me they have 'a lot of things' going on right now and that they'll get someone out as soon as possible. I can hear fights in the hallway outside the booth, and people aren't even supposed to be up here. I've locked the door, and I'm turning out the lights, so I don't draw attention to myself."

There's a loud pounding in the background much closer than the noise coming from the arena.

"Fuck! Someone's trying to get in. I'm cutting this off. If you're watching this, please see if you can get help. I've never seen anything like this."

The video ends and Keith returns his phone to his

pocket. "Isn't that fucked up? I wonder how he got that many people, let alone the school, to go along with that. I've tried texting him a ton but no answer. You know this is going to be like his calling card to Hollywood. Like a *War of the Worlds* kind of thing. Dude, what the fuck is wrong with you?"

Ben can feel the color leaving his face. "Keith, we ran into a cop in, like, full riot gear on the way here. He said there'd been 'an incident' at Moby."

Keith is quiet for a half second before saying, "You almost had me. Tim clued you in on this, didn't he? You're such a douche!" He laughs as he grabs the tap back and fills his cup from the keg.

"Keith, it's no joke. They closed Laurel Street. He had a machine gun, and there was another cop there too, also in full gear." Ben is replaying Watts' video.

Keith gives Ben a hard stare and says, "And there was a man on a horse, and a man on fire, and Brick killed a guy with a trident! That escalated quickly!" He starts laughing at his Ron Burgundy reference.

"Dude, I'm completely serious. I think something really bad is going on." He holds the phone out with the image paused on the crowd in the arena.

"You better not be fucking with me. If you get me believing you, and it's all a joke, I'm kicking your ass!" Keith says.

"No joke, man. I swear."

They're interrupted by a commotion from the front room. The music has suddenly stopped and it sounds like everyone in the front room of the house is running for the door. They can hear angry yelling, but it's too jumbled to make out what is being said. Keith hands the tap back to the next person in line and sets his beer down on the counter. He gives Ben a backhanded tap to the chest.

"Cops must be here," he says. "C'mon, let's check this out."

They make their way back out to the now empty front room and see two of the guys who were playing football outside carrying a third guy inside, with one of his arms over each of their shoulders. The kid being carried is bleeding steadily from a wound on his head and on his arm.

"What the hell happened?" Keith asks.

The guy closest to them says, "Some assholes in a white van just pulled up, jumped out and started fighting with us. Seriously fucked up, man."

The other non-injured kid says, "Yeah, two of them just started in on us for no reason. The van took off, but these two they left behind just went frickin' crazy. Biting and clawing and shit."

Ben has been looking out the front door. There's a crowd of about thirty people circled around a half dozen or so who are punching, kicking, and wrestling with each other. A bearded kid in a bloody "The Dude Abides" t-shirt runs up the steps and shoves his way past Ben, trailing a string of curse words and disappears into the rear of the house.

"Keith," Ben says, "I think we should get Andy and the girls and go."

The Dude Abides kid comes storming back from the rear of the house with a baseball bat. "We'll see how fucking tough they are now," he says to no one in particular as he rushes past them and out onto the lawn.

"I think you're right," Keith says. They turn and weave their way through the house, finding the back door behind the kitchen. Toni and Danielle are headed toward the door as the guys walk out. Toni speaks up first.

"What the hell is going on out there?"

"There's a fight. Some dickheads in a van rolled up and started shit with the guys out front," Keith says.

"And that incident at the gym looks like a riot broke out. Watts posted a video, and it looked bad," Ben says. The girls immediately reach for their phones, but Ben stops them. "Hey—watch it in the car. I think we should get the hell out of here before the police show up, or one of us gets caught up in that crap out front. Is there a side gate we can use?"

Keith offers to check for a gate. Danielle goes and gets Andy and Natalie and quickly tells them what's going on. Off in the distance, they can hear the *pop-pop-pop* of fireworks going off.

"Guys, over here!" Keith calls out. He's holding a gate open, and they all hustle over to him. He and Ben lead the way through the opening. At the corner of the house, they look around at the front yard. Several people are prone on the grass, and the rest of the crowd has pulled back. A couple of people are crying, and others are vomiting. Someone screams, "I can't get through to 911!" Another person responds with, "I can't get a signal at all!" There are people straddling some of those who are prone, accosting them as they lay apparently unconscious. It looks like the some of the people attending the party have started fighting each other, not the late arrivals. The Dude Abides guy runs at one of them and swings his baseball bat, connecting with the assailant's head. After the blow, the assailant goes stiff and collapses. Two other people grunt angrily—or did they *growl?*—and tackle Dude Abides. His baseball bat clatters loudly on the sidewalk. In the waning light of the day, there appears to be a lot of blood on most of the people involved in the scrum.

Keith turns to Ben and says, "We are getting the fuck out of here. Where's your truck?"

"This way," Ben says. "Come on, guys!" And with that, he starts jogging toward the ancient Toyota. The group follows him. When they get to the old SUV, Keith goes around back and opens the rear door. He helps Danielle get in and turns to Natalie, offering to help her climb in.

Andy waves him off. "I'm not leaving my car here. We'll drive separately. C'mon, Nat." Andy goes to a PT Cruiser across the street, and Natalie follows him.

Keith gets in the rear of the Land Cruiser and pulls the door shut. Ben starts the engine and begins backing up. In his mirror, he can see Andy back out of his space and point the car south, toward Laurel Street, and toward the gym where there's apparently a riot in progress. Ben calls out to him.

"Andy, no, don't go that way! The cops have Laurel closed!!" he shouts, but it's too late, the PT Cruiser is speeding off. Ben backs the old SUV the rest of the way out of the parking space and heads after Andy, putting distance between them and the melee in the yard. With the window down, the distant sound of fireworks is more persistent now.

"That sounds like ..." Ben says, trailing off.

"Gunfire," Keith finishes the thought.

They round the corner onto Laurel Street and can see the flashing lights from police cars at the far end of the street—about six blocks ahead—where it intersects with Shields Street. Four blocks beyond that is their apartment complex.

The noise they hear is now unmistakably that of gunfire. He presses harder on the gas so he can catch up with Andy. They pass a row of four-story dormitories before getting to "The Towers," which are twin twelve-story dorms. Durward and Westfall Halls are the tallest buildings on campus and overlook Moby Arena. There are dozens of people wandering between the buildings, and several in the street as well. They see a cop running from a crowd of about twenty people. He turns, raises a rifle, and fires a volley of shots.

A couple of the people fall and don't get back up. Others go down, but get up and immediately rejoin the pursuit, some of them injured and moving much slower than the others. The main group is still gaining on the cop, who fires a few more shots, dropping a couple more people, and then swaps magazines on the run.

Andy stops his PT Cruiser in the street and Ben rolls up behind him. No one in the car talks for a second.

"That did NOT just happen. Please tell me that didn't just happen," Danielle says.

Keith has his phone out and is filming the chase. The cop has made it across the street and turns again, firing his gun into the crowd until the magazine is empty. There are only about four people left in the main group, but they are enough to overpower him. They tackle the officer and begin beating and tearing at him, the assault bathed in the light of a street lamp. Andy, in the PT Cruiser ahead, has rolled down his window and is shouting at someone.

"What is he doing?" Toni asks.

Ben sticks his head out of the window and listens for a second. As the cop's screams die down, Andy can be heard more clearly.

"It sounds like he's yelling 'Watts,'" he says.

One of the people who was pursuing the cop, but much slower than the rest, turns toward Andy. It's Tim Watts, their friend who posted the video from inside the arena earlier. Visible in the cars' headlights, Tim is still carrying his cell phone in his right hand. As he turns toward them, they can see that his left arm hangs limp at his side. His shirt is ripped, and the muscle and skin from the upper arm are gone, leaving the bone exposed from just below the shoulder to just above the elbow. Most of his left hand is missing, and he has multiple gunshot wounds to his torso and left leg, which lags behind the right as he limps along; it seems barely able to support his weight. His abnormally pale skin is spider webbed with black veins. His pupils are blown, and his black eyes lock in on Andy. He opens his bloody mouth and screams in an eerie, disembodied fashion. It reminds Ben of Donald Sutherland at the end of *Invasion of the Body Snatchers*.

"What. The fuck. Is going on?" Danielle asks.

"Dudes, those people are eating that cop," Keith says, still filming the assault on the officer with his phone. They all look over and can see the people pulling at arms and legs, sinking their teeth in and pulling away, long strings of gore stretching from the body to their mouths.

"WHAT THE FUCK IS GOING ON??!!" Danielle is getting hysterical, so Keith stops filming and pulls her close to him. She buries her face in his shoulder and starts sobbing.

Up ahead, Watts, or rather the ragged body that used to be Watts, is shambling closer to Andy's car. Ben honks his horn and screams out the window, "Andy, GO! Let's get out of here!"

The four people who were ripping the cop apart have stopped their attack, turning their attention to Ben's horn and the people inside the vehicle. They scream in that same weird way as Watts did, and they all stand up almost in unison. Andy starts to pull forward as the gruesome foursome begin running at their vehicles, two of them drawn by the moving PT Cruiser and the other two focused on the Toyota. Ben puts the car in gear and gives it gas, pulling away, but not before the fastest of the creatures slams into the front fender. Ben keeps the gas pressed down, and the SUV lurches as the unfortunate ghoul falls under the rear wheel and gets run over.

"Fuck!" Ben shouts and slows down, instinctually worried about hitting a pedestrian.

"Ben, don't stop!" Toni yells. "Get us out of here!"

Ben presses the gas pedal again, pulling away from the bloody scene. Andy is roaring off in the PT Cruiser, dodging around the police cruiser at the inter-section. In his rearview mirror, Ben can see three of the people chasing them, but dropping back quickly. The fourth one, which he ran over, is trying unsuccessfully to stand up on broken legs.

They're going more than sixty miles per hour by the time they reach the Village Apartments. Their building is adjacent to the pool in Village West, farthest from the campus, so they pass the first two parking lots and pull into the third one. Ben drives up on the sidewalk and stops at the base of the staircase that leads to their apartment. He jumps out and takes the stairs two at a time, unlocking the door and getting it open as Toni catches up, followed by Danielle and Keith, with Andy and Natalie bringing the rear after sprinting from the parking lot.

Ben follows them in, turns, shuts the door, and

locks it. He turns around and can see by everyone's face that they feel like he does. They've just escaped from a nightmare, and they don't know how to process what they've just witnessed. They also don't know that there's no escaping this nightmare and that it's only just begun. The age of man is ending; it's Zed's World now.

ZED'S WORLD BOOK TWO

PROLOGUE | THE END OF THE WORLD AS WE KNEW IT

A'Ishah Maloof was one piece of a terrorist organization, the extent of which only a few people knew. Her motivations—and those of her father, known to his co-conspirators as "The Scientist"—were, in her eyes, pure. The governments of the West had taken her family from her. Her mother. Her brothers. Aunts, uncles, cousins—all dead because someone in a dark room somewhere in the United States made an error inputting coordinates in a computer. The missile strike blew her family to pieces, right in front of her, at her cousin's wedding. She was covered in blood, some of it hers, but mostly that of her relatives. She found a finger in her hair later that night. It's an image that would haunt her dreams for years.

Two years later, after she and her father had been accepted into the United States as refugees—fast-tracked in part as compensation for the "friendly fire" deaths of her family in 2002—her father confided in her his role *in a plot that was then in its infancy. He asked her to join him in it, to join him in getting revenge, not just on the government directly responsible for the murder of their family members—for that's what it was; murder— but on the culture that allowed such a government to exist. It would be a long time coming, he told her, maybe a decade or more. It would require her to participate in a marriage that would be a ruse. It would be such a ruse that even her husband would not know it wasn't real.*

The pieces were all being put into place, but there was much research to do before any concrete plans would be made. There was a real chance, he said, that this initiative would fail, and their efforts would be for nothing. She was eager to help and told her father she would do anything to avenge their family.

Her husband, Almahdi Maloof, was told a similar story by his handler, only he wasn't to know of his spouse's involvement. He was only told he would be wed to an orphaned Afghan refugee. They would court for six months, be wed, and raise a family. It would help throw any lingering suspicion off of him.

Almahdi himself was the son of Afghan refugees, people who fled the Soviets long before the Americans and the British came. They lived in Europe for a decade, then moved to the United States in the 1990s when Almahdi was just a boy. He didn't know that his father was considered a radical who preached Jihad. He just knew him as his father.

Almahdi had been radicalized at home without

knowing it and was put in place as a sleeper Mujahidin in the late 1990s. His father ran a furniture store, and after his death in 2001, mere weeks before 9/11, Almahdi inherited the business. His marriage in 2004 to the beautiful young A'ishah completed his cover. He believed she loved him, and after a time, he loved her too.

Though he had been coached to be as assimilated into the American culture as he could, Almahdi secretly hated the Americans and all of their excesses, their wasteful ways, the way they took all of their good fortunes for granted. After his father's death, however, his impressions and beliefs began to change. The outpouring of sympathy from his neighbors for the loss of his father was immense and genuine. For the first time, he saw his neighbors as people, not as enemies.

They were kind, and giving, and even if they were wasteful and ignorant about the injustice in the world, they weren't malevolent. By the time his children were born, Almahdi was still attending his weekly "briefing sessions" at the Fort Collins Islamic Center, but he was going through the motions. The moment he saw his son's face, he knew in his heart that all life is precious, and he knew that when the time came, he would choose life over death, for himself and others.

In 2005, he first met The Scientist. He was also Afghani, and also Mujahidin. He had scars on his face from a battle he had been part of in 2002. He was missing a finger on his left hand and had piercing blue eyes that touched the depths of Almahdi's mind. The

Scientist terrified him, and at one of the weekly briefings, he joined Ahmadi's handler.

Almahdi was reminded that he was going to be called on to participate in something glorious, something that would bring the nations of the West to their knees. Participation was not optional; if he wanted his family to remain safe, he must play his part, no matter what was asked of him. His son was the only thing that mattered to him more than life itself, so Almahdi kept playing his part.

The nature of the plot was so monstrous that Almahdi would not have guessed it in a thousand lifetimes. Always in his mind were his son (and by this time his daughter) and, of course, the lovely A'ishah. He had to play his part to keep them safe. It wasn't until the final moments of the plot that he knew doing what was right may not be what was best for his family, but the alternative was the complete destruction of mankind. The risk to his family notwithstanding, he had to try SOMETHING to stop the horrors that were about to be unleashed on humanity.

The Scientist was a step ahead of him, however, and A'ishah took care of the rest. When he arrived home, he was about to tell her that something horrible was coming, that he had taken steps to stop it, but she shot him with a CO2-powered tranquilizer gun before he could get a word out.

At 6:30 PM on Friday, May 17th, 2013, A'ishah Maloof wheeled her unconscious husband into Moby Gym in Fort Collins, Colorado, injected him with a serum that caused a quick but painful death, followed by a brief period where the virus in the serum hijacked the central nervous system of Almahdi's corpse, reanimating it and using it to assault others and propagate the strain.

Minutes later, after being shot by the police, A'ishah fired a dart into her neck, felt the serum burning in her veins and arteries. She believed as she died, in the final moments, she would see her lost relatives bidding her welcome to heaven.

She lay on the grass, fire burning through her veins, and as her consciousness slipped away, she saw nothing.

CHAPTER 1

At the same time that A'ishah Maloof wheels her incapacitated husband into Moby Gym, Kyle and Naomi Puckett are escorted to their table in a new restaurant called Fedora in Longview, forty-five minutes south of Fort Collins.

It's the start of their Date Night, a sacrosanct ritual with a few unbreakable rules: no phones, no TV, no talk radio; just each other's company. Their focus is on each other and nothing else. They've had Date Night every week for the better part of two decades. Neither one can remember exactly when they started, but once they started, they've never missed one. The time Naomi spent the evening in the hospital while Kyle passed a kidney stone, they both agree, counts.

This week, they've moved it from Saturday to Friday night because they're expecting their son Ben to come home from his freshman year of college sometime the next day. They will, no doubt, be spending the evening with him.

At 6:45, as Almahdi Maloof's undead corpse begins tearing into the sixty-five-year-old man across the aisle from the wheelchair where A'ishah left him, Kyle tears into a ten-ounce fillet, one of Fedora's specialties. In cities across the nation, riots have begun, but without their smartphones, Kyle and Naomi are unaware. People around them talk in hushed whispers, and a few ask for the check and leave after hearing reports from Europe indicating thousands of deaths from similar riots, but the pair remains blissfully ignorant of the growing chaos.

By 7:25, emergency rooms at hospitals in major cities around the country, and in fact around the world, begin to be overrun with the living dead. A'ishah Maloof has died and resurrected and has already infected five more people on the campus of Colorado State University. Kyle's son, Ben Puckett, and his friends are drinking their first beers in a house party on Whitcomb Street in Fort Collins, just a few blocks from Moby Gym. Sergeant Foster of the Fort Collins Police and the handful of officers with him enter Moby Gym through a side door to find hundreds of the undead wandering the interior of the building. Their gunshots only attract more of them, and soon they're overrun. At Fedora, Kyle and Naomi finish a piece of tiramisu. Kyle enjoys a glass of port and Naomi a cup of coffee.

At 7:50, Ben and his friends shut the door to their apartment, having escaped a group of zombies too small to call a horde, but large enough to run down a policeman and tear him to pieces in front of them.

In larger cities, widespread looting starts as the police are too busy dealing with the dead. Governors have activated the National Guard, but in cities like Denver, where the metropolitan area covers massive expanses of land, there is little hope of containment. In Fort Collins, the joint task force cobbled together consisting of the police, the county sheriff, and the National Guard begin working out a plan to block the major arteries in and out of the town to try to contain the violent residents of the town within its borders.

An Emergency Alert System message is broadcast warning all Fort Collins residents to stay in their homes, turn out all lights, and not to open their doors for anyone. Similar messages are being broadcast across the country. Kyle and Naomi are almost home in his Ford Explorer.

At 8:30, the President of the United States makes a speech to the American people authorizing martial law and handing the Department of Homeland Security control over all local law enforcement. Kyle and Naomi miss it. They've opted not to go to a movie after dinner as originally planned. Instead, Naomi tells Kyle she has a lot of tight muscles and needs to see her masseur, Sven.

Her decision to get to the sexy part of Date Night

early likely saves both of their lives. Kyle breaks several traffic laws getting home, and in no time, he has her lying face down, naked, on their bed. He methodically massages her from head to toe. He takes a painstaking amount of time pretending to be a professional masseur, whose accent he clearly lifted from the Swedish Chef on the Muppet Show. The professionalism (and the accent) ends when she turns over, opens her legs and pulls his head toward her. Kyle begins enthusiastically performing another kind of service for his randy wife.

At 10:00, pundits on MSNBC are blaming the riots on the Tea Party, the President is on Air Force One en route to a secure location, more than 100,000 people have died, and most of them re-animated, nationwide. Kyle and Naomi collapse in each other's arms in a sweaty heap, completely content and blissfully unaware of the epidemic or that it has spread out of Fort Collins and is working its way south. Hordes of the undead are coming north from Denver and trickling northeast out of Boulder.

In essence, Longview, considered a smallish city with just 80,000 people, is about to be surrounded. They don't know that their son and his friends are about to risk their lives trying to get to Kyle & Naomi's house. They don't know that a man named Jason Bowling, who will feature prominently in their future, is fighting for his life in his apartment building in Denver. Instead, they drift to sleep with orgasmic smiles on their faces. For them, Date Night has been a rousing success. For the rest of the world, it was the start of Armageddon.

KYLE'S EYES pop open at six the morning of the eighteenth. He has a deal with himself; on days where he wakes up early with no alarm, he MUST go out and run. He's not a perfect physical specimen, but at forty-three years old he does all right. He's run three marathons and has designs on a fourth. His best time is just under 4:30, but he feels like he has the potential for a 4:10. He rolls out of bed and reaches for his iPhone but realizes he left it in the charging station in the kitchen, having turned it off for date night. He grabs his iPod instead, puts on his running clothes, and after giving Naomi a gentle kiss on the forehead, he heads out the door.

He heads south to the end of his subdivision where the streets stop and farmland starts. He loves living on the edge of the small city, where you can still smell the cut hay before it gets baled. The air is fresher than in the center of town, still crisp in the mornings this early in the year. The street loops south past several vacant lots, left unused since the housing market collapsed in 2008, then winds through a couple of curves before turning back north. Here Kyle switches from the road to a concrete path. This loop adds a half mile to his run, but with little traffic, it lets him find his stride before he gets into the busier streets to the north of the Sunny Meadow subdivision where he and Naomi live.

His playlist leads off with "Savior" by Rise Against. It's a good song to start his run with, and he gets into his groove quickly. He's feeling good, so he pushes the pace and by the time the four-minute song is over, he's gone a half mile. He sees something out of the corner of his eye, and when he looks to his right, he sees three military helicopters speeding north, toward Loveland or Fort Collins. He's no expert on military vehicles, but even he recognizes that the lead two copters are Black-hawks and the one in the rear with the two rotors is a Chinook. The trio is moving very fast, he thinks, compared to normal air traffic he sees passing over the town.

He crosses Ninth Avenue to the strains of "Want You Bad" by The Offspring. The lyrics make him smile, reminding him of last night. He doesn't notice the suspicious lack of cars on the road. Even at this hour, there should be several cars on this stretch of Ninth but today there are none. He clocks one mile about a minute into "Rescue Me" by Buckcherry. He's making good time, having turned the first mile in about eight and a half minutes. The first mile is usually his slowest, so he thinks he'll finish his run in about fifty-three minutes total. *Yes,* he thinks, *I am totally doing another marathon this year. Maybe PF Chang's in September.*

Just over two miles into the run, he comes to Seven-teenth Avenue, turns west for a half mile, then turns back south on Price Street. This mile is uphill, so he shortens his stride a little and focuses on his breathing. He can feel his heart rate increase with the steepening incline. He passes a supermarket and the accompanying strip mall and out of habit, he glances down the eighteen-inch wide gap between the cinder block wall that marks the boundary of the receiving area behind the stores and the wooden fence that marks the edge of the housing development that butts against the commercial area. He has looked down this gap a thousand times on his runs, always wondering why it's there; who decided to leave this narrow boundary open to catch all manner of wind-blown trash? It's always littered with small cardboard boxes, newspapers, tumbleweeds, and a woman.

Wait, what was that? he thinks. *Did I just see what I think I saw?*

He stops, for the moment forgetting about the fast pace he's been running. He backtracks a few strides and looks down the small space between the two fences. Sure enough, there's a female figure in there, about twenty yards from the sidewalk. She has blood on her legs and seems to be wedged in between the fences. Kyle takes the headphone out of his right ear.

"Miss? Are you okay? Miss?" he calls out to her.

He sees her body stiffen. She pivots to her right to turn toward him. He notices that her shirt is torn open, and she has a bad chest wound. As she turns, Kyle can see that most of her left breast is missing, and several ribs are protruding from the left side of her chest. One of them gets stuck against a fence board and pulls away from her body as she turns, opening the hole in her chest a little wider. A blackish ooze runs down her abdomen.

At first, Kyle doesn't know what to think. Is it a costume? Is this a prank? Is she hurt? She didn't react to the sticking rib—and all logic dictates that she cannot be mobile if the wounds he sees are real, so he's leaning toward a prank. He glances around for cameras or people hiding and filming him but doesn't see anything of the sort.

"Miss, you look like you're hurt. If you're hurt I can call for help." He reaches for his iPhone but remembers that he left it at home. "Actually, I'll have to run for help. Can you tell me what happened?"

She begins to move toward him, walking awkwardly in the narrow space. At one point, she stumbles and scrapes the right side of her face on the cinder block wall, leaving a nasty strip of road rash on her cheek. Again, this doesn't seem to faze her. Kyle is beginning to have serious misgivings about this girl. He thinks she may be on meth. Her skin is gray and mottled with blackened veins, and she reminds him of the girls in the "Meth: Not Even Once" commercials that air on TV. Not that he's ever considered doing it, but those commercials have scared Kyle away from meth forever.

It's not until the girl is about ten yards away that she screams. It's a horrible, rasping sound that immediately reminds Kyle of someone screaming while breathing in rather than out. He starts backing away from the opening, and as he does so, she starts reaching her arms out toward him. He decides to do something he's good at: run. He puts about fifty yards between him and the opening in the two fences before he slows and looks back.

A few seconds pass, and the girl emerges from the gap in a stumble and regains her footing on the sidewalk. She turns her head and spots Kyle. She releases that hideous scream again and starts coming at him. Fast.

Kyle turns and starts running. He's able to run a mile at a sub-seven-minute pace, but that's about as far as he can go that quickly. After about a minute and a half, the run tracking application on his iPod interrupts the music in his headphones with its stilted, mechanical female voice. *Time: Twenty-three minutes. Distance: Two. Point. Seventy-five. Miles. Pace: Six minutes. Thirty seconds. Per mile. Workout average pace: Eight minutes. Nineteen seconds. Per mile.*

The pacing timer tells Kyle he just ran the last quarter mile at a 6:30 pace. He knows he can't keep that up for long. He steals a glance over his shoulder and sees the girl still coming, only she's closed the distance from fifty to about thirty yards. Kyle is baffled. Whatever she's on, clearly it makes her oblivious to pain, but there's no way she should be able to keep this pace up with a rib sticking out of her chest. He forces himself to go a little faster.

Time: Twenty-four minutes. Twenty-six. Seconds.

Distance: Three. Point Zero. Miles. Pace: Five minutes. Forty-five seconds. Per mile. Workout average pace: Eight minutes. Fifteen seconds. Per mile.

Kyle can hear his heart beating in his ears. His last quarter mile was sub-six minutes. He's never run at a sub-six pace before, let alone uphill, and his lungs are burning. His legs are hurting, and he knows he can't keep this up much longer, but a glance over his shoulder tells him the girl has closed the gap to about fifteen yards.

How can this be possible? he thinks, and he forces his legs to move a little faster. He's nearing the top of the hill and can see the stoplight at Ninth Avenue. There's a telephone/DSL control box at the corner; maybe, if he makes it there, he can keep it between the two of them so he can catch his breath.

Time: Twenty-five minutes. Forty-five seconds. Distance: Three. Point. Twenty-five. Miles. Pace: Five minutes. Fifteen seconds. Per mile. Workout average pace: Seven minutes. Fifty-five seconds. Per mile.

The corner is only a few hundred yards away now, but Kyle can feel the girl closing in. She must be within about twenty feet of him. He's focused on the big silver box with the phone company's logo on it when a police car roars into view, making a hard left turn off of Ninth Avenue and onto Price Street. The driver hits the gas and points the car directly at Kyle. A voice comes over the car's loudspeaker, startling him.

"Keep running," the voice commands him. "Do not slow down and do not change directions!"

Kyle listens to the man and keeps going as fast as he can. He is out of gas, though, and that big silver box is the limit of his increasingly rubbery legs' ability to sprint like this.

The car roars past him, missing him by two feet. He hears a thump as the car's tires hop up onto the sidewalk just behind him, and then another thump that he can only assume is the car hitting the woman a nanosecond after that. Then the police car is braking hard, stopping, and backing up. It grinds to a halt a couple of seconds later.

Kyle makes it to the four-and-a-half-foot-tall silver box and turns around to see what's happening behind him. The girl has been hit by the police car, and her broken body is contorted in directions the human body is not meant to bend. Her right leg is completely severed, and her left has a ninety-degree sideways bend at the knee. Her spine has to be broken as well, based on the angle of the new joint in the middle of her back. Kyle can't believe it, but her arms are still working, dragging her battered form toward him while her jaw snaps at the air.

The passenger door opens, and the cop gets out. He walks over to the girl, draws his gun and fires a shot into the back of her head. The body convulses once and lies still. Kyle, partly from the exertion and partly from the scene he's just witnessed, throws up. The cop walks over to him, gun still drawn, trigger finger resting on the slide.

"Sir, are you okay?" he asks.

"Yes. I think so. Have to. Catch breath," he says, gasping for air.

"Are you bit?" the cop asks.

"Am I bit?" Kyle doesn't know why the cop would want to know that. *Well, she was kind of like a mad dog; maybe she had rabies,* he thinks and then says, "No, I'm not bit."

"Good, because if you get bit, it's game over," the cop says, holstering his pistol. "What the hell are you doing out? Haven't you seen the news?"

"No," Kyle says. "It was date night."

The cop ignores the last comment and is interrupted by his radio.

"Paul 207 what is your twenty?" the voice on the radio says. Longview police designate their unit number with "Paul" for patrolman, unlike the Fort Collins police department who just go by their unit number.

The cop presses the button on his mic. "Paul 207 and Paul 220, Ninth and Price, Code 2. Subject code black." Code 2 indicates that they've made contact with the person they sought, and like the Fort Collins police, code black means the subject is dead.

"Copy Paul 207. Next contact; subject seen at Seventeenth and Alpen View. Green shirt and red hat."

He clicks the button again. "Paul 207 en route," he says. The police cruiser backs up next to the cop, who turns his attention back to Kyle.

"How far to your house?"

Kyle points east on Ninth Avenue. "About a mile and a half that way."

"We'd give you a ride, but we have another one of"—here he gestures with his thumb at the body on the ground behind him—"*these* fuckers to deal with. Listen to me; get home as quick as you can. Turn on the fucking news and get caught up on what's happening. Lock the doors, pull the shades, and don't do anything to draw attention to your house. Turn off your sprinklers. Turn off your light timers. If you have a gun, load it and be ready to use it. DO NOT go near these fuckers, do not offer to help them, do not try to talk to them. Whatever they've got has shut off their brains and all they do is attack and bite. And if you get bit, you're done; you become one of them. You read me?"

Kyle reads him but is having a hard time reconciling what he's just been told with what, until a few minutes ago, was a reality where people with massive injuries don't outrun uninjured people, police don't run those people down, and they definitely don't tell the town's residents to barricade in their homes and load up their guns. Out loud he says, "So you're saying these are zombies?"

"I didn't say that. I don't know what the fuck they are. Call 'em what you want, just don't get near them. We have to go—oh, and one more thing; to stop them you have to hit them in the head! You saw the damage she took," again he jerks his thumb at the twisted body behind him, "and was still coming for you. You gotta hit the head."

With that, the cop slides into the cruiser and the car speeds away to its next encounter.

With adrenaline pumping through his system like nitrous oxide in a street racer's car, Kyle has no problem running a sub-seven-minute pace all the way home.

CHAPTER 2

Fort Collins. Friday, May 17th, 2013, 8 PM - Zpoc plus 90 minutes

Danielle sits on the couch crying while Toni consoles her. Keith leans on the kitchen counter and watches the video he took of the zombies attacking and eating the policeman. Andy looks over Keith's shoulder.

"That's disgusting. I never want to see that again," Natalie says as she takes a glass of water to the sobbing girl on the couch.

Keith rolls his eyes and pockets his phone.

"Dude," he says to Ben, "we need to find out what the hell is happening. Let's check the TV." He looks at the girls on the couch and adds, "In my room."

The three guys make their way upstairs. Ben signals to Toni what they're doing, and she nods. In Keith's room, he has the TV on and turns it to one of the Denver news channels. The anchor has a graphic that reads "RIOTS" over his shoulder. The word "riots" has a cartoonish brown beer bottle breaking on it. He's in mid-sentence when the speakers on the TV come to life.

"... *again are asking people to stay in their homes, lock their doors and draw as little attention to themselves as possible. If you're not seriously injured you should not try to get to any of the area hospitals, as they are running over capacity, and they're asking people to avoid calling 911 unless it's absolutely necessary.*"

Keith clicks a button on the remote and switches to another channel.

"... *similar activity has been reported across the country. Governor Hickenlooper has mobilized the Colorado National Guard to augment the police forces trying to deal with this unprecedented level of civil unrest.*"

The video cuts to stock footage of Guardsmen loading gear into a Humvee. The anchor's voice runs over the stock video.

"*The United States has about 400,000 members in the Air and Army National Guard units, and it is expected that all of them will be called up by the state governors before this is over.*"

The video switches to Governor Hickenlooper in what looks like a hallway at the state capitol.

"*Our primary concern is the safety and health of the people of Colorado. Therefore, I'm issuing orders to all members of the Colorado National Guard to report for* duty. Our local police departments have called up all their officers, and they're doing all they can, but this has gotten so big there just aren't enough of them to go around."

Keith changes channels, this time to FoxNews. It's the top of the hour, and Greta Van Susteren is taking over from Sean Hannity. They've caught her in mid-sentence.

"... around the globe," she says.

The screen starts splitting into different views as she goes through a list.

"London."

The upper-left part of the screen shows a mélange of people on a darkened street, running and fighting. It's not immediately obvious in the small image, but individual people are being tackled by groups of attackers. The three boys watching know too well what happens next.

"Paris."

Greta goes on, and another section of the screen shows a similar scene.

"Berlin. Buenos Aires. San Jose. New York, Washington DC, Beijing, Moscow, Delhi, Melbourne, Manila—the list goes on and on. Masses of people have been rioting for more than an hour and a half, and no one knows why, no one knows how this was so coordinated, and no one knows how many have been hurt or killed. Hospitals everywhere are overrun with victims, riots have destroyed some medical facilities, and police and other first responders are just not able to keep up.

The President, we're told, will be speaking about this situation at 10:30 PM Eastern Time. Now, let's go to ..."

The boys are startled by a screech from the TV as the Emergency Alert System begins a broadcast. The screen goes black and "EAS" flashes across the top of the screen. The overbearing voice blasts at them.

"This is a broadcast of the Emergency Alert System. Authorities in your area have issued the following emergency warning. All residents of Fort Collins, Colorado, and surrounding communities are urged to stay indoors due to pockets of civil unrest occurring throughout the city. Residents should remain indoors with their doors locked. Do not open your doors to anyone you do not know or anyone who appears to be violent. Police are working in conjunction with the Larimer County Sheriff's Department to gain control of the affected areas. Local National Guard units, at the request of the governor, are mobilizing to assist in containing the situation."

The voice stops, and then the screeching noise repeats and the message begins to play again. Keith hits mute on the remote.

"What did it say?" Toni asks from the doorway.

The three boys jump at her interruption.

"Goddammit, Toni!" Keith exclaims. "You scared the shit out of me! We need to put a fucking bell on you or something so we know you're coming."

"Dick," she says, giving him a look. She turns to Ben. "We heard that God-awful emergency alert noise downstairs but couldn't understand what the warning said."

"Stay indoors, the police, sheriffs and National Guard are controlling the situation," Ben says.

"Like they controlled the situation over at Moby?" she exclaims. "They're not controlling shit! They're getting slaughtered!"

"Babe ..." Ben starts to say.

"Don't 'babe' me, Ben! We just watched a cop get EATEN! Watts was torn to pieces, somehow still able to walk, and screaming that horrible sounding scream! Danielle is just now getting herself under control, and I think all of us are in a state of shock. We can't get any calls out, either. We're scared, Ben! What are we going to do?"

The EAS alert is over, and Keith changes the channel to another local station and unmutes the sound. The anchor is talking while a map of Colorado displays on the screen. It has red dots pulsing over Fort Collins, several over the Denver metropolitan area, Colorado Springs, Pueblo, and Grand Junction on the western slope of the state.

"As you can see on this graphic, the affected areas are all the larger cities along the front range, and cities with interstate access running through them. The I-25 and I-70 corridors are, for the most part, affected, and on the Western Slope, Grand Junction is experiencing this violence as well. Whatever is driving this series of attacks has so far stayed out of the mountain communities, with no reports of violence in towns like Aspen and

Vail, and so far smaller cities to the north like Loveland, Longview, and Greeley seem to be fairly calm."

Keith mutes the TV again. "Let's get the fuck out of Dodge," he says.

Ben considers this for a moment. "We were headed home tomorrow anyway," he says, and then pauses for a second, thinking. "I'm sure the folks wouldn't mind if we brought a few more people. Not with all this shit going on." He looks at Toni. "What do you think?"

"Let's ask the others," she says. "But if it gets us out of here, away from those whacked-out people, I'm all for it."

Keith turns the TV off, and they all go downstairs to the living room. Danielle has stopped crying and looks over as they file down the stairs.

"So what is it?" she asks.

Ben takes a deep breath. "Well, there's good and bad news. They're saying that this," he gestures east, toward the campus, toward where they just came from, "these riots or whatever they are, are going on all over the place."

"Worldwide," Keith interjects.

"Right," Ben says. "It's global. But they're saying that it's focused on the bigger cities. They just said on Channel Nine that Longview hasn't been affected yet."

"Yet. But it will be," Danielle says.

"We don't know that," Keith says. "They're calling in the National Guard. I'm sure they'll get this under control. There's a Guard armory in Longview. I bet they're geared up and get this back to normal in no time."

"Keith, we just watched people kill and eat a cop," Danielle replies. "Rioters don't do that. Watts was torn to pieces but was still moving. That's not normal. Christ, Ben ran over one of them, and it just started pulling itself along with its arms, like nothing happened. I'm no expert, but that's NOT normal rioter behavior. That's not even normal HUMAN behavior." Danielle is getting upset again and once more on the verge of tears.

Ben speaks up again. "Look, we don't have a lot of information, but based on the news, Longview hasn't been affected, neither has Loveland or Greeley. We think Longview is our best bet. It's a few miles away from I-25 and close to the mountains, and according to the news, those are both good things." He gestures at Keith. "Our folks are there. They'll have an idea of what to do." He turns to the others. "My dad's neighbor is a big survivalist nut. He'll for sure have some ideas on what to do and where to go."

"Oh, yeah—Danny!" Keith says. "Danny can arm the whole lot of us! He's been hooking dad up with all kinds of shit as payment from when he fixed that financial fraud deal! Shit, I forgot about him. Done deal, let's go!"

"I'm graduating tomorrow!" Danielle protests. "I'm supposed to be on a plane to San Diego Sunday! I'm not going to head off to Longview on some stupid hunch you have."

She reaches for the remote to turn on the TV.

"What are they saying about California?" she asks. "Is this happening there too?"

"We didn't see anything about California," Ben says.

"So how do we know there are any problems there?"

"Try calling your folks," Keith says to her.

"I've been trying. All circuits are busy."

"That's a pretty big sign that things are fucked, Danielle," Keith says. "The phone lines are overloaded because everyone's trying to call their families to check on them. They didn't say 'it's affecting every major city in the world *except* the one you're running away to.'"

"No," she says. "I'm too close. I just fucking finished school! I'm supposed to be starting my LIFE after graduation tomorrow! This isn't fucking fair!"

"Well, you can do whatever you want. I'm not going to end up like Watts. I'm going to Longview," Keith declares.

"Let's vote on it," Ben says. "I don't want to force anyone to do anything, not when it could be life or death. Everyone for going to Longview?" He holds up his hand. So do Keith, Andy, and Toni. After a minute, Natalie raises her hand.

"I'm not staying here alone," she says.

"Well, if you're all going to abandon me, I guess I have no choice," Danielle says.

"You have a choice. If you come with us, though, don't bitch the whole time," Keith says.

"Fuck you, Keith! I should have broken up with—" Danielle starts.

"Okay, it's settled. We're going," Ben says, cutting her off before she starts an argument with Keith. "Let's grab the stuff we want to take and get moving. I don't think we should waste any time."

"At least I have clothes here to pack," Danielle says.

Ben looks at Toni and Natalie. "We'll pack the stuff you all have here," he says, referring to the drawer each of them has in the boys' respective rooms for nights when they stay over "unexpectedly." They each have some of the essentials—clean underwear, hair ties, t-shirts, toothbrushes, and other critical sundries— stored in the apartment. Ben continues, "And you two grab some food and water from the kitchen. When we get going, we'll see how it looks out there, and if it's clear we'll go by your places and get a real bag packed, okay?"

The girls agree, and the guys and Danielle all go to pack their bags. Toni grabs Natalie, and they hit the kitchen, getting bottled water from the fridge and some protein and cereal bars from the cabinets. It's only forty-five minutes to an hour from the apartment to Ben's and Keith's parents' houses, but Toni doesn't want to take chances on getting stuck somewhere and letting thirst or hunger cause them to make a bad decision. Natalie agrees, and they get the essentials packed in red and blue plastic milk crates and wait for the others to come down so they can start their exodus.

CHAPTER 3

In Denver, Colorado, Jason "D-Day" Bowling returns to his apartment building just after 6:30 PM and goes straight into a hot shower to wash the dirt from a hard day's labor off his tired body. He stays in the shower for a full thirty minutes. After returning from Afghanistan in 2012 and getting his discharge papers, he's never missed a chance to take a long, hot shower. It's a luxury he seldom had in his deployments.

Jason had been deployed to Iraq almost a year to the day after enlisting in the US Army. He served a tour in 2004, back-to-back tours from 2006 through 2008, and then deployed to Afghanistan in 2010, where he stayed until 2012. His unit's base had been relocated from Fort Hood in Texas to Colorado's Fort Carson as part of a reorganization in 2009, so that's where he returned. What time he'd been able to spend in Colorado outside of his deployments convinced him to remain there after his discharge, but the recession has taken its toll on the job market, and Jason is working for a landscaping company until he can find something better.

The apartment is quite nice, just off of Denver's Park Avenue, and it would normally be out of his price range, but after ten years in the military with no wife or family and no real expenses, he'd saved a lot of money. He plans on riding out his lease here and finding something cheaper in the fall. For now, though, he enjoys the south facing view from his living room window. From his tenth-floor vantage point, he can see downtown Denver and the Rocky Mountains beyond it.

He gets out of the shower just past 7:00, throws on jeans and a t-shirt, and puts dinner in the microwave. That's another thing he doesn't miss about the Army— the food. The frozen dinners he microwaves are ten times better than the Army food he's eaten for just shy of a decade. He grabs an India pale ale from the fridge and takes dinner over to the little table he has set up by the windows. It's about an hour and a half before sundown and Jason loves watching the transformation as the huge buildings downtown cast the streets into shadow and the buildings themselves slowly light up as the sun descends behind the mountains to the west.

As he eats, he notices a lot of emergency vehicles going in and out of the downtown area. His apartment is only a mile from the massive medical complex that houses Children's Hospital, Presbyterian St. Luke's

Medical Center, and the Exempla St. Joseph Hospital, so he's used to seeing a fair amount of emergency traffic, but this appears to be worse than normal. He turns on the TV and sees an emergency alert scrolling across the bottom of the screen. It's in the middle of a sentence when he starts reading it.

... 16TH STREET MALL and the surrounding area. Denver police are asking that people stay out of the area for their protection, and people in the area should remain sheltered in place and stay where they are until it is safe to leave. The wounded are being taken to Presbyterian St. Luke's Medical Center. Anyone searching for a friend or relative who has been taken away by ambulance should contact them at the following numbers...

THE MESSAGE STARTS over at this point.

DENVER POLICE HAVE CONFIRMED that a civil disturbance in downtown Denver has resulted in multiple fatalities this evening, including several people who were shot by the police. Multiple policemen have been injured and the violence continues to rage through the 16th Street Mall and the surrounding area. Denver police ...

THE PHONE RINGS, interrupting Jason's train of thought. He picks it up and scowls at the caller ID. Fort Carson.

He presses the button. "Bowling," he says, using his last name out of habit.

"D-Day?" the voice on the other end of the line says. Jason recognizes the voice—Martha Cowher. They've had a few flings together here and there over the last ten years, though her feelings ran much deeper than his did. Like him, she's unmarried and happy that way—mostly—but unlike him, she'll never leave the Army if given a choice. They parted on good enough terms, although he knows she's pissed that when he was offered the chance to get out, he took it. He feels guilty he hasn't called her since getting out, but he's trying to forget a lot of bad things, and she'll never understand or believe that it's not all about her.

"Hey, Mar, yeah, it's me. It's good to hear your voice!" *This can't be good*, he thinks to himself.

"I'm just going to get right to it, D-Day. They're recalling everyone, and before you say 'I've completed my full-term of service,' an emergency session of Congress has authorized this. They want you—everyone, not just you—to report immediately. This call serves as your official notice. If you're not here by 8 AM tomorrow, you'll be considered AWOL." She says all this with a flat official tone. Jason—D-Day since an early age, owing to his birth on June sixth—can tell she's reading from a script.

"Mar, what's going on? Does this have anything to

do with the stuff happening downtown? If the cops can't deal with it, isn't that what the National Guard is for? The regular army doesn't get involved in domestic stuff."

She didn't answer his question. "Just do yourself a favor and get down here ASAP. I have other calls to make, D-Day. Just get here."

He looks at the phone as the connection goes dead. He has a familiar, but unwelcome, feeling in the pit of his stomach. It's the same feeling he got in Afghanistan before his unit's last mission went all FUBAR. It's the same feeling that made him pull his lieutenant behind a cement barrier just before the homicide bomber flipped his switch and turned himself and fourteen other people—including three in D-Day's patrol—into red mist at the checkpoint in Iraq. It's the same feeling that kept him alive multiple times in combat, the feeling that told him things were about to get really, really bad.

He looks out the window and from the elevated vantage point, he can see that the amount of flashing emergency lights traveling up Eighteenth Avenue toward the medical complex has increased at least tenfold. He turns back to the TV and turns on the local NBC station. The info screen says the show should be Dateline, but the reporter on screen is local to Denver and is reporting from downtown.

"WE'VE BEEN TOLD *that the riots are spreading out*

from Sixteenth Street throughout the lower downtown, or Lo-Do, area. The police have confirmed that they've seen people getting attacked by groups of five or six assailants, and a short while later these same victims have actually joined the mob in attacking others. We even saw what looked like policemen in one of the mobs before we were told in no uncertain terms to move to another spot for our safety."

THEY TOLD them to get the fuck out of there, D-Day thinks. He mutes the TV and grabs his binoculars from the bag in his bedroom. He trains them toward downtown, and though he can't see directly to the Sixteenth Street Pedestrian Mall, he can see between the buildings enough to glimpse some of the cross streets. He sees pandemonium—people running through the streets, cars driving up onto sidewalks or even driving backwards to get out of traffic. He sees a yellow Hummer H2 pushing vehicles out of the way as it tries to get clear of an intersection. The feeling in the pit of his stomach gets worse.

He goes back into the bedroom and changes out of his jeans and into a pair of khaki cargo pants and tan tactical boots, a tight-fitting polyester undershirt and a black long-sleeved shirt over that. Now dressed in more combat-ready clothing, he checks out the window again.

He sees people running down the street going from east to west. Cars going by are driving way too fast, and he sees one clip a pedestrian. The car doesn't stop, and the three people running behind the pedestrian pounce on him and attack him mercilessly. D-Day sees blood spurt from a wound into the face of one of the assailants, who doesn't notice or slow his attack.

From the corner of his eye, he sees the TV flash to the Emergency Alert System message, and he unmutes it right at the end of the irritating, braying noise.

"THIS IS a broadcast of the Emergency Alert System. Authorities in your area have issued the following emergency warning. Civil disturbances and riots are taking place in downtown Denver and cities across the greater Denver Metropolitan Area. All people living in or near downtown Denver or any of the affected areas are urged to remain indoors with the doors locked. Do not open your doors to anyone you do not know or anyone who appears to be violent. Police are working in multi-jurisdictional task forces to gain control of the affected areas. Local National Guard units, at the request of the governor, have begun mobilizing to assist in containing the situation."

D-DAY MUTES the TV again and goes back to the window. The three men who were attacking the pedestrian have moved on to attack someone else directly in front of his building. In the waning light, D-Day can see a massive pool of blood under the pedestrian. He trains his binoculars on the victim. He sees a hideous, ragged neck wound from where much of the blood has poured forth. Other equally vicious wounds are peppered up and down his arms and chest. D-Day has seen enough carnage in Iraq and Afghanistan to recognize a dead body when he sees one.

Except, this man isn't dead. Despite the ragged hole in his neck, despite the spreading pool of blood that screams out "this guy is dead," the dead man twitches. First his legs move, and then his arms and then he opens his eyes. His mouth opens, and he coughs out a black, oily glob, and then sits up. His eyes are little more than black orbs. The man rises and spots the three people who attacked him. He sprints— sprints!—over to them and momentarily joins them in savaging the body of a young woman. Mere seconds later, in unison, they all stand up and look around. They spot a young hipster running to the gated pool area of the building across the street. The four of them give chase, bringing the young man down before he can get his ID card in the gate's lock.

D-Day looks to the east, toward the hospitals, and sees people like these, some in hospital gowns, barefoot, some in scrubs, here an EMT, over there a policeman. All are covered in blood, all bearing hideous wounds, all of them looking for people to attack.

He looks back to the woman who was attacked on the grassy area in front of his building. She's wobbling to her feet, leaving a bloody pool behind her. She has a wounded leg which doesn't allow her to move with the speed of the others, but she still moves with surprising agility for someone who should be dead.

D-Day thinks through his options. He knows he's not going to make it to Fort Carson tonight. As if to punctuate that point, a Ford Taurus comes speeding the wrong way up Twentieth Avenue and hits a group of five of the bloodied assailants. The driver loses control trying to make the sharp turn and sideswipes an older Nissan pickup. The pickup spins nearly 360 degrees, and then the driver rights its course and hits the gas. The Taurus appears to have stalled, and a crowd of attackers descends on it. An elderly man in a hospital gown is pounding on the driver's side window, his IV tubes flailing around wildly, not caring that his bare ass is hanging out in the breeze.

D-Day knows the AR-15 he has in the closet and the few thousand rounds of ammunition he has on hand will not be enough to fight through this growing crowd, not with the speeds at which they're moving. He grabs his phone, scrolls through his contacts, finds one and hits send. He's greeted with a message stating that all circuits are busy, try again later. He hangs up and hits the number again. Again, all circuits are busy. He continues to watch the carnage unfold outside his window. Finally, on the tenth try, the phone rings.

"D-Day, I don't have time for this," Martha says, already irritated as soon as she answers. "I've got about a thousand calls to make and it's getting harder and harder to get through to people."

"Zombies, really?" he asks. "Because that's what

they look like to me. Is this why they want everyone back? Why didn't you say something before? And I have news for you. I'm not going to make it out of here. Not tonight, not in one piece, Cowher. They can list me as AWOL if they want, but if I try to get down there tonight, they'll be listing me as KIA."

"D-Day—Jason—they're not telling us everything, I'm sure, but we're mounting a counterattack right now. We have squads out in the Springs as we speak, and when I'm done here, I have to help load out the trucks for resupply and reinforcement. If things go to plan, we'll be hitting Denver by morning. Hang tight and do what you can where you are. We'll get there, and you can link up with us then."

He ponders for a moment that there are regular army troops on the streets of Colorado Springs right now. This is unprecedented. But then, so is what he's witnessed in the streets outside his building. "How big is this, Cowher? And please tell me this isn't something WE started."

She pauses for a long second before replying. "I'm not authorized to say anything; you should know that. But ... it's massive. Global. And no, it's not ours, at least not that I've been told. I've told you more than I should. I have to go. Jason—please be careful. Hopefully, I'll see you in the next day or so." She hangs up without saying goodbye. Either that or the line cut out; either way, she's gone, leaving D-Day alone with his thoughts.

The last time she called him Jason was more than a

year ago in Afghanistan, when she was the driver on what was supposed to be a non-combat supply run, and they were caught in an ambush. Alone and outnumbered, she had been convinced they were going to die. She was not combat seasoned like D-Day and the others with them, but she was brave and fought as well as could be expected. Their situation was dire, though, and there was no way she was going die without telling him she loved him, and there was no way she was going to tell him she loved him using his nickname. Of course, they lived, and he didn't reciprocate her feelings, not in the way she wanted. While he liked her company and found her easy to talk to and fun to be with—and he *definitely* enjoyed being intimate with her—he just didn't feel the same gravitational pull toward her that she felt toward him. After that things became awkward between them.

Now she'd used his given name again. Twice. It's like a "tell" in poker. It's her subconscious way of dealing with a serious, life-threatening situation. She's stiffer, more formal. *It must be even worse than I think it is,* he says to himself. *And I'm thinking this is pretty damned bad. Maybe it's an extinction-level event. Well, I'll be as ready as I can.* With that cheerful thought bouncing around his head, he goes to his bedroom to do something he never thought he'd have to do again; prepare for combat.

CHAPTER 4

Fort Collins, Colorado. Friday, May 17th, 2013; 8:30 PM

The FJ Cruiser weaves its way down Shields Street, navigating around abandoned cars and undead bodies. The undead fly at the side of the old SUV with wild abandon, bouncing off with a loud thud every time. There are bloody streaks on some of the windows, where ruined body parts have slid across the glass while gore-covered fingers try to find purchase.

Whether they're getting used to it or are just desensitized, the noises no longer bother the six people inside the vehicle. After the first few elicited screams from some of the occupants—notably Danielle—once they realized that the tough old Toyota was capable of navigating the melee around them, they settled down and either kept their eyes away from the windows or stared out of them with morbid curiosity.

All along the stretch of Shields from the campus south, the undead have been busy running people down, attacking them, and turning them into creatures like themselves. One sorority house has the door ripped from its hinges; blood-covered coeds roam around both in and out of the house. The lights are all on, and the carnage inside is plain to see for those driving past.

The group decided to take the main route out of town, thinking that it would be the fastest. They didn't think there'd be as many crashed and abandoned cars as there are, but they're already several blocks into the journey, so Ben keeps the FJ pointed south.

The vehicle approaches the intersection of Shields and Horsetooth where, a few hours earlier, a delivery van dropped two of its human vectors of death at a graduation party. Ben, Keith, and the rest of the group have no idea that it was the same van that stopped by their party. For that matter, they don't know that Saji Masun Safar, using his Facebook alias "Brian Hansen," found and targeted the party because multiple people had been posting about it and said he should come. This party was the first location to experience the living dead, and it is the one the police had responded to first. All officers reporting to this site were killed.

As they draw near to the intersection, Ben sees hundreds of the undead swarming the parking lot of the apartment complex, the green spaces in between the buildings, and even on the balconies of the upper units.

"Check it out," Keith says, pointing to the parking lot. "They're swarming the cop cars."

They can see what he's talking about. There's about thirty of them surrounding and climbing on one of the empty cruisers that sits with its overhead lights still running. As they watch, the horde pulls the light bar off of the car and the lights go dark. With no lights flashing, the undead begin wandering away.

"They're attracted to the lights!" Keith exclaims.

"So? What does that matter?" Natalie asks.

"Well, it's probably good to know what draws them, so we know how NOT to draw them," he replies.

"Like it matters in the world's loudest vehicle," Natalie says. She's scared and tense, and Andy gives him a subtle head shake, so Keith holds his tongue.

Ben turns off the headlights in response to Keith's observation. Natalie's right too; the FJ is loud. The street starts to slope downhill, so Ben pushes in the clutch and lets the big vehicle coast, letting the engine idle. For the next quarter mile, they pick up speed. He coasts through the intersection with only a handful of the horrible creatures taking notice. They give chase for a few seconds but lose sight of the vehicle and turn their attention to other things. The slope begins to lessen, and when the FJ starts to slow, Ben lets the clutch out and gives it gas.

South of Horsetooth the population thins out, with a long stretch of open fields on the west side of the road and mostly churches and businesses giving way to single-family homes on the east side. While they still see the occasional zombie, they don't see the hordes like they did back in the center of town, so he keeps his foot on the gas. Toni, from the passenger seat, sees people peeking out of their windows then closing the blinds or curtains after they had their curiosity satisfied.

They cross Harmony Road, which marks the edge of town. Only one subdivision remains, and then there's only open space for a few miles until they'll hit the north end of Loveland; which, according to the last news reports has not been affected by the violence yet. With no street lights illuminating the road, Ben turns the headlights on again.

The mood in the car lightens as they see the lights of the city fading away behind them.

"Yeah, buddy!" Keith reaches up and grabs Ben's shoulder, giving him a shake. "We made it out of crazy town!"

Even Danielle smiles now, the weight of the horrors she's witnessed left behind them with the zombies.

"What the hell ..." Ben says, trailing off at the end of his question as he tries to decipher what lies in the road ahead of them. There's a massive shape in the middle of the road, just out of reach of their headlights. Everyone squints into the darkness ahead, trying to see what it is. *It looks like a huge rock,* Ben thinks. *No, it's—*

A second later, the interior of the Toyota is awash in light and Ben is blinded by a spotlight blasting them in the face. He hits the brakes and brings the beast to a lurching stop in front of a pair of vehicles, one a full-sized Humvee and the other an MRAP, though Ben doesn't know that acronym. He's just focused on the huge gun in the turret on top, which is pointing its barrel at them. The hole in the end of the barrel looks massive, and Ben can only imagine the damage the bullets coming out of that thing would do to them.

Several figures rush up to the car on both sides with rifles trained on different spots on the vehicle. One of them raises his M4 and points it at Ben.

"Out of the car, NOW!" the man yells. Either the light has dimmed, or Ben's eyes have adjusted to it because now he can see that the man is wearing Army fatigues. He can't read the patches on the man's shirt, but with the muzzle of the gun trained on his face, Ben isn't going to ask a lot of questions.

"NOW!" the soldier repeats.

Ben pulls the door handle and pushes it open.

"Hands where I can see them!" the man shouts as he takes a step back from the opening door.

Ben raises his hands in the air and pivots in the seat. He glances back at a terrified Toni and smiles at her, trying to be reassuring, then hops out of the SUV. His feet touch down on the pavement, and a trio of gunshots rip through the night.

Toni screams but cuts it short when she realizes that Ben has not been shot.

"It was hanging onto the ladder on the back door," says the soldier who fired his gun. The name patch on his uniform reads "Bentley."

Ben opens his eyes, which he involuntarily shut when the shots rang out. Lying on the ground by the rear tire is a dead (again) woman. She's leaking black ooze from holes in her neck and head.

"Oh, Jesus, that stinks," Bentley says, wrinkling his nose in disgust. "These things are disgusting."

"Stow that, Bentley, and get that thing off the road," the man who ordered Ben to get out of the car says. He turns back to Ben, and as he does, Ben can see his name is Ordonez. "What the hell are you doing out and about, kid? Don't you know martial law has been declared? We could have just mowed you down and not thought twice about it!"

"Thanks for ... um, *not* doing that. Mister ... Ordonez," Ben stammers.

"Stow that 'Mister Ordonez' bullshit. It's Lieutenant Ordonez, but don't get used to that either. There's a mandatory curfew in effect, or had you not heard? We have very strict instructions. No one gets past this point. No one leaves the city. Now, get back in your vehicle, turn around and go back home or where ever you came from."

"Lieutenant, you can't make us do that," Ben pleads. They were so close to getting out! He can't drag the group back through all that carnage. Danielle is barely holding it together, and the others aren't doing much better. Except for Keith, who seems to be taking it all in stride. "You haven't seen what we went through to get here. You can't ask us to go back through that. We won't make it. You have to let us through."

"What's your name, son?" Ordonez asks.

"Ben."

"I have orders, *Ben*," Ordonez says with a heavy inflection on "Ben." "These orders are very specific: Do. Not. Let. Anyone. Leave. Fort. Collins. Can you guess what I'm not going to do?"

"Let anyone leave Fort Collins?" Ben says with more than a trace of sarcasm, his patience wearing thin as the man condescends to him.

"You're smarter than you look, Ben. Get back in your vehicle, turn around and go back the way you came. Do it now, before I lose my patience with you and your frat pack." Ordonez gestures at the group looking through the windshield at them.

"Please," Ben says. "You're sending us back to die!"

"NO MORE DISCUSSION!" Ordonez points a finger at the Toyota while he yells. "Get in your vehicle, NOW. I need to see taillights fading in thirty seconds or Sullivan gets to let the fifty take over the conversation!" Ordonez retracts his finger and jerks his thumb over his shoulder.

Ben follows the thumb to the soldier standing in the turret of the MRAP with the .50-caliber machine gun trained on the Toyota. Ben turns, gets back in the FJ Cruiser, starts the engine, and pulls the old SUV into a Y-turn. Without looking back, he starts heading north on Shields, back toward the mouths of the monsters.

BENTLEY APPROACHES ORDONEZ. "Sir, we could have let them through. The kid was right, we just sent them back to their deaths."

"I didn't ask your opinion, Bentley. You know our orders. If one of them were bit, we'd be unleashing this on the next city. I don't want that on my head. Do you want it on yours?"

"No sir, it's just ..." Bentley hesitates. As a National Guardsman he's not used to blindly following orders outside of his two-weeks-a-year, one-weekend-a-month duties with the guard. "We could have inspected them, only let the ones through without bites. They made it through all that crap in town ..."

"Are you a medical expert, Bentley? Because I'm not. I don't know the difference between a scratch from an infected versus a scratch from a rusty nail. Do you? Do they need a tetanus shot or bullet to the brain, Bentley? If one of them was injured, would you know whether they were infected? Maybe in some people, it takes a while. Maybe they make it to Loveland, or Longview before they go gray, and then we've lost the only uninfected cities on the front range."

Bentley looks unconvinced.

"Look, I get it, Bentley," Ordonez continues dressing him down. "This is a fucked-up situation. Neither of us," he gestures to the other men watching them, "and none of them ever imagined this is what we'd be called up to do. But here we are, so let me make it simple. We have orders. No one leaves Fort Collins. The orders are clear, the orders are simple, and we will follow those orders until we're dead, the orders change, or we are relieved. If you can't do that, you'll end up next to your friend there." Ordonez points to the dead woman Bentley has pushed off the road. "You got me, Bentley?"

"Yes, sir!" Bentley replies.

"Good. End of discussion. Man. Your. Post." Ordonez turns to the man running the spotlight. "Sweep the fields, check for movement."

Bentley sighs and goes back to his assigned position while the spotlight searches around the fields on either side of the road, looking for anyone—living or dead—trying to sneak past their position.

IN THE TOYOTA, Toni is furious.

"These guys work for *us*, dammit! How can they refuse to allow us to leave?" she asks.

Ben can't tell if the question is rhetorical or not, so he answers.

"All I can tell you is that if I pushed him any further, he was going to have the guy in the huge truck-thing open up on us with that giant gun. No way was I going to see if he was bluffing."

"But this means that all the other exits out of town are gonna be blocked too," Keith says.

"The main ones, yeah, probably. But the side roads, maybe not. I don't know how many Army guys they have up here. Andy, did you bring that night vision thing you used in the paintball free-for-all-in March?" Ben inquires.

"Yeah, but it's super cheap, dude. You can only see about thirty, maybe fifty feet with it at the most," Andy replies.

"That will have to be enough. Get it out," Ben says. They're getting back into zombie territory. He notices that the larger crowds of the dead have moved a few blocks farther south, so either the population of undead is getting larger or, like mice following the Pied Piper, they followed their earlier path south on Shields. Or a combination of both.

"Everyone hang on," he says. "This is going to get bumpy."

CHAPTER 5

D-Day's Building, Denver

There are now hundreds of zombies in the street below D-Day's apartment window. The waning light makes it hard to see everything clearly, and given the nature of what he's observing, that's probably for the best. Even the street lights, activated by their photo sensors, don't afford him perfect visibility, but he can see enough. He's learning a lot about their behavior by watching them. For instance, he notices that they're attracted to lights—particularly lights changing, as the stop lights, or turning on, like in most of the buildings around the area.

Second, they have a herd mindset. When the traffic light at the intersection changes, some of them head toward the green light, and some toward the red. Each faction draws a dozen or so followers. These few dozen zombies have spent fifteen minutes going back and forth in the intersection as the number of victims out and about to draw their attention has dwindled. Occasionally a car plows through the horde; sometimes it makes it through and keeps going toward the interstate. As more cars have crashed and the road has become more clogged with both vehicles and bodies, Park Avenue has become more impassible. Now most cars are getting stuck, and in these cases, the zombies don't take long to get to the human cargo inside.

D-Day watches as a couple of the zombies run after one car, and at first a couple of others follow; then a few more, and then several dozen are on their trail in a stampede. Definite herd behavior. The car is headed west in the eastbound lane. It jumps the curb and rides the sidewalk for a few hundred feet, takes out a handful of the undead, drops back onto the roadway and disappears around behind the next building over. Twenty zombies are still chasing it.

The police presence is mostly concentrated in lower downtown, but there have been occasional squad cars that have come through the area. One had three officers in it. They fired into the crowd of zombies as it converged on their car, then sped off to get clear of the horde, then fired on a few more. Through his binoculars, he notices that only head shots put down the creatures permanently. Anything else just slows them down, or in some cases, cripples them. The police car continued this pattern all the way down Twentieth Avenue until it disappeared, leaving a few dead zombies in the road, a few wounded, but mostly just drawing more in with their gunfire. The next car was not so lucky. It used this same engage-and-evade tactic, but this time, the horde was either too large or too fast, and the car was swarmed. No one made it out alive.

He also notices that several of the zombies, aside from the ones who have been shot, have already begun to slow down. One sprints after a man who has escaped from his car after crashing. Like all the other runners he's seen, this one seems to be impossibly fast. They seem to have no medium speed; if they're running, it's all-out with no regard for what they hit or what they're doing to their bodies. The zombie is in full stride when his—*its?*—left leg gives out, and it tumbles onto the street. It gets back to its feet and now has a severe limp; instead of running, it moves at a fast walk, the left leg dragging behind. Jason surmises that it has torn a muscle, and though it doesn't look like it feels pain, physically it's incapable of moving the way it had before it fell. He's reminded of a line from The Terminator Two. In response to being asked if it hurts to get shot, the T100 says, "I sense injuries. The data could be called pain."

They're just like the Terminator, D-Day thinks. *Physically, injuries impact the zombies, but they don't acknowledge the pain. It's just data that causes them to change their method of attack. But they will not stop. Ever ... unless their CPU (the brain) is destroyed. I guess that makes the rest of us John Connor.*

D-Day decides he needs to check the security of the building. The ground floor is an open design, with a security guard behind a central desk. The front entrance consists of a set of four doors, the first two of which are open to the public. They open outward, so you have to pull them to open them. Nothing D-Day has observed indicates that the undead have the mental capacity to do so. Smash car windows, yes. Smash the ballistic glass of which the doors are made? Probably not, but enough of them in a mob could break them off of the hinges.

The second, inner, set of doors is only accessible with the access all residents have that replaces a physical key, or by being buzzed in by a resident. In short, no one can get in unless they live in the building or know someone who does. In addition to the doors, the panel windows are made of ballistic glass, so the odds of a zombie breaking them is remote, but in sufficient numbers—100, 500, 1000 zombies pressing against them—it's not out of the realm of possibility they could push them out of their sealed frames. Jason dons his tactical vest and puts four magazines for the AR in the pouches. He holsters his .40 pistol and pockets two extra mags for it too, then grabs his rifle, and after checking the peephole, he heads out into the hallway.

The hallway is quiet but well lit. There are only two windows, one at either end, by the entrances to the stairwells. The elevator is in the middle of the hallway, but Jason decides not to use it in case the power goes out. He hasn't seen so much as a flicker yet, but all it takes is one car hitting a pole with a transformer and the electricity is gone. Instead, he goes for the stairs at the east end of the hallway.

He opens the door and listens for a minute, but hears nothing. He enters the stairwell, taking the time to close the door quietly. He goes down to the ninth floor and cracks open the door to the hallway. Everything looks quiet. He works his way down floor by floor until he reaches the ground floor. He peeks out into the lobby, but aside from the green EXIT sign over the main entrance, the lobby is dark. He curses himself for leaving his night vision goggles in his room. *Nothing I can do about that now,* he thinks. He slips into the lobby and lets the door ease closed behind him.

There's no sign of life in the lobby, which is unusual for this time of night on a Friday. Of course, no lights is unusual too, but it's a good sign. There are no hordes of undead clamoring to get in, but D-Day can see the street teeming with them beyond the wide windows and glass doors.

The hairs on the back of his neck stand up. He wheels around to see what has set off his internal alarm and finds himself staring into the barrel of a gun.

"What do you think you're doing?"

The security guard's question hangs in the air a moment, somewhere between the gun he's pointing at D-Day and the spot-on D-Day's forehead that would be concaved by the bullet fired from that gun.

"Cortez, I'm just checking the security of the lobby. Put the gun down, or least point it somewhere other than my head. Please," D-Day says, silently cursing himself for being too focused on the monsters outside to notice Cortez was behind him.

"You're going to open the doors and let them know we're in here! I can't let that happen," Cortez replies.

"Cortez, listen to me," D-Day says. "I can see you've got the lobby handled. I just wanted to be sure that we weren't getting overrun down here. Believe me, the last thing I want to do is let those things know we're here. Come on, man, lower the gun."

Cortez the security guard wavers for a second, lowering the barrel of his gun just a bit, then raising it again. D-Day sees the indecision and knows he'll lower it for good, and when he does ...

BLAM! The noise startles them both, and it's a miracle that Cortez doesn't pull the trigger. Instead, he pivots the gun toward the window to the left of the entry. D-Day turns, dropping down to a knee, raising his rifle, and sighting it in all in one motion. A zombie has slammed into the glass and is peering around the lobby. The reflective glass in front of the darkened lobby probably doesn't afford much of a view inside. Cortez was smart to turn the lights out.

Both men remain still as the zombie loses interest in the window and turns back toward the growing crowds in the street. D-Day rises, letting his rifle hang by its sling. Cortez has momentarily forgotten his mistrust of the former soldier.

"They do that now and then. I think something reflects off of the window, and they come charging. I've been watching all this shit on the TV, and when it started getting dark I turned off all the lights on this level, so I don't think they can see inside." Cortez says all this without looking at D-Day, but rather staring out the windows. "I've been in the back office watching the cameras. It's almost like watching a movie, except it's real, you know? I know the security guys in the apartment building across the street, and I saw one of them attacked and killed by these things. Now he's out there roaming around and waiting for someone he can attack. Robert. His name is—was—Robert Paulson."

D-Day lets that hang in the air for a moment. Cortez has at least been thinking strategically, even if he's a little off balance.

"Cortez, how long have you been here?" D-Day asks.

"Me? About six years," he replies absently.

"No, I meant today. How long today?"

Cortez looks at his watch, doing some mental math.

"I've been on for sixteen hours, give or take," he says, reflecting on his thoughts. "I guess the next shift ain't coming in. Like, ever."

D-Day nods. "What if I help you out?" he offers. "You can get some sleep; I can watch the cameras and you can get some rest."

"You serve?" Cortez asks.

"Fourth Infantry, 1st Brigade. We captured Hussein."

Cortez's eyes widen. "Were you there for that?"

"No. It wasn't my unit that actually laid hands on him. The guys who did were insufferable after that."

Cortez keeps pressing. "You see a lot of combat?"

"I saw my share," D-Day says and leaves it at that, though he suspects Cortez wants more detail.

"Ever see anything like this?"

"No, nothing like this. I don't think anyone has seen anything like this." He's tempted to tell Cortez that the Army is planning to be in Denver tomorrow but thinks better of it.

Cortez regards him for a minute, and then turns and opens the door to the security office, giving D-Day a nod to follow him.

D-Day enters the office and shuts the door behind him. Once the door is shut, Cortez turns on the lights and switches on a bank of monitors. He pulls two chairs up to a console and motions for D-Day to take a seat, so he can give him a rundown of the equipment.

"We pride ourselves on keeping the building secure," Cortez begins, "from the decorative barricades to keep any Tim McVeigh wannabes away, to the ballistic glass in the windows, to the airlock security entrances, this building is designed to keep people out unless they have proper authority to be here." His mental autopilot has kicked in, and he's repeating something he's said to a thousand trainees.

D-Day has heard all of this before. "Cortez, I read the brochures. It's partly why I moved here. Tell me about the cameras."

"Okay, okay. We have sixty-five cameras on the interior of the building, ten on the exterior, and eighteen in the parking garage. We can see every hallway, every public space like the gym and rec room, every side of the building, every emergency exit, every stairwell entrance, and every parking space in the parking garage."

Cortez gestures to the bank of LCD flat-panel monitors three wide and four high mounted on the wall in front of the console. "We have twelve monitors, and we can subdivide them into quarters, so we can watch up to forty-eight views at once. These four," he waves his hand over a separate set of screens built into the console itself, "are the only ones we record from. We always record the front entrance, we always record the entrance from the parking garage, and then the other two we rotate as needed."

Cortez fiddles with a few buttons and the third screen changes. D-Day sees "10-W" in the corner next to what is obviously a date and time stamp.

"This is the tenth-floor camera on the west end of the hallway," Cortez says. He moves a joystick, and the camera rotates. Next, he turns a dial and the camera zooms in on a doorway. D-Day's apartment. "See, we can see anything happening in the public spaces, right up to your doorstep. We've got about a half a million wrapped up in this system." Cortez is proud of his workspace.

He shows D-Day how to change cameras on the monitors and manipulate them. Cortez is right; there's not a single viewpoint that D-Day can't access, but there's only a few he really cares about. He queues up the emergency exits as Cortez goes to the security manager's office to stretch out on a cot and, he hopes, get some sleep.

D-Day settles in. The front entrance seems secure, with only the occasional zombie investigating the building's facade. He zooms several of the external cameras on the surrounding landscape and buildings. The Safeway and strip mall across the street to the east is overrun with the undead. Every store that still has lights on is filled with the creatures. The cameras can't penetrate the darkened storefronts, so D-Day can't tell if there are any survivors in them. *If only these cameras had FLIR,* he thinks to himself. *Infrared would be nice to have right now. Easy to spot people in the dark.* He wonders if the zombies show up on FLIR, or if they are ambient temperature. He changes cameras.

The apartment building's parking garage to the north has thirty to forty of the creatures milling around, mostly on the first level. He's not as concerned about this access point because it has an airlock design like the front, and it only grants access to an elevator that requires a resident's access card to operate. Once inserted, the resident's card opens both the front and rear elevator doors. First-floor residents simply pass through to get to their apartments, and upper-level people take the ride to the appropriate floor. It's unlikely a zombie, even if it had an access card, would be able to operate it. *If they're that smart, we're fucked,* he thinks. Nothing he's seen thus far leads him to believe that there's anything other than animal instinct in these reanimated human shells.

He changes cameras again. To the west, he can see the four-story apartment building across the street has undead throughout.

Another camera change, looking south. The building Cortez referenced, where he knew Robert Paulson, the security guard, has a pool and party area that is rife with the undead. D-Day zooms the camera in and can see the parking area's entrance that leads under this neighboring building has dozens of revenants inside. They've breached the access door to the main building. Panning up, D-Day can see them through the windows of several of the units on the first few floors. How they got up there, he has no idea since he doesn't have a schematic of the interior. He can see one unit with its door open. Light from the main hallway shines on blood that has sprayed the door and has run in streaks before congealing.

He pulls the camera's view back and focuses it on the street in front of the building, then on the sides and rear. The undead are everywhere in the streets as far as he can see. He's surrounded. Behind enemy lines. Outnumbered several thousand to one. And he has no plan on how to get out of here.

He pulls his phone out of his pocket and checks it. No messages, no texts. He tries calling Martha Cowher at Fort Carson, but the call doesn't connect. Instead, he's told that all circuits are busy; please try again later.

The monitor he left connected to the camera on the west side emergency exit of his building catches his eye. Someone has left their apartment and peeks out the exterior door. On another monitor, he pulls up the first-floor interior west camera, and he can see the door to the last apartment, 103, is open. A woman lingers in the doorway of the apartment while a man has the door to the stairwell open and the third person, also a man, looks out the side exit door. This third man, the one who first drew D-Day's attention, steps outside, pushes the door completely open and holds it there.

"What the hell is he doing?" D-Day says out loud. A second later, a figure on a motorcycle enters the frame and jumps onto the sidewalk from the street then gooses the motor to climb the five stairs leading to the emergency exit. The figure bails off of the motorcycle, and it slams into the door, wedging it open. The man rushes over to the biker and tries helping him up. The biker removes his helmet to reveal long dark hair and a woman's face. She gets to her feet and starts limping to the doorway. The image on screen begins to fill with the undead, rushing toward the pair from the street.

Inside the building, the man at the stairwell door gestures frantically at the pair to hurry up. A half dozen or so people have opened their apartment doors to see what's happening. The trio—the older man, the younger man, and the woman from the motorcycle—get into Apartment 103 and shut the door a few seconds before the first of the undead begin running into the hallway.

"Cortez!" D-Day shouts. "We've got problems!"

CHAPTER 6

Fort Collins, Colorado

"Andy, tell me you have your iPad," Ben says as he maneuvers the old FJ Cruiser to hit as few zombies as possible. Still, every few seconds there's a *thump* as he either runs one over or one of them runs headlong into the side of the vehicle.

"Yeah, I have it," Andy says from one of the bench seats in the rear of the 4×4. "Why?"

"You still have that maps program we used when we went camping last fall?" Ben asks.

"Um ... yeah, I think so."

"Good. Check on there for a connection from Overland Trail to the utility pole access road," Ben says.

"What are you cooking up?" Toni asks.

"Overland Trail dead-ends at Southwest Community Park, so I'm hoping there's no military there. I did temp work last summer for the parks department at Dixon Reservoir, remember?" Ben asks as he steers around a group of three zombies feeding on some unfortunate soul in the middle of the road.

"Yeah, so?"

"Well, there's a series of walking trails and bike paths that connect the park and the Dixon Recreation Area. There's also an access road used by the Poudre Valley Power Authority for line maintenance that follows those big hundred-and-fifty-foot power poles south out of town. If we can get to that road from the park, we can get out of here," Ben says.

"So, you're betting that the Army isn't going to be watching that road? What if they are?" Toni asks.

"Why would they? It's not named or labeled on any map. It's all land owned by the power company. I only know about it because I worked at the reservoir last year and the power lines pass the east side of the res. We used a section of the access road to get around that side of it," Ben says.

"If you know how to get there, just go the way you know. I don't trust Gadget Boy there and his electronic maps," Keith says.

"The way I know takes us there on Dixon Canyon Road, which leads west out of town. There's nothing else that gets you out of town that direction until you're way north. If they're trying to seal off the town, I'm sure that road is guarded. Plus, Andy's app is not just a map, it's got a satellite view. Like I said, this road isn't on any map. Andy, how you coming?" Ben asks.

"Got it. As long as nothing has changed since these images were taken, you can turn right into a neighborhood just before the park. It dead-ends in a cul-de-sac. There's a dirt trail there that connects to the park's trail system, so you just have to jump the curb, veer to the right, and you're on that access road. There's just one problem—it looks pretty wide open to the east. Any Army checkpoints like the one we just left will be able to see us," Andy says.

"That's why I need that night vision rig of yours. I'll turn off the lights and go slow, keep my foot off of the brake, and use the parking brake to slow down. Even if I only get fifty feet of visibility from your goggles, it's better than nothing. If anyone has a better idea, now's the time to bring it up," Ben says.

"I trust you," Toni says. "Besides, I've got nothing better."

"Just get us away from this place. I don't care how," Danielle moans from the back seat.

"Vamanos!" Keith says.

Andy and Natalie offer their agreement, and Ben dodges another zombie, and at the next intersection heads toward Overland Trail to set their plan in motion.

The further west they go, the fewer zombies they encounter. The houses are dark, though occasionally they see someone peek out of their blinds, a horizontal slit of light appearing and disappearing just as fast. After a few minutes of silent, zombie-free travel, they reach the end of Overland Trail and the access point to the park.

Everyone in the FJ40 holds their breath. Ben turns off the lights before hopping the curb at the end of the cul-de-sac, to which Andy had navigated them using his iPad. He dons Andy's night vision goggles that, though they are little more than an expensive toy, are effective enough to let him see a few dozen feet in front of him. Their speed has slowed to a crawl, but they're still moving forward.

They've gone about a mile when the trail gets rough. Ben depresses the clutch and pulls on the parking brake to bring them to a stop. He shifts the old SUV into four-wheel drive.

"Talk to me, Andy. I can't see where I should go next," Ben says.

"We can't see shit," Keith says. "Next chance we get, we're getting more of those night vision goggles."

"We need something better than these, man. Like I said before, they're better than nothing, but these were not made for driving," Ben says.

In the back seat, Andy hides inside a sweatshirt with his phone and his iPad to keep the light from giving them away. He's checking their GPS location on his phone and checking the more detailed map he has downloaded to his iPad.

"Okay, I think I've got it," Andy says. "If you go to the right, you should see a clearing that goes up a hill just past the next power pole. You'll be going over a bunch of scrub brush. When you get to a huge rock, go left. You'll see a couple of trees, and you'll have to go around them. You should be under the power lines at that point. Make a couple of lefts and you're back on a real dirt road. Keep on that road and we will hit County Road 38."

"Okay, I'll never remember all that. I can see a hill on the other side of this pole. I'm heading there. Here goes nothing," Ben says.

He turns the wheel and steers up the hill. The FJ lurches and bumps over bushes and smaller rocks but has no problem scaling the hill.

"I see a boulder bigger than the FJ," Ben says. "Which way now?"

"Left," Andy says, "then right around two big pine trees."

Ben turns the FJ left, downhill, and continues to drive through bushes and rocky patches. He pulls the parking brake again as they get close to a couple of large trees. The FJ slides on the loose rocks, turning sideways. Ben steers into the skid and gets the SUV under control, then maneuvers the vehicle around the trees. He spins the wheel a couple turns to the left, bounces the 4×4 over the drainage gutter on the side of the dirt road, and brings it to a stop. Danielle gets tossed off the bench in the rear, and Andy falls on top of her, unable to catch himself with his arms inside his sweatshirt hideaway.

"Get off of me, Andy!" she cries out. "And Ben,

what the fuck? Can you keep it on four wheels, please?"

"Holy shit!" Keith says. "That was wild! I thought we were going to crash there for a minute. Nice driving, Tokyo Drift!"

"Sorry guys," Ben says. "It's not easy without the brakes. If we can stay on this road for a while, it will be easier going."

They all breathe a collective sigh of relief. Ben shifts the FJ out of four-wheel drive and gets them moving again.

"Are we sure that there's no easier way?" Danielle asks. "If I get tossed around like that again, I'm going to be sick."

"Every other way takes us closer to Taft Hill Road or Shields," Andy says from under his sweatshirt, back on his spot on the bench seat. "We know Shields is blocked at Trilby Road because that's where we met the Army dicks, and I'm willing to bet that Taft Hill is blocked there as well."

"Ugh. I wish we brought some Dramamine," Danielle complains.

"I wish I brought some Rohypnol," Keith says.

"Real fucking funny, Keith," she says. "Date rape is hilarious. Dick."

"I'll try to keep the fishtailing to a minimum," Ben says before Keith can respond to his angry girlfriend. "Andy, I'm at County Road 38. What do I do now?"

Andy gives Ben directions, navigating them south through a country neighborhood for just over three miles. The distance takes about twelve minutes since they're still driving without any lights.

"This next bit gets dicey," Andy says from the back seat. "This road dead-ends at someone's house, but there's a broken trail just before their house that gets us most of the way through Loveland. We just need to get to that trail, and we should be home free."

"I don't like this," Danielle says.

"What else is new?" Keith responds.

"Seriously, ass!" she says. "We're in the middle of nowhere on a road that dead-ends at someone's country house. We're in the middle of Night of the Living Dead, and we're driving right into Texas Chainsaw Massacre."

"Dani, ease off the drama, all right?" Keith says. "It's not like you've had any other ideas."

"I didn't even want to fucking come on this ride," Danielle says. "I want to get home to San Diego, but you guys were going to bail on me."

"Oh, give it a rest ..." Keith starts to say.

Ben stops the FJ, hitting the brakes hard enough to make everyone slide forward in their seats and startle Keith into silence. For a second.

"Dude, what's up? What is it?" Keith asks. In the back seat, Andy pops his head out of his sweatshirt and looks around the darkness in vain.

"No one do anything," Ben says. He's looking around with his night vision goggles. "No sudden moves. Just sit still."

"What's the deal? I can't see anything!" Toni says.

"We're surrounded," Ben says.

Toni gulps out loud. "By zombies?"

"Not exactly."

CHAPTER 7

Cortez and D-Day look at the monitor, watching the recorded replay of the people from Apartment 103 getting their door shut a second before the dead reach it. With the outer emergency door blocked open by the wrecked motorcycle, nothing stops the zombies from getting into the building. A steady stream of them comes in, so the inner door never has a chance to close, and now about forty of the creatures occupy the first-floor hallway. Several pound on the door to 103, trying to get to the people they've just seen disappear behind the rectangular barrier.

The other people who were peeking out of their apartments have withdrawn, but not before a couple of zombies spotted them, so they're now pounding on their doors as well. In the stairwell, more zombies come in, and with the inner door proving to be a bottleneck of the undead, many of them stumble up the stairs like water following the path of least resistance, rather than waiting to gain access to the first-floor hallway. Once in the stairwell, they only need to lean against the push bar to get the doors on each floor to open. There's nothing stopping the zombies from overrunning the building.

Cortez turns on the camera to the second-floor west stairwell and sees zombies already walking around on the landing. It's clear that they need to secure the entrances to the west stairs.

"Cortez, I need you to get to the intercoms for the apartments on the first floor. Tell the people to stay inside, keep quiet and we'll get to them. Make a note on which apartments answer and which ones don't. Then start on the second floor—be sure to tell them the west stairs are closed—certain death if they try to get out that way. They should stay put, and we'll let them know when we've got it secured. Every ten minutes radio me so we can sync statuses and plan our next steps," D-Day says.

"Where are you going?" Cortez asks.

"As soon as you show me where the maintenance room is, I'm going to secure the west stairs," D-Day replies as he grabs one of the security team's walkie-talkies.

Cortez shows him the way to the maintenance room, which thankfully isn't behind the lobby doors where the undead are roaming free in the hallway. He goes back to the security console, grabs a notepad, and goes out to the front desk, where he starts working on contacting the first-floor residents.

In the maintenance room, D-Day looks over the supplies. He's lucky; the maintenance crew is well organized. The toolboxes have all the drawers labeled. The cordless tools are lined up under a bank of batteries that are on their chargers. This will make things a lot easier.

D-Day grabs a canvas tool bag and puts in two cordless drills and four batteries. He locates drill bits and grabs several 3/32" diamond drill bits and loads one into one of the cordless drills. He grabs several Philips head screwdriver bits, loading one into the other cordless drill. He throws a couple of boxes of three-inch screws into the bag as well. Looking around, he spots a couple of large rubber doorstops and a pair of wooden ones; he adds them to his kit. He grabs some rope and, of course, duct tape for good measure and heads for the east stairwell.

D-Day opens the second-floor door a crack and peeks through the gap. No one is visible; most important, there are no zombies.

He trots down the hall to the west stairs. On the other side of the door, he can hear the zombies grumbling and stumbling on the stairs. He takes one of the wooden doorstops and wedges it under the door on the side that opens, giving it a kick to ensure it's wedged in there good and tight. Then he pulls out the cordless drills and starts to work.

He starts drilling a hole through the metal door jamb into the steel door at eye level. Right away he can hear the zombies on the other side get more active and start vocalizing more. It's a terrifying sound, but not as bad as when he hears the push bar get depressed from the other side of the door. The latch is released, and the upper half of the door moves about a half inch inward, but the wedge at the bottom holds the door shut. D-Day switches to the drill with the screwdriver bit in it. He pushes against the door with all his might and manages to get the screw started with his free hand. The door buckles inward again, and again D-Day pushes it back.

He gets the cordless drill working and drives the screw home. The door doesn't move again. He repeats the process on the lower half of the door, and a final time just below the latch in the middle. Satisfied the door isn't going to budge, he puts the tools back in the bag and heads for the east stairs again. He thinks about using the elevator to save time, but he's still concerned about an untimely power outage, and he doesn't know if the third floor has been breached. It would be bad to have to doors open to a dozen man-eaters, so he makes the trek all the way down the hall to the stairwell and advances to the third floor.

He sees two zombies at the far end of the hall, but the door to the stairwell is shut. D-Day shifts the canvass bag around to his back and brings the AR15 up, thankful he remembered to secure the suppressor to it before leaving his apartment, and sights in on the first zombie. He pulls the trigger and sees a puff of oily blood mist through the air behind the zombie's head. It drops in its tracks like someone cut the strings on a marionette. Even suppressed, an AR15 still makes a fair bit of noise—about as loud as a car door shutting— and the other zombie, a woman, or rather it *used* to be a woman, keys in on the source of the sound. It locks eyes on D-Day and starts sprinting toward him.

He squeezes the trigger again. A spray of black fluid jets from the creature's left shoulder just above the collar bone. It doesn't even notice; it just keeps coming. D-Day drops to one knee and exhales. He squeezes the trigger again, and the dead woman goes down, sporting a new hole in her forehead.

He gets up and runs toward the west door. As he does so, he hears the walkie-talkie crackle but can't understand what Cortez is saying. His primary concern is to get a wooden wedge under the door so no additional undead can get into the hallway from the stairwell.

"Not from ... tairs ..." the walkie-talkie crackles. Cortez's voice sounds stressed. *"Apart ... oh-four!"*

As D-Day passes Apartment 304, he puts together what Cortez is saying, but not before a zombie hits him full force as it sprints from the open doorway of Apartment 304.

The zombie knocks D-Day off balance but doesn't take him to the ground. The dead child only reaches about four feet tall, and D-Day gets his AR15 between himself and the little zombie's mouth. The creature bites down hard on the magazine, damaging it but at the same time breaking several teeth. D-Day gives the kid a hard shove, knocking it a couple of feet backward. He pivots the rifle and puts a round right through the kid's head. The pint-sized monster goes down in a heap.

The latch on the door to the east stairwell clicks, and D-Day can see the door start to open. He sprints the final twenty-five feet down the hall, slams into the door and smashes a female zombie between the door and the door jamb. He can hear her ribs break, and she vomits a stream of black bile onto the carpet. The odor makes D-Day retch.

On the other side of the door, he hears several zombies clattering on the staircase. He must have knocked them backward when he slammed the door shut on the woman. His AR failed to cycle a round because of the damage the kid caused to the magazine, so he draws his pistol and lets the door loose for a second. The woman starts to fall inward, so he grabs her and throws her into the hallway then leans his back against the door and closes it all the way this time.

The zombie gets back to her feet, her torso caved in on one side. She's unable to draw fully upright but still manages to turn toward him, her hands reaching out in anticipation, teeth clacking together. Unlucky for her, he's ready with his pistol and fires two rounds. The first one passes through her cheeks and hits an apartment door behind her. The second hits her just under her left eye, the bullet penetrating her skull and flipping the off switch. The force of impact pushes her left eye out of the socket, and her forward momentum brings her to rest at D-Day's feet.

The undead pound at the door again. D-Day can hear the push bar getting depressed over and over as the dead are pressing themselves against the door. Each time it clicks, the door buckles inward before he pushes it back. His tool bag lies on its side, too far down the hall for him to reach before the door will spring open.

He looks at the magazine the child zombie bit. The bottom plate is gone, and the plastic is smashed together. He releases the magazine from the receiver and drops it to the floor. With one foot, he moves it over to the edge of the door on the latch side and pushes the smashed end under the door. It just fits, and he gives it two good solid kicks, wedging it in place. He checks the rifle to ensure it's clear of any jams, puts a fresh magazine in it, and cycles the charging handle. He releases his pressure on the door and takes a cautious step back. It holds. He sprints to the tool bag, and when he gets back to the door he puts one of the wood wedges in place for good measure. It takes him less than three minutes to get two screws in place. He decides not to bother with a third one; he'd rather get to the fourth floor and secure it before any zombies can get in up there.

After he retrieves the wedge and the broken magazine from the bottom of the door, he radios Cortez to find out how he's coming on reaching the residents of the building, but he gets no answer. As he turns to head back toward the east stairwell, he sees several of the doors are cracked open, curious residents peeking into the hall.

"We're secure out here for now," he says loud enough so the people can hear him. "Please do not try to go outside tonight. You won't last long. Right now your best defense is to stay in your apartments."

The door to 305 opens and a middle-aged woman stands in the doorway. "Who are you?" she asks, eying his AR with caution.

"Name's Jason, but I go by D-Day. I live on ten," he says. "The west stairwell's overrun with these"—he pauses for a second, unsure if he should use the word or not, then decides he might as well get used to it —"zombies. I'm trying to get the stairwell doors locked, so the rest of the building doesn't get overrun too."

He sees her looking at the open door to 304 and the four bodies in the hallway. He notices for the first time that there's blood on the door and a real crime scene inside the apartment. He's expecting the woman to introduce herself, but she doesn't. She just stares at the open doorway.

"Did you see what happened?" he asks, breaking her out of her reverie.

"I heard him come in a while ago. Jim. Jim was his name, the father." She's already using the past tense. "Hanson was his last name. He was shouting and pounding on the door. He was frantic. A few minutes before you came, I heard screaming again and the door opened. By the time I got to the peephole, the screaming was over, and I didn't see anyone, just that open door. I thought about poking my head out to call out to them, but the TV told us not to open the door for anyone. I just kept looking out there and then Jim came walking down from the end of the hall. If I had opened the door ..." she trails off. After a couple of seconds, she says, "There were four of them."

"What do you mean there were four of them?" D-Day asks.

"In the apartment. There were four of them living there."

He turns to the open door. He could just shut it and seal the fourth resident in the apartment, but they would try to get out if they turned. Maybe whoever it was hadn't been bitten. Maybe they weren't even home. He turns back to the woman.

"Ma'am, do you know if all four of them were home?" he asks.

"I think so. It's Jim, his wife, his daughter from another marriage, and the son they have together. Jim, Betty and John, you've ... taken care of," she says, choosing her words carefully. "But I heard two different women screaming, so I think Nancy is home."

Overall, this gal is taking things pretty well, he thinks. Out loud he says, "The daughter. How old?"

"I'm not sure. Fourteen or fifteen, I think."

"You should go back into your apartment. I'll take care of this," he says.

He turns and enters Apartment 304. He hears a moaning sound coming from the bathroom, so he knows what waits for him. Taking care not to slip in the pool of blood in the hallway, he moves forward to clear the threat.

CHAPTER 8

Somewhere south of Fort Collins

"What do you mean 'not really'?" Toni asks.

"I can only see so well with these goggles, but there's a bunch of armed people outside the car," Ben says.

"Oh shit, is it the Army?" Natalie asks from the back seat.

"No, it's not the Army," he says.

Ben reaches for the window handle and starts turning it.

"What are you doing?" Toni asks.

"They want to talk to us," Ben replies.

Outside, one of the armed people is making the "roll down your window" sign. Ben rolls the window down the rest of the way. He can see the man has night vision goggles on as well, but his look like the real deal. He approaches the side of the car as another person, also wearing night vision, moves so they can keep their rifle trained on Ben.

"I'd feel a lot better if I could see some hands," the man says. "I'd be a lot less jumpy with the iron, if you understand me."

Ben raises both of his hands, so the man can see them. Everyone else in the car follows suit.

"We're unarmed," Ben says.

"Well, maybe you are and maybe you aren't. I don't know you enough to take your word for anything. In fact, I don't know you at all, except that you're on my property on a night all hell is breaking loose. The National Guard is locking down the countryside, and here you are creeping along in the dark with your car full of people looking to do Lord knows what," the man says.

"We're just trying to get to Longview, to my parents' house," Ben says. "I'm sorry about the trespassing, but we can't take the main roads, and the longer we stay in Fort Collins the worse it gets. We're afraid if we don't get out now, we'll never get out."

The man regards Ben for a minute. "Can you see well enough to get this old beast into that shed down there?" The man points to a building too big to be just a shed and too small to be a barn. It lies ahead just to the right of the trail that he believes Andy wanted them to take.

"Yes, I can," Ben says.

"Put her in gear and ease down there. Try to take

off and you'll have trouble." The man taps his rifle for emphasis.

Ben pulls the FJ into the big shed as the man and three other figures follow them and shut the doors to the building after they've entered.

"Watch your eyes!" the man says to them. Ben takes the night vision off and a second later overhead lights illuminate the space.

The man opens the rear doors on the FJ, with two other people behind him, guns trained on the passengers.

"You all come out slowly, please. Keep your hands where we can see 'em. March yourselves up to the front of the car," the man directs them.

They all file out and move to the open area in front of the SUV.

"Now you, driver and passenger, join your friends. Same drill, move slow, keep your hands where I can see 'em and we'll all be happy."

The man looks at them for a long couple of moments.

"Well," he finally says, "you don't seem like a bunch of desperadoes. You mind telling me who you are and what you was planning on doing?"

They look at each other for a few seconds, and then Ben starts talking. He introduces everyone in his group and proceeds to tell the man about their experience at the party, the horrors of driving back to their apartment, and the newscasts they saw. He tells him about their attempt to leave town via Shields, the encounter with the Army, Ben's idea to take the power company's access road, Andy's navigation with his iPad and phone, and their eventual arrival at their host's property.

"That's not bad, kids, not bad at all. Right up until you crossed the boundary of my property and broke the infrared sensors I have set across the road. It rings a buzzer up at the house, lets us know someone's coming up the drive. You're on the right track keeping to the back roads. What you all ran into was Army National Guard, not regular Army. On the news, they've said that the Guard is stretched pretty thin, but they've got the major intersections covered. Denver is a mess, and most of the Guard units have been called there to support the police. Colorado Springs is having a hell of a time of it too. The Army units in the Springs out of Fort Carson are fighting in the streets but from what we've seen, they're not faring too well. If you can keep away from the big intersections, you're likely to be okay."

"Have you heard anything about Longview?" Keith asks.

"No mention of it, other than from the maps they've been showing on TV. It looks pretty clear. Most of the focus is on Denver; that's where most of the people are. Colorado Springs, Boulder, Fort Collins have all been hit hard. Grand Junction over on the Western Slope has taken a beating. Whatever this thing is, it's worldwide, and it's spreading. They've said that if you come in contact with the body fluids of these people, you become like them. Violent beyond control. I don't think the police are asking too many questions now. They're just shooting if someone doesn't look right. It's bad, kids.

"Now, all this considered, Longview probably ain't a bad place to be right now. I know it pretty well, had a cousin that lived there for a bit in the nineties. You have access to any number of side roads to get out of town, close to the mountains, several connections to major highways within ten miles of the town, assuming they're passable within the next few days. I expect once this settles a bit you won't have a problem getting out of town, if that's what you want to do."

He looks at them for a minute, then says, "My name is Henry Sims, the three back here are my nieces Annie and Stephenie, and my nephew Robert."

The trio nods and waves to them. Robert signs to Stephenie. Henry answers the question he knows the other kids will ask. "Stephenie is deaf. She lost her hearing to a fever when she was not yet four. She can talk well enough, can read lips a little, but mostly she uses sign language."

The kids all murmur their hellos to the trio. Now that they can see their faces they can tell their ages range from late teens to mid-twenties, much like their group, with Annie looking like she's the oldest.

"Listen, I don't know you kids from Adam, but I have an offer for you," Henry says.

"Henry, this isn't necessary!" Robert says. "We aren't leaving you!"

"Dammit, Robert, you have no choice! Fort Collins is going to fall, and we can't hold them off forever. There are more than 150,000 people in that town. We'll get overrun if we stay. You three are capable, but your best chances of survival are with a larger group, and we don't have a lot of choices right now. Besides, I still have to deal with the other ..." Henry trails off.

Stephenie signs to Robert, who translates. "She says she doesn't want to go; or that if we go, you should come with us."

Henry signs while he talks to Stephenie. "Honey, you kids need to go. This mess is going to get worse. Ben here will give me his address, and I'll be down there when I've taken care of things."

Stephenie signs to Henry again.

"No, Stephenie. We don't have another choice. The clock is ticking," he says. He turns to Robert. "I want you to lead them off of the property using the south trail. You know the back roads better than anyone. Get them around Loveland and down to Longview." He turns his attention to Ben. "And you—I need you to take them in. They have good skills. They know how to hunt and fish, and they all have good skills with a rifle, especially Stephenie. They'll earn their keep. Once things settle down, or the Army gets things under control, then you all can go your separate ways as you see fit. But I need to know that they're going to be sheltered."

"They're not going to be able to shelter us!" Robert protests. "They don't have any weapons. They don't have any real supplies. They're indoor dogs, Henry! You're talking like you aren't coming down there! If you're worried about us making it here with you, what chance do you have without *us*? This is crazy!"

Henry speaks in a steady, calm voice, which is more chilling than if he were to yell. "Robert, when your parents died we took you kids in as our own. We never had kids, and we never asked for any, but we got you anyway. We'd rather die ..." his voice wavers when he says this, "than see anything happen to you. I will be damned if I will see you killed—or worse—by one of those *things*. You'll do as I say and you will lead these folks out of here. Stick with them and earn your keep. You will not survive this alone."

Henry hands his night vision goggles to Ben. "Here," he says, "you're going to need some real NVGs, not them toys you drove in here wearing." He points to a pad and paper on a bench in the rear of the shed. "Write your address on that for me."

Annie, the oldest of the three of Henry's kin, speaks up while he pauses. "Uncle Henry, why don't you let one of these kids do it? They don't know her. It won't be as emotional for them. Then we can all leave together. Please."

"Annie, girl, it's not their place. I'm responsible. I owe it to her to be the one. Your truck is loaded with your gear. You all need to be gone before I get to the house."

With that, Henry turns and walks away, turning the light off before he leaves through the access door on the side of the big shed. That he left without getting the address from Ben is not lost on any of them.

"What's going on? What does he have to do?" Keith asks.

"Our aunt got bit in town, in the King Soopers parking lot," Robert says. "They came home, but she got sick on the way. She turned into one of those *things* in Henry's truck, but she can't get out because of the seat belt. It's a miracle that he didn't get bit by her."

Stephenie says something that none of Ben's group can understand, but the two others, used to her communication style, hear her perfectly: "Let's get him."

"Look, you need to get south. I'll lead you out of here, but we need you guys to help us convince him to come with us," Robert says. "Help us with that and then we'll all get the hell out of here."

Ben agrees, seconded by everyone else, and they all exit the side door through which Henry disappeared. They're walking at a quick pace when Robert notices his truck's door is partially open. He mutters "what the hell?" not quite under his breath and trots over to it. The others hustle over as he opens the door and finds a piece of paper on the seat. He shines a small green filtered flashlight on it.

"NO!" he screams, turning and running for the house, dropping the paper as he rushes past everyone. Annie picks up the paper and shines her light on it. It has two sentences written on it:

"I'm sorry, but I can't go on without her. Take care of each other."

AS ROBERT NEARS THE HOUSE, a gunshot rings out and a flash of light bursts through the windows in the garage. A moment later a second shot rings out, and the two sisters, knowing what just happened, start to cry.

CHAPTER 9

D-Day finishes driving the last screw into place. That's it, twelve floors, twelve doors, all secured. Wait—eleven, he reminds himself. They still have to deal with the door on one. After he killed Nancy, the last member of the Hanson family, he's had no more encounters with the living dead. If they're going to secure the first floor, that's going to change.

He takes the stairs to the tenth floor and stops at his apartment. He grabs his night vision gear, stowing it in a backpack, into which he also puts some extra ammo, some zip ties, some protein bars, and a couple of bottles of water. He drinks a glass of water in the kitchen, shoulders the pack, and heads back into the hallway. He decides to risk the power going out and rides the elevator down to the second floor, where he gets off and heads for the east stairs. He still hasn't been able to reach Cortez on the walkie-talkie, and he fears the worst. He knows there's only a pair of doors that separates the first-floor hallway from the lobby. He never checked to see if they were secured, but Cortez had said he locked all the doors on the first floor. D-Day took him at his word and didn't check them.

He eases the stairwell door open and confirms his fears. There are three zombies in the lobby; two are dead on the floor, and one is going back and forth in front of the windows. D-Day recognizes her as a woman from his floor—1006 or 1008, he thinks. She was an attorney or accountant—some profession that required her to wear expensive suits to work. She spent a lot of time in the gym on the fifth floor of the building. D-Day had thought about asking her out a few times, but she had a general air of unapproachability, so he never did. He's glad for that now; if they had a relationship, this would be more distressing than it is. She bears wounds on her arms, shoulders, neck, and right calf. The calf wound has her limping, but she's mobile enough to be a threat. Fortunately, her attention is focused on several dozen zombies outside the building, some pounding on the windows and the outer doors, trying to get in. With the suppressor affixed to the rifle, D-Day takes aim and with one shot, he drops her to the floor. He scans the lobby, but she was the only moving threat inside.

He moves quickly to the security office door and finds it locked, so he knocks on it twice. The knob turns, and a pale, sweaty Cortez opens the door.

"D-Day, sorry I dropped out on you, man. I was contacting people like you said, and tried to warn you about the zombies in 304. I didn't notice Tamara from the tenth floor coming in the front door until it was too late. She drove her BMW right up to the bollards and then sprinted to the door. She almost made it, but two of those things got through with her, and they took her down in the lobby. I got one with my Beretta, but the other one got me, bro."

Cortez holds up his right hand to show the blood-soaked bandage before he continues his story. "He just nicked me with his teeth, but it was enough. I dropped my pistol, so I started hitting him with the only thing I had handy—my walkie-talkie. I caved in his head but destroyed the walkie, and the others aren't working." He winces in pain. "It really, really hurts, man. My arm is on fire."

D-Day looks at his arm and from the site of the wound to the cuff of his golf shirt, the brown skin has faded to an ashy color. The veins are black, and the wound itself smells gangrenous, even though D-Day knows it can't be infected this quickly.

"Cortez, this doesn't look good. I'm a no-bullshit kind of person, and I have to tell you the reality of the situation ..." D-Day says.

"No need, bro. I know the score; I've seen it on the cameras. I'm going to turn. I wasn't sure until I saw the black shit start spreading up my arms. I should have just left them alone out there and radioed you to come help, but I thought I could pop them both. That second one was just too fast for me. I'm sorry, man, you're going to have to finish this without me. I do have a plan, though," Cortez says.

"Plan for what?" D-Day asks.

"To get the first-floor stairwell shut. I can help get the last part of the building secured before I go out," Cortez says. "But we need to move fast because I don't know how much longer I can take this." He points to a bloody piece of paper. "I wrote my address and number on there. If you get through this shit, please try to find my girlfriend. I've not been able to reach her, and if she makes it, I want her to know I was thinking of her before I died. I want her to know I went out fighting."

D-Day looks at the paper, feeling a little ashamed that he never asked Cortez about his family or friends. Since leaving the military, he's so used to being alone that he never thinks about other people's situations and how they may have close ties with their people. He shakes the thoughts away and takes the paper, folds it, and puts it in a pocket.

"If I get through this thing, I promise I'll try to find her," D-Day says. "Now, you said you have a plan?"

"Yeah. I've been talking to the people in 103, the ones who let all these things inside, you know?" Cortez asks. D-Day nods and Cortez continues. "We've got an idea. It gives them a chance to redeem themselves and lets me go out as a hero. Who could ask for more, right?"

Cortez tells D-Day the details, and without a better idea, D-Day agrees to do his part.

"You're sure about this? You know what you're in for?" D-Day asks.

"I know. I'm in so much pain right now I can barely see straight anyway. At least this way it will be over quickly."

D-Day checks the rifle and pistol to make sure they're both ready to go.

"One more thing, D-Day," Cortez says, handing him a keycard and key on a lanyard. "These open any door in the building. You're going to need them, I expect. The building is yours now, my friend."

D-Day goes over to the intercom panel and presses 103. A voice comes back a few seconds later.

"Cortez?" a woman's voice says.

D-Day presses the button. "My name's D-Day ... I'm here with Cortez. You guys were talking to him before?"

"Yes, that's right," she says. "Are you guys ready?"

"Yep. Be ready to move," D-Day says, and then releases the button and walks away.

Cortez is in the lobby by the security doors that lead to the hallway overrun with the infected dead. He's breathing hard and wincing in pain. He's retrieved his pistol and holds it in his left hand.

"You sure you can do this?" D-Day asks.

"No going back, bro. But I need to go, like, now," he says.

"Okay," D-Day says. He swipes his security card through the card reader and unlocks the doors. Cortez pulls the left door open and goes through, and D-Day pushes it shut behind him and starts counting.

On the other side of the door, the undead immediately take notice of Cortez. He charges right at them, going as fast as his pain-riddled body will go. He screams like a banshee, and the undead hurl their disturbing howls back at him as they, too, rush headlong down the hall to meet him.

At the end of the hall, as the undead leave to pursue Cortez, the door to 103 opens. Two women come out with baseball bats. One, the one who crashed her motorcycle, kicks a zombie in the chest as it comes through the open stairwell door. The other woman, older, bearing a strong resemblance to the dark-haired woman, hustles to the stairwell door and starts shutting it. The first woman swings the bat like a club and cracks another zombie in the head, and then she kicks that one back through the doorway like she did the first one.

Some of the zombies have noticed them from down the hall and turn back to get at the fresh meat. The main horde, however, has reached Cortez. He's aiming his Beretta and fires a shot, hitting the closest zombie in the head, sending oily fluid into the air and the zombie to the carpet. His second shot misses wide and hits the wall just above the women at the end of the hall. And then the horde is on him.

Behind the security door, D-Day has counted to fifteen and pulls the door open. He draws the AR up and starts firing, hitting the head of a zombie maybe every third shot. With the shots suppressed and Cortez screaming, it takes a few seconds for the creatures to notice him, and the zombies who don't have a hold of Cortez turn their focus to D-Day. His magazine is empty, so he drops it and cycles a fresh one into the rifle.

At the end of the hall, the two men from 103 have hauled a large safe out of the apartment. It's about three feet tall, two feet wide, two feet deep and has to weigh 250 pounds. They set it down in front of the stairwell door while the two women hit zombies with their baseball bats.

"Now!" one of the men screams and the women back their way toward Apartment 103, where the men slam the door shut the second the women clear the doorway.

D-Day drops his second empty magazine. He's fired fifty-nine rounds (the sixtieth having dispatched Tenth-Floor-Tamara in the lobby), and he has ninety left, plus forty-eight rounds for his pistol. With the stairwell door shut, he only has to deal with the dead that remain in the hallway. He estimates he's got about forty to deal with, and most of them are coming his way. Many of them stumble over the bodies on the floor, sometimes falling. D-Day notes that they don't avoid obstacles well, and they don't put their arms out to stop their fall the way living people do, so when they fall, they fall hard. They seem to home in on their prey, and that's all they see. He backs toward the security doors, thinking he needs to choke their flow somehow, so he can shoot slower and with more accuracy. He opens them and heads for the east stairwell.

He holds the stairwell door open and waits for the first zombie to clear the security doors. When it does, he runs into the stairwell and turns around when he's halfway up the first flight. The zombie comes through the doorway and is instantly met by a .223 round to the head. It drops in the doorway and blocks the door open. D-Day climbs the remaining stairs to the first landing and turns as the next zombie comes through the door. He fires two shots, the second one hitting the mark, and the creature goes down in a heap. He lets the next few through the door and onto the stairs before he drops them. He doesn't want the doorway to get so congested they stop coming through; rather he wants them to continue their pursuit. He's in a good position now, he figures, because he can shoot at will. If he runs low on ammo, he can always keep going up the stairs to the next floor and resupply from his backpack. He's wrapped his way around the stairs to the second-floor landing, and the zombies have slowed to a trickle. He hasn't kept careful track of how many he's put down, but he knows the number is north of thirty. He can see through the clear window on his magazine that he's down to the last few rounds for his rifle. He drops one more zombie and waits a few seconds. He neither sees nor hears any others. He doesn't want to chance wading through the bodies; some may not be fully dead. He could trip and injure himself, or worse, he could be in the middle of them, and a straggler could come in and leave him little room or time to get a shot on target.

He goes through the second-floor access door and jogs to the elevator. It's still on the second floor so when he presses the down button the doors open right away. He steps back just to be sure there's nothing undead inside, and then steps in and presses '1.' As the doors shut, he slings the rifle and draws his pistol, and waits for the doors to open.

The elevator stops on the first floor, pauses, and then the doors slide open. D-Day hears the sound of wet thumps and breaking bones. He peers out of the elevator and to the right he sees three zombies. The people from 103 have re-emerged to attack them with baseball bats. The dark-haired woman swings her bat, and there's a wet crunch as she connects with the side of the zombie's head. It lurches sideways and hits the wall, leaving a black, brackish smear behind. She kicks another zombie in the chest, knocking it backward. She comes close to losing her balance, and then recovers and deals the death blow to the first zombie. One of the men has finished off the zombie he had been fighting, and then he starts swinging at the one that the woman kicked.

A moan to the left gets D-Day's attention. Two zombies run back at them from the lobby. He raises his pistol and with three shots, he drops them both. He looks back at the people at the end of the hallway, and for a minute they all just breathe, taking in the silence of no undead moaning and trying to rip their flesh from their bones.

The silence is momentary. The pounding on the stairwell access door resumes, and despite the weight of the safe sitting in front of it, the door moves inward a couple of inches.

"Get down there and get the door shut, NOW!" D-Day shouts. "I'll get the tools!"

He runs down the hallway, stepping around the fetid bodies lining the floor, does a quick check of the lobby, and retrieves the tool bag from the security office. A few tense moments later and he's got three screws driven into the door to secure it. The pounding continues, but the door doesn't budge one iota. Everyone looks relieved, for about a second.

Then the man with the bat starts screaming.

They all turn to look at him, and to D-Day's horror, Cortez's reanimated corpse, pinned under a pile of bodies, sinks his teeth into the man's calf. The man tries to pull his leg away from Cortez, but his jaws have a firm grasp on his bare leg. Cargo shorts were clearly a bad idea for fighting zombies. He continues his struggle, and as he pulls his leg away from the gnashing teeth, a large piece of the calf muscle tears free from the Achilles' tendon and stretches between the leg of the man and the mouth of the creature. D-Day sights his pistol and two pops sound in the hall. Cortez's head jerks back, his jaws go limp, and his forehead sports two new holes. Black ooze from the wounds sprays the man's legs and wounded calf. He screams even more when the oily substance makes contact with the exposed muscle.

"Bill!" the woman yells and runs down the hallway to his side. She grabs one of his arms and pulls it over her shoulder to support his weight. "Help me, please!" she shouts at D-Day.

He goes to Bill's left side, and the two of them take the wounded man to Apartment 103. The other couple is inside the apartment, and D-Day gets a good, close look at them for the first time. They're older, perhaps in their mid sixties, while the other two are late thirties or early forties. Based on the resemblance of the two women, D-Day guesses they're mother and daughter. Bill must be the son or son-in-law; based on his lighter complexion, D-Day guesses son-in-law.

"Oh my God, what happened?" the older man asks.

"There was one still alive in the pile. It bit his leg," the young woman says.

"Oh, God, it hurts!" Bill's face contorts with agony, and D-Day can see the veins in the leg turning black. The ruined muscle has contracted and leaks black fluid on the floor.

The older woman has gone to the kitchen and now she returns with an old dish towel that she puts over the wound. She's trying to stop the bleeding, which would be a good idea, but when she touches the wound, Bill thrashes and kicks, screaming louder than ever. He knocks the woman backward and flings blood all over her and the flat-screen TV behind her.

The younger woman turns to D-Day. "Do something!" she yells. "This was your stupid plan! We risked our lives to get that stupid door shut! Help him!"

"Yeah, the door your stupid ass blocked open with your bike? All of these monsters got in because of you," D-Day points at Bill, writhing in agony and bleeding all over the couch, "and him. So don't go laying this off on ME! And besides, there's nothing we can do for him. You'd best make your peace with that and decide who's going to take care of him when he turns."

The woman's face contorts, and D-Day expects her to explode at him, but instead, he gets tears.

"No, there has to be something we can do. There has to be," she says through sobs.

D-Day takes a more conciliatory tone. "Look at that leg. You see the black veins? That's the way Cortez's arm looked after he was bitten. My guess is that with the way its spread through his veins, by now it's spread into his torso. If we could have amputated the leg immediately, maybe that would have stopped it, but he probably would have bled out. I just don't think there's anything that can be done."

"But you don't know that, right? He could still be okay if we stop the bleeding?" the older woman asks.

"All I can tell you is that I've been watching these things since this started," D-Day says. "They attack someone, that person dies, they move on to the next poor bastard they can get their hands on. A few minutes later, the person they attacked gets up and joins them. Every time. Every one of them. Not one of them has recovered or stayed dead."

On the couch, Bill coughs and emits a hollow-sounding moan then sinks into the cushions, finally lying still. He's still breathing, but death lurks nearby.

"Look, I don't want to be insensitive, but the clock's ticking here. We need to be ready for what comes next," D-Day says. He looks at Bill writhing in pain on the couch. He knows that it's a matter of time before he dies and comes back. He needs the three remaining people to understand that.

"I need the three of you to understand this," D-Day says, speaking in a deliberate tone. "He is going to die. He will come back as one of them, and he will try to attack you, kill you, and turn you, just like what's happening to him. The only thing that will stop him is that" —he points at the bloody baseball bat— "or this," and he pats the pistol on his hip.

He seems to have had an effect because he can see the hope drain from their faces. He turns to the dark-haired woman. Now that he's closer to her, he can tell she's younger than he thought. She's in her early thirties, maybe, and quite attractive.

"What's your name?" he asks.

"Carmen," she says, and nods at the other two. "My parents, Elizabeth and George."

"Carmen, I know this has to be tough to deal with. But this is reality." He glances at his watch and does a mental calculation. "What I've seen over the last ten hours is like a nightmare. If I didn't see it happen before my eyes, I'd never believe it. But there it is; it's happening, and we can't stop it. And here's how you deal with a situation you're immersed in that's going to unfold whether you want it to or not; you either accept it, fight and do whatever you have to, or you keep saying 'there has to be something else we can do.' Deny reality and you'll die."

George clears his throat. "It's easy to say that when it's not your son-in-law on that couch."

"George, right?" D-Day asks. George nods. "Him being your son-in-law doesn't change the situation. He's going to die. He's going to come back. He'll have to be put back down. I'm trying to be gentle here, but you need to understand this much; either he gets put down, or all four of you do. I'll do it for you if you can't, but you guys need to make that decision. It's going to be light in a couple of hours, and we have a lot of work to do. We need to get the mess in the hallway cleaned up, get supplies gathered, figure out how many people we have in the building and how long we can last. I can't have four new zombies running around causing havoc."

"I'll do it." Carmen says. "If I can use your pistol."

"Carmen, you shouldn't have to ..." George starts to say, but Carmen cuts him off mid-sentence.

"Dad, I'll do it. If he doesn't have much time left I want to spend it with him. Right up to the end. I owe him that."

"Are you sure? Honey, this is too much for you to deal with ..." George says.

"George, it's her decision," Elizabeth says.

"I just ... she shouldn't have to take this on, not when this guy's volunteered to do it. She's been through enough tonight already." George is protesting, but the strength has left his voice.

"I'd like to be alone with him please," Carmen says. "Can you guys wait in the hall?"

D-Day takes his pistol out of its holster and holds it out to Carmen.

"Do you know how to use this?" he asks.

"I've shot before. Bill has a .45 ... at home," she answers.

"Okay, well, this is a .40. Still has some kick to it, but if you can handle a .45 you can handle this. It's suppressed, so it won't be real loud. Just don't miss the headshot."

She nods and ushers the three of them out into the hallway. The zombies in the stairwell still pound on the door. Elizabeth flinches a tiny bit with each thump, but George and D-Day tune out the noise. D-Day scans the hallway, looking for any zombies that may not have been completely dispatched, but he sees nothing amiss. George breaks the silence first.

"It was an accident, you know," he says. "The door, the motorcycle. She was meeting us here for dinner. Bill was here helping us set up a new computer, and we decided to order pizza. Of course, the food never got delivered, and Carmen barely made it here after she got off of work. She went through a lot to get here, and now she's about to lose her husband. You should go easy on her."

"I didn't mean to be hard on her, George," D-Day says. "It was an accident, but it still put the entire building's occupants in danger. We have to deal with the threat first and grieve later. Emotions have no place in this situation. Emotions will get you killed."

"Where did you serve?" George asks. "With an attitude like that, you must have been in combat. Iraq? Afghanistan?"

"Both," D-Day says.

"Wow. You must have seen some bad stuff," George says.

"I did. And this stuff," D-Day gestures to the mess of dead zombies in the hallway, "is worse than anything I saw over there. These things can't be reasoned with. They aren't afraid. You can't intimidate them. Point a gun at them and they don't even flinch. I don't know what's going on, how this started, or what happens next, but I do know that we still have a lot to do this morning before we can let down and grieve for what we've seen and done."

"Okay, you've made your point," Elizabeth says. "We get it, and we'll help you with whatever you need. We owe you that. We wouldn't be here if you and your friend hadn't taken these things on like you did."

Before D-Day can say anything, they hear a scream from the apartment, and then the muffled whump of the gunshot. George has the door open and is inside before D-Day can get his rifle into firing position. He follows George and finds Carmen standing over the transformed body of her husband, Bill. Black fluid leaks from a hole in his forehead just above the left eye.

She turns around and holds out the pistol. The slide is locked back, the magazine empty.

"One bullet?" she asks. "What the hell was that?"

"I told you not to miss," D-Day says.

"What, were you afraid I was going to kill myself if you gave me two bullets?"

"Frankly, yes," D-Day replies.

She presses the gun against his chest, lets it go without checking to see if he had a grip on it, and walks past him to her father, who gives her a long hug.

D-Day takes out the empty magazine, puts in a fresh one, releases the slide, and holsters the gun.

He looks down at the body and thinks of the forty-plus other bodies littering the first floor, and then the five bodies he left up on the third floor. They need to clean this mess up before it starts to smell worse than it does. It's going to be a long morning.

CHAPTER 10

South of Fort Collins, Colorado

R obert runs toward the garage, toward the flashes of light that just lit up the closed space. Annie and Stephenie are crying because the intent of the note Henry left is clear; he intends to kill himself after shooting his zombified wife. While Stephenie couldn't hear the gunshots, she saw the dual flashes from the garage and has assumed the worst.

Robert enters the garage and turns on the light, making the house visible for miles. A few seconds later the light goes dark, and Robert emerges from the side access door.

"Robert ..." Annie says but trails off. Robert just shakes his head. He walks back to the others, who are standing by the Ram pickup truck.

"He did it. The son of a bitch did it," he says, and he grabs the driver's door and slams it shut. He opens it and slams it again, and again and again. Finally, he leaves it shut and drops to his knees and begins sobbing.

"Sorry, man ..." Keith says.

"Don't! Don't you dare say anything!" Robert screams through his sobs. "If you assholes hadn't come along, we would have been fine! He was looking for the first excuse to punch his ticket and you motherfuckers gave it to him!" He gets up and takes a couple of angry steps toward Keith.

"Robert!" Annie yells, stepping in front of him. "Stop this! We have to figure out what to do next. The world is still crashing down around us. If we're going to go, we need to do it soon. We can't do anything about Henry or Aunt Lynn if we get caught up in a horde of those things. Live today, grieve tomorrow, right? Isn't that what Henry would say?"

"Henry's not going to say anything because he fucking bailed on us! I don't care what he wanted; I'm not going anywhere with these assholes," he says. He turns toward Ben and the rest of the group. "You all can get moving, find your own way out of here."

Everyone is unsure what to say or do next. It's Stephenie who breaks the silence. Though she's deaf and her speech isn't clear, everyone understands when she says, "We need to bury them."

Annie and Robert look at her silhouette in the darkness. They have just realized that in the dark she can neither read their lips nor see sign language, yet somehow, she's chosen the right moment to speak. It's almost as though she can hear the conversation.

"I need help digging the hole. Who will help me?" she says. Keith immediately raises his hand, and the others follow suit.

Annie latches on to the concept. "Robert and I will get some sheets and wrap them up. Get them ready," she says. "Okay, Robert? Steph's right, this needs to be done. Whether we stay or go, we can't leave them as they are and it doesn't seem like a funeral home is going to be able to get them any time soon."

Robert, still glaring at Keith in the dim light, pauses for a long moment and finally agrees with his sister. He and Annie head to the house to find something suitable to wrap the bodies of their aunt and uncle in, and Stephenie leads the group to a shed on the south side of the house. She opens it, walks in, and comes right back out with a trio of shovels. She extends one to Keith and another to Ben. Keeping the last one for herself, she walks over to a gate that opens with a loud squeak that she doesn't hear and walks past a massive garden to a bare patch of ground. At the end of the patch is a headstone, barely visible in the darkness.

"Our dog is buried there," she says, pointing at the headstone. "This is a good place for them. They'd like being close to Charlie."

She starts digging a hole, and Keith moves a few feet to her right and starts a second hole. Stephenie tugs at his sleeve. "No, they'd want to be buried together. One hole," she says.

They work for about thirty minutes, with Andy, Danielle, Toni and Natalie taking turns with the shovels when one of the others gets tired. They've got a hole about two and a half feet deep, four feet wide, and six feet long when Annie shows up.

"We could use some help," she says. "It's harder than you would think, trying to move a ... well, a body." She chokes on the last word. Andy and Natalie offer to help them while the rest of the kids keep digging.

A couple of minutes later, the four of them are walking into the garden area, carrying the first of the two bodies. The smell of the oily fluid leaking from the wound tells the kids that this is Aunt Lynn. They place her as gently as possible in the hole and head back for Uncle Henry. Soon he's lying in the hole next to his beloved wife, without whom he was unwilling to face the changing world. Robert has put a diffuser on the end of a Fenix flashlight, so it acts as a lantern instead of a spotlight. Annie signs for Stephenie while Robert talks.

"Um ..." Robert says, clearing his throat. "I don't know what to say, exactly. These two have been my parents as long as I can remember. Henry always said that while he never asked for kids, if he could have put in an order he never could have hoped for three kids as good as us. He was a plain-spoken, honest man who said pretty much what he was thinking. Some people thought that was rude, but I admired it. And Lynn was ... was ..."

"Our mom." Annie finishes his thought. "Even

though Robert and Stephenie don't remember our real mom, Aunt Lynn was every bit as good of a mother to us. She loved us unconditionally and never thought twice about taking us in and raising us as her own. I know this is going to hit me—hit *us*—real hard later, but whatever happens next I hope that we make her proud."

Stephenie starts signing and Annie translates for the others, almost out of habit. "Blessed be the God and Father of our Lord Jesus Christ, the Father of mercies and God of all comfort, who comforts us all in our affliction, so that we may be able to comfort those who are in any affliction, with the comfort from which we ourselves are comforted by God," she says.

Everyone looks at Stephenie with surprise that she had scripture already prepared for this event. The next part she says out loud and either she's speaking more clearly, or they're all getting accustomed to her mode of speech because they have no problems understanding her.

"Henry taught me that after I went deaf. He said it meant that no matter how bad we have it, someone else has it worse. He said that no matter what happens, I should never feel sorry for myself and always think of the people who have it worse than me and be glad that I got the hand I was dealt. He never let me have a pity party when I was growing up, and I'm not going to start now. Bad things happen to people, and there's nothing we can do about it. I hope God is comforting him and Aunt Lynn tonight."

With that, she throws a shovel full of dirt onto the two bodies, wrapped with love in their best linens. Robert and Annie also begin shoveling dirt into the grave and in a few minutes, the hole has been filled. The group files silently back around the front of the house.

"We appreciate your help with that, but you guys can get in your Landcruiser and get on your way now," Robert says. "You're welcome to go across Henry's land to avoid the blockades, but you need to go."

"Robert don't be rude. We haven't even discussed what we're doing," Annie says. "Henry wanted us to leave."

"Well, he's not here now, and I never wanted to leave in the first place. We have plenty of food and ammo. We can hold out until this thing blows over," he says.

Stephenie walks up with a large backpack on her back. She stands in front of Ben and hands him the night vision goggles she had been wearing earlier. "Let's go," she says.

Robert grabs her sleeve and pulls her toward him. He signs while talking to her. "What do you think you're doing?" he asks.

"I'm not staying here. You saw the TV. You saw what Lynn turned into. I'm getting away from here," she signs, though no one except Robert and Annie can understand her sign language.

"I agree, I think we should go," Annie says out loud

while signing. "And if Steph is leaving with these guys, I'm going with her. I'm not letting her go by herself."

Robert stares back and forth between the two girls for a few seconds and realizes that he's outnumbered by his sisters. He knows from experience that once they've aligned on something and set their minds to it, there's no turning them around. He sighs and says, "Okay, I'm with you. But you two ride with me. And like Henry said—once this dies down, we go our separate ways."

The girls nod their assent.

They hear the staccato of gunfire in the distance, and everyone starts throwing nervous glances back and forth.

"That was probably at the barricade on Trilby Road," Robert says. He grabs the backpack and pulls it off of Stephenie's shoulders, grunting when the weight falls against him. He puts it in the crew cab of his pickup, then turns back to Ben and the others. "I'll lead the way. I've pulled the brake light fuse, so we can run dark. Try not to rear-end me. Before we go, let's get your brake lights disabled so we don't give any Guardsmen we cross paths with something to shoot at."

"Or zombies something to chase," Toni adds.

In the shed, Robert wastes no time with the lighting configuration of the FJ.

"Time is of the essence," he says. "And it's not like you're going to get a ticket."

Before Ben can protest, Robert swings a hammer and smashes the left brake light, then the right.

"Hit the brakes," he says to Ben.

Ben presses the brake pedal and the light still works on the passenger side. Robert whacks it with the hammer, and it goes dark for good.

"Here," Annie says. "So we can keep on the same page." She holds out a walkie-talkie.

Ben takes it and hands it to Toni. "You're the co-pilot," he says. She takes it and the night vision goggles that Henry had handed over earlier and heads to the front seat.

Robert turns and gets in the cab of his truck. Stephenie smiles at them, and Keith could swear he saw her wink before she, too climbed into the truck.

"I guess that's it," he says. "Let's mount up." The group climbs into the SUV and Ben backs the FJ40 out of the shed. From the back seat, Keith speaks up.

"Dude, that Robert guy is a dick," he says.

"Not now, Keith. I just want to get us the fuck out of here," Ben replies.

"I'm just saying, we don't need any of his shit. We were doing fine until they hijacked us. It's not our fault their people got bit and killed themselves," Keith says, then punctuates his statement with, "Fuck him."

"Okay, enough!" Ben snaps. "Can we please focus on not dying tonight? Jesus."

Keith sulks while Ben puts the FJ in gear and rolls up on the rear of the Robert's pickup. Annie's voice crackles over the walkie-talkie she gave them.

"Take off the night vision and look behind you. It's a good thing we're leaving," she says.

They all turn and look back to the northeast. A giant fireball is rising in the air, and a thunderous BOOM follows a few seconds later. Ben rolls the window down and can hear gunfire again. It sounds like automatic gunfire, which means the soldiers at the barricades are either engaged with people or zombies. Either option is not good.

The walkie-talkie crackles again. "Time to go, kiddies," Robert's voice says from the speaker. Ahead, he's already pulling away from Ben in his pickup.

Keith mutters something, but Ben can't hear it, so he ignores it. He's put on the night vision goggles that Stephenie gave him and he's impressed that he can see clearly about seventy yards with them instead of the nine or ten yards of vision that Andy's gave him. Ben puts the FJ40 in gear and hits the gas, spinning the back wheels in the dirt for a second, then accelerates down the dirt trail after Robert's black truck. Annie comes back on the walkie-talkie.

"We're going across Henry's land for a while. He has a lot of land from when he used to graze cattle and sheep. We have trails like this one all over the land to get to the fences, the water troughs, and all of that stuff. Henry sold off the last of his herd a couple of years ago and now we mostly just ride our four-wheelers on it. We used to come out at night and hunt coyotes. That's what all the night vision stuff is for. Coyotes would kill the sheep and sometimes even the cattle, though that was rare. It cost Henry a lot of money. Besides, it gave him a lot of quality time with us; Stephenie in particular. She loved coming out on hunts, and she's the best shot. Better even than Henry."

Annie continues the narrative for a while, directing them to watch out as they cross a buried culvert, so they don't drop a wheel in the gully on either side or warning them about a large washout on one side of the trail. Eventually, she stops telling them the history of the land they're traversing and just gives directions when needed.

They come to one of several long, steep ridges of rocks jutting up into the night. These ridges mark the end of the great prairie and the beginning of the Rocky Mountains. Annie advises them to put the FJ into four-wheel-drive as they get ready to traverse the ridge in one of only a handful of spots a four-wheeled vehicle can pass through. They slow to a crawl as the two vehicles zigzag up the trail and creep their way through a narrow opening in the rocks, and then they zigzag down the steep slope on the back side of the ridge.

Annie comes on the walkie-talkie again. "We're going to be on a regular road in a few minutes. Robert says even though it's a paved road to keep your lights off. We'll only be on it for a bit and then it's on more trails. We'll cross Highway 34 and cut across the Buttes Golf Course. From there we hope you know where you're going because we run out of backcountry trails to follow."

From under his sweatshirt, Andy says, "Hand me the walkie-talkie."

Toni passes it back to Natalie, who slides her hand

under the hoodie and hands off the Motorola device to Andy. He clicks the button. "When we get to Highway 34 let us take the lead. I've got a course mapped out that should get us there with minimum time on the roads."

"Okay, you got it," Annie says.

They ride for another thirty minutes without incident. Ben takes the lead and follows Andy's directions, eventually taking a dirt road that follows an irrigation ditch.

"You're sure this takes us to Longview?" Ben asks.

"It looks like it goes all the way to Venison Road, and from there we can cut through a farm and cross Gypsum Highway right by the Gypsum Creek Golf Course," Andy replies.

"That's perfect! If we can get to the golf course, that's only like two miles from my folks' place. I know exactly where to go from there!" Ben exclaims.

"And the last time we tried crossing farmland worked out so well for us," Danielle says. It's the first thing she's said in hours, and of course, it's negative.

"We're out of Fort Collins, aren't we? See any zombies?" Ben asks. "Can we just celebrate something going right tonight? For once?"

Danielle resumes her silence, which is fine with Ben. For the first time he feels hopeful their overly long journey is nearing its end.

Just as he's thinking this, he rounds a corner on the road and hits the brakes hard. Robert, in the Ram 1500 reacts quickly and avoids rear-ending the FJ40.

"What's the deal?" he asks over the walkie-talkie.

Ben is staring at a gate made of thick steel pipe, set on massive hinges. The gate opens toward the vehicle and stops against a large steel plate that runs the full length of the five-foot steel pole on the right side of the gate. A thick chain wraps through the gate and around the pole and is secured by a massive padlock.

"Something that wasn't on the map," Ben says into the walkie. "Something we're not prepared for."

Ben, Robert, Toni, Annie, and Keith get out and walk over to the gate. Ben gives the lock a tug to verify that it's actually locked. It is.

"Anyone have bolt cutters? So we can cut the chain?" Robert asks. "No? Then I'll just shoot the lock."

"I don't think that will do it," Keith says. "Look at the size of that thing!"

"I don't care what you think. Unless you have a magic key that opens this thing, we don't have a lot of other options." Robert is openly hostile to Keith.

Stephenie walks up to the group, takes Andy's night vision goggles off of Keith's head, puts them on, and kneels down in front of the lock. Unseen in the darkness, Danielle gives her a crusty look.

Stephenie takes a small black pouch out of the pocket of her jacket, and after looking at the lock, she pulls a couple of pieces of thin metal out of it and inserts them into the key slot.

"Is that a lock pick set?" Annie asks.

Robert taps Stephenie on the shoulder and signs while he asks her.

"Yes," she says. "Now shut up and give me a few minutes. I can get this open."

"When the hell did she start picking locks?" a surprised Annie asks.

"And when did she get so bossy?" Robert says back. "She's full of surprises tonight."

Ben scans the area around them, nervous that a zombie will come after them, or a farmer will shoot at them. This road has taken them uncomfortably close to some farm houses, but so far there are no signs of life from any of them.

"Got it!" Stephenie says. She stands up and pulls the lock from the chain, removes the chain from the gate, and pushes the gate open. She puts the lock picks back in the kit, zips it up, and puts the night vision goggles back on Keith's head, but gets them crooked. She smiles at him, lightly slaps his cheek and says, "Thanks."

"Uh. No problem," Keith stammers.

"She can't hear you, dick," Robert says. Annie smacks Robert in the back of the head, and they walk back to the truck.

Keith waits while the two vehicles drive through the gate, then closes the gate and wraps the chain around the post a couple of times. He doesn't put the lock on the chain just in case they need to come back this way in a hurry. This way, they can ram the gate to open it with minimal damage to either vehicle. Keith runs up and jumps in the Toyota, and Robert puts the Ram in gear and starts after them.

"I don't like that smart-assed kid, Keith," he says.

"Really? I thought you wanted to be besties," Annie says. "And you should be nicer. We might be with them for a while."

"Not if I can help it," he says.

In the back seat, Stephenie misses the conversation, but she knows how Robert feels. She sees him tense up every time Keith is nearby. Or says anything. Or exists. She smiles at that last thought. Robert is uber-protective of her, but he's going to have to let her do her thing, especially now that the world is ending. She's not going to live under his thumb forever.

Up in the FJ40, Keith is clearly becoming smitten with Stephenie.

"Does anyone else think the deaf chick is kinda badass?" he asks. "I guess you'd have to be, what with not having all five senses."

"We get it, Keith. She's cute. She shoots. She can pick locks. She smiled at you. She's Supergirl," Danielle says.

"What?" Keith protests. "What did I say? I'm just pointing out she's pretty badass. I don't know anyone else that can pick locks. And, I never said she was cute."

"It's just like you to be flirting in the middle of the freaking zombie apocalypse—in front of me, no less," Danielle says with a chill in her voice.

"Oh, Jesus, here we go," Keith says. Even in the dark everyone can tell he's rolling his eyes.

"GUYS! Please, knock it off. I'm stressed enough as it is; I don't need to hear this right now," Ben says, and then a second later he adds, "Oh, God dammit!"

"What is it?" Toni asks.

"Another gate," Ben replies.

"Cue Supergirl," Danielle snarks.

CHAPTER 11

D-Day grunts as he drops the body off of the roof. Five full seconds elapse before he hears the thud of the corpse hitting the pavement.

George Bustamante, Carmen's father, is helping him dispose of the rotten bodies of the undead they've killed. They've decided to drop them off the roof into the cordoned-off area that houses the numerous trash dumpsters for the building. The last one on the utility cart is that of George's deceased son-in-law, Bill.

"I'm sad that my Carmen had to deal with this, but between you and me, I never really liked this guy," he says.

"Really?" D-Day says. "You guys seemed really broken up over it."

"Don't get me wrong, this is terrible. But given

what else has happened tonight, it could have been worse. They were getting divorced, you know."

"No," D-Day says. "I didn't know that. I just met you people a couple of hours ago. In case you forgot."

George smiles at him. "You remind me of a guy I knew in the service. Said whatever he thought. No filter. You always knew where you stood with him."

"Yeah? What happened to him?"

"Killed in Vietnam. The same day I shipped out home. My tour was over. He re-upped. Got killed while I was on a plane to Germany."

"That's too bad," D-Day says.

"He made his choice," George says, shrugging. "We all do, and we have to live with the outcome. Anyway, Carmen thinks we don't know about it, but Bill has been talking to us, trying to get us to take his side against Carmen, to get her to withdraw the papers. Like we'd do that."

"Why hasn't she told you?" D-Day asks.

"Don't know. She will, in time. Or maybe not now, not since this has happened." George gestures at the body under the sheet. "She has her reasons, whatever they are."

"So—how do you want to do this?" D-Day asks. "Wanna say something? Or just over the edge?"

George looks at D-Day for a second, and then looks down at Bill's body and says, "Ashes to ashes, dust to dust. May God have mercy on your soul and grant you passage to heaven."

He looks back up at D-Day.

"Grab his feet," he says. Together they heft the body to the edge and pitch it over with the other fetid corpses.

They push the cart back over to the maintenance room that sticks up from the roof. It's a twenty-foot by twenty-foot building that encloses the elevator and the UPS batteries that run the building's core features—like the emergency lighting and the electronic locks—in the event of a power outage. The power cells are kept topped off by dozens of solar panels covering most of the roof's surface.

D-Day turns around. "Look at that," he says, waving his arm out over the Denver Metro area to the south and west of their building. Smoke, even in this pre-dawn gloom, can be seen rising from dozens of fires, some with flames extending hundreds of feet into the air. Outside of the downtown area, few buildings are over ten stories, and the farther out you look, the flatter it gets. There are wide swaths of neighborhoods consisting of single-family homes where the power is out, creating black holes in the normally well-lit landscape. The glimpse of I-25 they can see from the roof shows a road clogged with cars. None of them are moving. A far off scream breaks the silence, but it's not repeated. D-Day wonders what happened to that person. He can guess, but hopes they made it.

"It's the end of days," George says.

"We're not getting off that easy," D-Day says. "Come on, we have more work to do."

The two men head to the maintenance room and

press the button for the elevator. It opens right away. D-Day pushes the cart inside, and then he and George get in. George presses "1" and the doors close. D-Day holds his breath, but the power stays on, and they make it all the way to the ground floor.

Carmen and her mother, Elizabeth, have been going through the building's roster, kept in the security office, and calling the apartments on the intercom to see who's home and who's not. They're on the last floor when D-Day and George return.

Carmen hustles over to her father and gives him a big hug.

"Thank you," she says and looks at D-Day. "And thank you, too. I could not deal with that."

"No problem," D-Day says. "How's it coming?"

"We're about done. So far about half the building is here, half isn't answering."

"Okay. We've got a lot of work to do," D-Day says. "I think the people on the lower floors need to relocate to apartments higher up. The fewer floors we have to keep secured, the better." He looks at George. "Can you help coordinate that effort, George?"

"I suppose," he says. "But what if people don't want to move?"

"It's their choice, but they're on their own if they stay separate from the group."

"What if we move people into an apartment, and the person who lives there comes back?"

"You've seen the city. What do you think the chances are of that happening?"

"I guess you're right," George says with a sigh.

"And don't do it all yourself. When you meet someone who seems competent, recruit them to help," D-Day instructs him.

"Okay, can do," George says.

"Elizabeth," D-Day continues, "you stay in close contact with George. When someone picks a new place to hang their hat, update that roster so we know who's who in the building. We need to know the names of everyone in their family, how many there are, etc."

"Got it," she says.

"And you," he says to Carmen, "I want you to start going through the vacant apartments and grabbing all the food you can find. We'll use the common room on the twelfth floor to consolidate it. We need to know how many people we have, how much food and how much water we have. Then we'll have an idea of how much trouble we're in. Grab people to help when you find someone who's competent."

"Should I fill the tubs and sinks in the apartments I search?" Carmen asks.

"Great idea! Water will eventually get stagnant, but we can boil it for cooking and drinking, and we can find other uses for it. The more we have stored up, the better. Lack of water—clean water—will kill us faster than anything else. Other than the zombies, of course. I'll get some people to help me move the rest of the bodies."

D-Day looks around at the three of them.

"This is it, folks. We're going to be stuck in this

building for a while. We have to get everyone coordinated and on the same page with us, or we won't make it very long. The Army is planning to come north from Colorado Springs. They said they'd be here tomorrow —today, rather—but I have my doubts. The point is, they'll be here. We just have to make it until they show up."

"Okay," George says. "Let's get to it then."

They get busy with their respective tasks. D-Day makes a copy of Elizabeth's updated building roster, marking the people he knows, denoting them with a plus sign or a minus sign, depending on if he thinks they'll be an asset or liability. It strikes him how few people in the building he knows. That's going to change soon.

CHAPTER 12

North of Longview, Colorado

"What's taking so long?" Robert signs to Stephenie. "The last one took you like two minutes!"

"Do you want to do it?" she says out loud so he can hear her frustration. "It's a better lock."

Robert holds his hands in the air in a sign of submission and steps back, away from her. "Sorry!" he says to her back.

"She can't hear you, dick," Annie says, smiling. Robert shoots her a look that she misses in the dark, nor can he see her grinning.

It takes Stephenie more than ten minutes to get it picked, switching to different configurations on the picks until she finally finds one that works. She waits while the trucks drive through, wraps the chains through the gate like the previous one, and then she jumps into the Ram, and they're moving again. They're near the north-south running Highway 287, the main artery into Longview from any of the towns to the north. Robert speaks up through the walkie-talkie.

"If we keep running into these gates, this is going to take us forever. We're out of the hot zone; do you guys think we should just take 287 into town?"

Ben stops the FJ40 a hundred feet short of the road. He grabs the walkie-talkie.

"Hold tight. Something's coming," he says. He sees flashing lights through the trees, and then the headlights of two vehicles. They're going well over a hundred miles per hour toward Longview. It looks like an Escalade in the lead being chased by a state patrolman. The sirens from the trooper's car wail and then fade as it speeds past them. A few seconds later, another state trooper races past.

"Any other night that would seem out of place," Robert says over the walkie. "Tonight it just seems kinda normal. I guess that answers my question about taking Highway 287 into town."

Ben puts the FJ into gear and creeps toward the highway. No other cars are visible, so he pulls up onto the highway and crosses to the dirt road on the other side. They're only a quarter mile off the highway when they run into another locked gate.

This time, the only people who get out are the Sims, with Robert and Annie standing watch while Stephenie works on the lock. In the east, the horizon has turned a light gray. Ben checks his watch: it's 5:20.

The sun will be up in another half hour. These locked gates hamper their progress but beat the alternative of running the gauntlet on the main roads, where the police are clearly active. They've got to get into Longview before daylight, though, or their odds bypassing any roadblocks are slim.

Stephenie recognizes the lock as the same one she just picked. She grabs the same pick she used on that one, and she gets it opened in a few seconds over a minute. She loops the chain around the gate, hops back in the truck, and they get moving again. Then things start happening quickly.

As they round a bend in the road, the passenger window on the FJ Cruiser shatters and the front tire goes flat. Ben hits the brakes, but Annie screams into the walkie-talkie from the truck behind them.

"GO GO GO! Don't stop, we're being shot at!" she yells.

Ben hears several thumps as bullets hit the side of the FJ and feels something burning his leg. Everyone in the SUV is screaming. From the black Ram, Stephenie returns fire with her AR15 while Annie gets hers ready. Robert hits the gas and accelerates around the right side of the FJ.

Floodlights turn on, and Ben sees several people outside of a farmhouse to their right, armed with rifles running up the hill toward them. A couple of four-wheeled ATVs come roaring out of a barn with armed men on them. Ben has a hard time steering with the flat tire and knows he can't go much farther with the car in this condition. He makes it around the bend, for the moment out of sight of the posse chasing them, and finds Robert's truck parked to the right side of the dirt trail. It's empty. In front of the Toyota is another locked gate.

"What the hell? Where did they go?" Ben says out loud.

Behind them, the beams of the headlights on the ATVs crest the hill and point in their direction. Any second now they'll round the corner and, Ben assumes, they'll kill them all. He can't believe the Sims took off like they did. He grabs the walkie-talkie and presses the transmit button.

"Hey, where did you guys go? What should we do?" he asks.

Annie comes back over the speaker. "Stay where you are," she says, "And stay down."

Gunfire erupts from multiple locations around them. To their left they can see Robert and Annie now, shooting from the concealment of the tall grass that grows along the irrigation ditch. Based on the direction of the noise, Stephenie is somewhere unseen to their right, and the trio has a decent crossfire set up, converging their fire from two different locations onto the people coming from the farmhouse.

Crouching in the back seat, Keith can't help smiling as he says, "Supergirl to the rescue."

"I NEED to cross over the trail. Steph shouldn't be by herself," Robert says.

"Robert, she's fine. Just keep shooting or none of us are going to be okay." Annie peers around the cover of a fallen tree trunk, sights in on the lead four-wheeled ATV and squeezes the trigger. The man driving falls off and the ATV veers off the path and stops in a thatch of weeds.

"How many are there?" Robert asks.

"Eight, as far as I could tell. Six now," Annie says, eyeing the two men who lie motionless in the dirt in the predawn twilight. Shots from their left tell them that Stephenie is fighting with someone. Robert wants to sprint over to her and help, but he knows he'd be a target, and he also knows she's stealthier than both he and Annie combined.

"Probably down to five now," Annie says.

A voice breaks the silence.

"You all are trespassing! Put your weapons down and get your hands up or this will go badly for you!" a man's voice calls out to them.

"We don't want any trouble! We're just trying to get through to Longview! Let us go on and no one else will get hurt!" Robert yells back.

"That's horseshit!" a different voice says. "They're here to sabotage our equipment. They're Milford men!"

"Shut up, DJ," the first man says. Then to the group, "Too late for that 'we don't want trouble,' my friend. You've already killed some of our people. No one takes up arms if they don't want trouble. I'll say it one more time, lay down your arms or you're going to die! And for what? So Milford can make another buck?"

"You fired on us first! What the hell is wrong with you?" Robert shouts back. He looks at Annie and mouths "Milford?" She just shrugs back at him.

"I'm giving you to the count of five! One ..." the man starts, but a shot from the left side of the trail, from Stephenie's position, cuts his count short. Several voices are talking at once, so Robert takes the opportunity to move to his right, behind a large cottonwood tree.

Once he's behind the tree, he stands and peeks around the trunk. He can see two men down on the path and two more on the left side; one isn't moving. The other crawls toward the other ATV. He can hear far-off, muffled voices coming from the direction of the farmhouse. Several large pieces of farming equipment sit rusting in the field, so he figures they're hiding behind one of them. He decides to try a bluff.

"Hey!" he calls out, "you're not faring too well here. You're outnumbered and outgunned. We're not trying to do anything but get to the road and get out of here. Unless you want more blood on YOUR hands, you all head back to that barn and let us pass. We see you coming, we'll shoot you down. We didn't start this fight, but by God we'll finish it!"

More murmuring and then Robert sees an open hand stick up behind the rusted hulk of an old harvester. A man steps halfway out from his cover. "Let us collect our guys and get them some medical attention," he calls to Robert. It's not the same man that was shouting at them a few moments earlier, nor is it the one they called "DJ."

Robert knows they have the upper hand for the moment, but they have to coordinate with the group or these farmers will shoot them in the back as they try to leave.

"No good. Let us get out of here and you can do whatever you want. But we need you down the hill and out of gun range so we can move out," Robert stands firm.

"Come on, man, our people need help!" the man pleads now.

"How about we just kill you all and take our time getting out of here? How'd that be? The quicker you get back, the quicker we're gone."

Robert hears more murmurs, and then the man calls out, "Okay, we're backing off."

Robert sees three of them jogging away from the harvester, back to the barn. He's still watching them when a red light flashes on his left eye. Startled, he ducks down and brings his rifle up, looking for a gunman with a laser sight. Instead, he spots Stephenie sitting up behind an old El Camino missing three of its four tires. She has a laser pointer in her hand that she slides into a pocket, and she signs to Robert. He can just make out what she's saying in the growing light.

He nods and tells her he's got it, thinking that sometimes it's good that they know sign language.

"You there, on your belly behind the old feed bin," he shouts. "Unless you want another hole in your head, you'd best get up and get moving with your friends."

A couple of seconds pass. Robert hears someone yell "DJ!" and a fourth man gets up and starts running for the barn.

Robert signs to Stephenie to look at the lock on the gate and returns to Annie's position behind the fallen tree.

"Well, that was fucked up," he says. "Are you okay?"

"I'm good, not a scratch," she says, though her hands are shaking. "You should check on the others. I ll stay here and watch the barn."

"I can watch the barn," he says. "You should help the kids."

"Go," she says. "I've got this."

Robert gives in and heads back to the vehicles. He finds the group digging through their gear, looking for something.

"What's going on?" he asks.

Ben looks up from the bag through which he's digging. Robert sees his right pants leg is soaked in blood, but the injury doesn't appear to register with Ben.

When he speaks, Ben's voice is strained with panic. "Toni's been shot."

ROBERT RUNS AROUND to the passenger side of the Toyota. There are multiple bullet holes in the side of the vehicle, and the front tire is flat. The passenger door hangs wide open, and Natalie stands next to Toni. Toni winces in pain, her face wet with tears.

"Where is she hit?" he asks.

"Her shoulder and her side, I think," Natalie says. "There's so much blood. I can't tell for sure."

Ben runs up with a medical kit. He takes out some gauze and reaches under Toni's shirt. He presses it against the shoulder wound while she cries out in pain. He repeats the process for the wound in the ribs. He wraps an elastic bandage around the wounds to hold the gauze in place.

"We need to get the tire changed so we can get out of here," Ben says.

"No time," Robert says. "It's only going to take so long until those farmers regroup and realize they have more guns than us. She's shot up and bleeding. Our best bet is to load your shit in the truck and get the hell out of here."

"And leave my FJ behind for them to steal?" Ben asks.

"Your girl or your car, man; you choose," Robert says. Ben nods and hangs his head in submission. Robert turns to the others, clearly in charge now, and says, "Come on guys, let's go, time is a factor here. Get your gear in the back of the truck. Everything you don't want to lose, because we're not coming back here."

Keith and Andy start grabbing their bags and everything else not bolted down and throw it all in the bed of the truck.

Robert comes back to Ben. "How's your leg?" he asks.

"What?" Ben says, genuinely bewildered, then he remembers the burning sensation he felt while they were being shot at. He looks down at his leg, and sees his pants are bloody. "It stings, now that you've mentioned it, but it doesn't bother me. I'm just worried about Toni."

"Okay, I got ya," Robert says. "Just keep an eye on that wound. We'll need to clean it as soon as we get a chance so it doesn't get infected. C'mon, I'll help you move Toni over to the truck."

They get Toni to swing her feet out, and she slides from the seat, crying out when her feet make contact with the ground. With Robert and Ben on either side, they help her walk over to the truck. Robert has Ben get in first and turns Toni, so her back is in the rear door frame.

"Lean back," he says. She leans back against the seat and Robert squats down and hooks his arms around her legs and lifts, pushing her into the truck and against Ben, who in turn helps guide her in by her good left arm. She cries out as he pulls her the rest of the way inside.

"Keep pressure on those wounds," Robert says to Ben. "That's your only job now."

Robert turns to Keith. "Where's the walkie you guys had? I need it." While Keith looks through the stuff they threw into the bed of the truck, Robert turns to Andy. "Go check on Stephenie, on the progress she's making on that lock. Tell her we need to go ASAP."

Keith hands the walkie to Robert, who presses the alert button. He knows this will vibrate the one Annie has with her.

"You ready?" she asks, her voice coming through the speaker.

"Just about. Checking on the lock. Any sign of our friends?" he says back to his sister.

"There's no offensive in the works, at least not that I can tell ... but there are more people down there now. Several women. Maybe the neighbors have come to see what all the shooting's been about? I'm worried that they're going to get stupid and come after us again now that they have more people," Annie says.

Andy comes running toward Robert, flashing a thumbs up. Stephenie is only a few steps behind him. Robert clicks the button on the walkie.

"Let's not be here when they do, sis. We're good to go," he says. He addresses the rest of the group. "We're out of here, folks. Everyone pile in the truck." He signs to Stephenie. *"You get in the back with Annie and guard the rear."*

She nods, goes around to the passenger side of the truck, and grabs a bag of magazines from her gear then climbs in the bed. She puts a fresh magazine in her rifle and sits down as Annie comes running toward the truck. She doesn't wait for directions and climbs right into the bed and takes a seat next to Stephenie, who hands her a magazine from her bag.

Robert has also put a full magazine in his rifle. He holds it out to Andy. "You're riding shotgun," he says. "Do you know how to shoot?"

"I've shot a Ruger 10/22," he replies.

"Same principle, just louder. One trigger pull, one shot, just like the 10/22. Here's the safety," Robert shows him how to work the fire select switch. "The scope has a green circle with a dot in the middle. Put that dot on what you want dead. Don't point it at anything you *don't* want to kill, and please, don't shoot any of us."

Robert pivots to Keith. "Loverboy, you're next to me up front. You're navigating. Forget this back roads crap; just get us to wherever we're going by the fastest route we can take."

Keith nods and climbs into the cab.

"Everyone have everything?" Robert asks. "Speak now or it's getting left behind."

No one says anything, so Robert climbs into the truck, starts it up, and drives forward, through the open gate, and Keith directs him to go right onto Wildcat Road.

It's 6:25 AM and they're only a few minutes from home. On Price Street, four and a half miles away as the crow flies, Kyle Puckett is in the middle of his all-out sprint away from the female zombie he stumbled upon by the supermarket.

Robert hits the gas and the black truck speeds away from Nelson Farms, though none of them knew that's where they were.

CHAPTER 13

Blankets cover the bodies of four men. Virginia Nelson rubs her hand across her daughter-in-law Vanessa's back in an attempt to comfort her; Vanessa's husband (Virginia's second oldest son) lies under one of the blankets. Virginia has her own grieving to do, but she's the matriarch of the family, so it will have to wait. Dale Nelson, her husband, is the CEO of Nelson Farms, LLC, and the CEO of the Nelson family itself. Virginia is his number two, and he doesn't make many decisions without her.

Correction, she thinks to herself. Dale *was* CEO. She looks again at the four blankets, one of which covers Dale. Together they have faced tough economies, droughts, sabotage and legal battles with massive pro-GMO corporations like Milford, and they managed to keep the farm intact and solvent. They helped their only daughter's husband and his family keep their dairy farm from falling into Big Corporate hands by bringing them into the LLC, which they've always joked stands for 'Little Local Company.'

When their neighboring farms were in financial trouble they leased their land from them so they would not lose their farms; some just sold the land to them outright. Every acre of land kept out of Milford's hands was a victory for the small farmer. Over the last five years, since the economic crash of 2008, their conglomerate has grown to more than 150,000 acres.

In addition to her husband, Virginia's children have all joined the company as it's grown. They raise corn, sugar beets, and wheat; they also raise a limited number of cattle, pigs and chickens, which they use to feed the family and sell to locally owned restaurants. After all their years of struggles, all their work, all the legal wrangling and, at times, physical confrontations with Big Corporate thugs, one night of civil unrest has brought it all down. Her husband, Dale; second oldest son, Roger; son-in-law's brother William; and the farm's foreman, Hector Martinez, all lie on the ground, dead, and covered with blankets. As she stares at the bodies, Virginia's mind goes back to last night's events.

WHEN BEN PUCKETT drove through the first gate, he tripped a motion alarm that, in turn, sent an alert to Dale's phone. His sons and daughter also get these alerts. Dale's phone rang within a few seconds. Dale Junior, or DJ, was on the other end.

"Are you getting this alert?" he asked.

"I am. Probably a coyote," Dale said. Coyotes often jumped through the gates rather than over the fence, tripping the motion sensors in the process.

"All this shit on TV, these riots and you're not concerned about this?" DJ asked.

"What, DJ, do you think the meth-addled miscreants down in Denver are going to come all the way north to our farm and use the gates to access our land? Don't get panicky, son," Dale Senior replied.

"All this shit going on gives those Milford bastards the perfect cover to sabotage our equipment again. You think the cops are going to come out for a trespassing complaint on a night like this?" DJ countered.

"We're not going to panic, Deej. Just keep your wits about you and let's see what happens," Dale said.

About fifteen minutes passed, and another alert buzzed on Dale's phone followed immediately by another call from DJ. He didn't even issue a greeting when Dale answered.

"You still think it's coyotes? Think they're going from gate to gate tripping the sensors? I'm telling you; it's Milford. They're pissed off that they lost in court last week, and they're going to sabotage our shit, Dad. It has to be them."

Dale pondered the issue for a minute. On the one hand, DJ has always been quick to anger. Growing up, he started more than his share of fights, always saying it was "pre-emptive." If he didn't strike first, he'd be at a disadvantage when—not *if*—the other guy started it, and Dale had, on more than one occasion, warned his boy that a quick fuse was liable to get him burned one day. On the other hand, Hector had seen several Milford trucks crawling past their land earlier in the day, lingering near the gates that accessed the irrigation ditches, and by proxy the pumping stations that kept the water flowing to the crops.

"Okay, son, it won't hurt to be ready. You organize it. Get your brothers, Hector, whoever else you can get to come over, and let's have a welcoming committee in case there is something bad going on. But let's be smart about this. The last thing we need is to wind up back in court with Milford. They'll end up bleeding us dry in that courthouse. They can afford to pay lawyers to harass us; we can't afford to keep paying to defend against it."

DJ and two of Dale's other sons, Roger and Tim, were at their house when the third alert hit their phones. Roger was beaming because he was the one who set up the motion sensors and the system that sent alerts to the family's smartphones. After a series of covert attacks—they believed by Milford employees, but could never prove it—damaged one of their harvesters and several pump stations, Dale okayed the expense and Roger had everything up and running in two weeks. They got a fair number of false positives from coyotes or deer, as Dale said. However, in light of more than $60,000 in damages from the sabotage, they all figured it was a good trade if it could prevent another attack, or offer proof of who was responsible.

This third alert also triggered an infrared camera, similar to the ones that hunters leave in the woods to capture evidence of game in their hunting areas. The camera sent the image to their phones.

"Holy shit!" DJ exclaimed. "They're armed!"

Everyone was pulling up the images, and sure enough, captured on screen was a trio of people in a truck. The barrels and handguards of what look like at least two AR15s were visible in the cab.

"We have to load up," DJ said.

"No!"

They all turned to see Virginia standing with her hands on her hips. She raised a finger and pointed it at DJ.

"That's the last thing you need to do, DJ; go out in the dark with your gun and get yourself killed," she said. "You have no idea what they're doing or what their motives are. This night has been bad all over, and we don't know what those people have been through. We don't need to be making it worse for them, just like we don't need to be making a bunch of trouble for ourselves."

A FRESH ROUND of sobbing from Vanessa breaks Virginia out of her mental replay of last night's events. Even though she feels like she's dying inside, she has to be strong for the rest of them. She won't let this tragedy stop her from providing stability for the remaining family. Dale would do the same thing, she knew, were the roles reversed, and holding the family together feels like the best way to honor him right now.

After the firefight with the trespassers, which she had warned her men not to start, she had the bodies brought down to the barn. She had no idea if they would rise as the people they'd been showing on the news, but she's seen enough on the news to know that it wasn't meth heads doing the rioting, and she wasn't taking chances by bringing the bodies into the house.

Once they had recovered the bodies, she sent DJ, her middle son, Tim, and her son-in-law, Steve, out to search the old Toyota the others had left. The kids were returning on the ATVs now, so she breaks her attention from the blankets on the ground and walks toward the men that she still refers to as "her boys."

"Tell me you found something," she says as they roll to a stop.

DJ swings a leg over the ATV and steps off of it.

"There's not much in there. Some clothes, girl's clothes by the way, so it seems like they weren't just a bunch of guys. And there's this," he holds out a piece of paper, which Virginia snatches from his hand.

The Colorado motor vehicle registration lists the owner of the FJ40 as Ben Puckett. His address is in Fort Collins.

"Puckett," she says the name like she's cursing. "He said they were going to Longview, right?"

"That's what the guy said, that they were only trying to get through to Longview," Tim says.

"Yeah, right before you let them get away." DJ snarls at Tim

"They shot Dad right in mid-sentence, Deej! Bill was hit, Hector and William were already down ..." Tim is cut off by Virginia.

"Your brother did the right thing, DJ. You and your father should never have picked that fight. Those people would have passed right on through if you had left them alone. You had no idea what they were doing, but they were sure as hell NOT sabotaging anything of ours. All you had to do was watch them and make sure they're weren't going after our equipment. Shooting at them cost us your father, your brother, Hector, Steve's brother, and Bill is all shot up. Tim kept us from having to bury more of our own." Virginia pauses and stares at DJ, who is still spoiling for a fight.

"So we're just going to let them get away with killing our people?" he asks.

"I didn't say that, but we're going to be smart about this. Puckett can't be too common of a name. We tell the Sheriff about this, and he goes and tracks them down. But remember, we shot first with no provocation ..."

"They were TRESPASSING!" DJ shouts, inter-rupting his mother.

"And we fired on them with no provocation! DJ, we may live in the country, but we don't live in the 1860s. You're not John Wayne, and there's no such

thing as frontier justice. The law may not side with us."
Virginia is trying hard to retain her calm exterior.

Steve Anderson, Virginia's son-in-law and owner of
Anderson dairy farms (now part of the Nelson LLC),
speaks up.

"You've seen the news, Virginia. There is no law
anymore. If justice is going to be done, it's going to have
to come from us," he says.

"Well, if that turns out to be the case, that's different. But we don't know that yet. We don't know much
of anything right now other than we have people to
tend to. Vanessa is a wreck, and we need to try to get in
touch with Hector's wife. Tim, take the truck up to the
ridge and you and Steve tow that FJ down here. DJ,
you get in the house and help tend to your brother Bill.
He took a bullet in this fight you were so keen on
having; you can help clean up the mess."

Virginia turns on her heel, telling the trio that the
discussion is over, and she puts an arm on Vanessa's
shoulder.

"Come on, honey," she says, "let's get inside and
get something to drink. I could sure use some coffee
right now."

Vanessa nods and they start walking to the house.

DJ points back toward the ridge where the FJ rests
just out of sight.

"This," he says, waving his arm, "isn't over. We're
gonna find these fuckers, and we're gonna make
them pay."

Neither of the other men objects.

CHAPTER 14

The black Ram pickup approaches Gypsum Highway at a crawl. Robert doesn't want to chance getting caught by any police or military personnel. They'd have a hard time explaining Toni's wounds to the authorities, and based on what the news on the radio has been saying, there's a good chance they'll just be shot rather than risking any infected getting into the city. He sees no activity in either direction, so he hits the gas, crosses the road, and enters the Shadow Valley neighborhood.

"Okay, we're on Alpen View Street," Keith says. "Just stay on this street until we come to the golf course. It cuts the neighborhood in half. You can jump the curb and take the cart path from the end of the street, cut across the fairway, and we'll be back on Alpen View. We'll come to a stop light, and we'll make a left there."

Robert nods his understanding and looks in the rearview mirror.

"How's she doing?" he asks, looking at Ben.

Ben has Toni leaning into his lap, holding pressure on the wounds in her back and her side.

"She's doing okay," Ben says, "but she's in a lot of pain." Toni has her eyes clamped shut and winces whenever she moves too much or they hit a bump in the road. "Can we go any faster? I don't want to put her through this any longer than we have to."

"I'm going to get us to your folks' place as soon as I can," Robert says, "but I'm going to keep the speed reasonable. I don't want to crash before we get there, or she's in real trouble."

"Shouldn't we be going to the hospital?" Natalie asks. She's in the seat next to Ben and has a hold of Toni's hand.

"You heard the radio, right? The news says that the hospitals were like ground zero for this stuff. The first responders were getting overrun with ..." Robert trails off.

"Zombies." Keith finishes the thought.

Robert flashes Keith a look and then softens his tone a little. "Yeah. Zombies. I guess there's no other word for them. Anyway, we should get everyone to safety and then we can find out if the hospital is okay or not."

"And if it's not?" Natalie asks.

"We'll cross that bridge when we come to it, okay? Let's just get to point B as soon as possible. I'd like to get this night behind us," Robert says, ending the conversation.

They come to the golf course, and Robert slows down, drives onto the sidewalk and then onto the cart path that winds its way through the golf course. He follows the path around the tee box with the big sign that reads "8" and has a crude map of the hole, which doglegs to the left. On the other side of the tee box, the cart path ends at the seventh fairway. He drives over the closely cropped grass, picks up the cart path again on the far side of the hole, and continues for a few dozen more yards.

Just past the seventh tee, there's a sign like a deer crossing warning, only it has a picture of a golf cart on it. This is where the golfers cross the street, and Robert exits back onto Alpen View.

In the bed of the truck, Annie and Stephenie watch the area around them with sharp eyes. Stephenie hits Annie's leg and points to a side street. Three houses off of Alpen View a trio of the undead feast on a man who has been pulled from a car that rests half on the street, half on the sidewalk and into someone's yard. The remains of a brick-enclosed mailbox are scattered around the yard in front of the car, and steam pours out from under the hood.

"Not good," Annie signs to Stephenie.

"You think?" comes the reply, which even though it's not said out loud, Annie can tell it drips with sarcasm.

They approach the intersection of Alpen View and

17th Avenue, where Keith has instructed Robert to turn left, and they can see something is amiss. A big black SUV lies on its side, broken glass strewn throughout the intersection, glittering in the morning sun. Robert slows the truck down and stops before entering the intersection.

"Looks like they tried to make a right off this street ..." he starts to say, pointing at the cross street.

"Seventeenth Avenue," Keith interrupts.

"Whatever. And they lost it, flipped over," Robert finishes.

Robert edges the truck into the intersection, turning against the red light, and creeps past the overturned SUV.

"It's an Escalade," Andy says from the far side of the cab. "You think it's the same one from last night? The one the cops were chasing on 287?"

Robert points at an empty state patrol car a few hundred feet before the intersection to the west. "I'd say it's a fair bet," he says.

The overhead lights are still flashing on the cruiser, but there's no one around, at least not that they can see.

There's a pool of congealing blood around the back of the Escalade, making some of the broken glass sparkle red as the early morning sun hits it. Black, oily fluid is pooled all around the vehicle as well. Everyone exchanges nervous glances.

As they crawl around the corner, they see another police car, this time, a City of Longview squad car. It sits half on the sidewalk, facing west in the eastbound lane. Both doors hang open, but the occupants are nowhere to be seen. Again, there's a lot of blood on the ground. Several spent shell casings litter the sidewalk, and a semi-automatic pistol lies in a pool of blood.

"This is not looking good," Robert says.

"No shit," Keith replies. "Let's get moving. At the next light, make a right."

Robert gets the truck up to forty-five miles per hour, and at the next road, he turns right. Off to the left-hand side of the road is a strip mall with a Safeway as its anchor. The gas station advertising twenty-four-hour pay-at-the-pump in front of the supermarket has a crowd of cars, all with people fighting to get gas. A couple of fist fights break out, and someone pulls a gun and starts shooting. As they drive past, a small horde of zombies—including one in a police uniform—comes streaming from a side street and heads straight for the crowd. Halfway across the street, one of the zombies, a portly man wearing a bloodstained t-shirt that proclaims "This IS my good shirt" turns and angles toward the truck.

A gunshot rings out, and the zombie's shoulder sprays oily fluid. Its body turns from the impact of the bullet, altering its course enough that Robert doesn't have to do much to steer around it, and the truck passes it without making contact. As the truck speeds away, the perforated undead man loses interest in it and turns back to the crowd at the gas station.

In the bed of the truck, Stephenie sits back down with her rifle at the ready. They're a mile and a half from the Puckett home, and it appears that things in the city are rapidly deteriorating.

At Ninth and Price—where Kyle Puckett's sprint from the female zombie ended a few minutes earlier—everyone except Stephenie misses the body of the zombie that almost caught Kyle. She points out the twisted and broken form to Annie, who simply shakes her head.

Keith directs Robert to turn left, and then after three-quarters of a mile, Keith has him to turn right into the Sunny Meadow Neighborhood (a covenant-controlled neighborhood, the sign says). They go past a row of condominiums and town homes, then into a neighborhood of single-family homes. The garages all face alleyways, and Keith points to one just past a roundabout and tells Robert to turn into that it. Halfway down the alley, he has him pull into a drive-way. They've finally reached the Puckett's house.

"Toni, babe, we're here. We need to get up," Ben says to the wounded girl. She cries out when she tries to sit up, but then Robert is there helping to get her out of the truck.

Keith runs to the back door of the house and begins pounding on it. It takes a few moments, but Ben's father, Kyle, finally opens the door. He's drenched in sweat, still breathing hard from his run-in with the female zombie a few minutes earlier. Keith, unaware of that encounter, thinks it's odd that the sight of nine young adults, two of which are women with AR15s in the ready position, and Andy holding Robert's rifle casually propped on his shoulder, doesn't freak him out more than it does.

Kyle sees Ben and Robert carrying Toni, who has passed out. He notices the blood with alarm and says, "Is she bit?"

Ben is taken aback. "Bit? What? No, Dad, she's been shot. You won't believe the night we've had."

"Oh, shit!" Kyle says. "Bring her inside. All of you, get in here, hurry!"

They file in, and Keith, Natalie, Andy, and Annie make a quick second trip to grab the rest of their gear from the truck.

Inside, a group of older adults is gathered. Keith sees his father, Marc Wallace.

"Dad!" he exclaims and runs to his father and hugs him hard. Marc hugs his son back, relief visible on his face.

Naomi Puckett comes out of the master bedroom, momentarily startled by the group filling her family room—a room that had been empty when she went into the bedroom moments before. Then she spots her son. "Ben! Oh my God, what happened?" she asks as she runs to him.

Danny Harris and his wife Elaine are in the kitchen. They each have a pistol on their hip, and a short-barreled AR15 slung over their shoulders.

Over the din of the kids' and parents' joy at seeing each other, Robert nods at the girl he and Ben hold and says, "We need to get her some medical attention or

I'm afraid she's going to die. Can we get her to the hospital?"

"Not a good idea," Danny says from the kitchen. "If anyone is still alive there, they're not in a position to offer us any help." He walks over to the black dining table and clears the centerpiece. "Get her over here and tell me what happened."

They bring Toni over and lay her on the table while the other kids start telling them about their flight from Fort Collins, but Danny cuts them off. "Just tell me about the wounds."

Before they can explain what happened, the house shakes and a thunderous boom rattles the windows. Keith and Andy rush to the back door and peer outside. In the distance, back toward the gas station in front of the Safeway, a massive fireball billows into the sky.

"This is the end," Danielle says.

Stephenie signs and Annie translates. "No, it's just beginning."

Danielle covers her mouth so Stephenie can't read her lips and murmurs to Natalie, "I fucking hate her."

CHAPTER 15

D-Day has recruited more help to police the dead bodies throughout the building. Wearing Tyvek suits and rubber gloves—found in the maintenance room—they've pulled the flatbed carts (also from maintenance) and loaded the corpses on them. Once they bring them to the roof, they swing them in one-two-three fashion, heaving them over the roof's edge on three. There were forty-eight in all, including Carmen's husband Bill, the family of four from the third floor, Cortez, and Tamara from ten.

He stares at the body on the cart. It's the last one, and D-Day told the others he'd take care of it, so he sent them below to clean up and see if they can help people relocate to higher floors. He stares at the body of Cortez, who had lived his final moments in an act of sacrifice that helped save the lives of perhaps everyone in the building. D-Day can only imagine the pain he was going through, and the fear, the terror, that had to be going through his mind, knowing what was going to happen to him. He's as brave a man as D-Day has known, and he didn't know him well at all. He wonders if Cortez was that selfless all the time, if he was one of those people who would be there for you, no matter what. He pulls back the sheet and fishes through the dead man's pockets. He finds his wallet and opens it.

According to his driver's license, Cortez's first name was Michael. He was an organ donor and had his motorcycle and commercial truck endorsements. He has three photos in his wallet; one of a woman D-Day assumes to be his mother, another of a pretty young woman who has to be the girlfriend he mentioned, and the third is a '68 Camaro RS. D-Day doesn't know the particulars of the car, but he can appreciate the classic lines, the black stripes over the gray body. His mom, his girlfriend, and his car. D-Day smiles.

"You had your priorities right, my friend," he says. "And you have real pictures, not just data on a cell phone screen. These three were very important to you."

He sighs. It's sad to dump the body like this, but they don't have any other options. It's not like the coroner, or a funeral home is going to get them. D-Day feels like he should say something. He doesn't know why; it just feels like the right thing to do.

"I wish I knew you better," he says. "But those last minutes where I did get to know you, you lived them well and you died a noble death. In my opinion, no one can ask for more than that." He pauses for a minute, and with more sadness than he expected to feel, he rolls the body over the edge. He takes the driver's license and the three pictures out of the wallet and tosses it after the body then starts pulling the cart back to the maintenance building.

While he's on the maintenance path, he sees a pair of planes coming from the southeast. He recognizes them from his time in Afghanistan. The stealth drones, called the X47-B, are known to the public, having been featured on various TV programs spotlighting military technology. They've been billed as "experimental," supposedly with only two test models having been built. D-Day knows from experience that they're not experimental, and the Air Force has, at least, a dozen of them in service. Like most things in the military, whatever is released to the public is well behind current technology—unless it's released to as propaganda to scare the enemy.

The fighter-jet-sized drone looks like a miniature stealth bomber, though at sixty feet across and with a payload of forty-five hundred pounds, there's nothing miniature about these unmanned aircraft.

D-Day lifts his binoculars and sees throngs of people in the downtown streets. As far as he can tell, the police have completely stopped any attempt to contain the crowds. The drones circle the Denver metro area in a loop several miles wide. D-Day has seen this before. The drones are lining up a bombing run. The pilots, probably in a dark room in Nevada, will fly the drones around the area to see where they can have the greatest effect with the least amount of damage.

He watches as they pass over downtown on the opposite side of the skyscrapers from D-Day's vantage point, the bombs leaving the drones well before they pass over the target. D-Day glimpses massive walls of flame erupt in between the tall buildings of downtown. He hears the concussion, louder than a gunshot even though the bombs hit more than a mile away. A few seconds later, a shock-wave rolls over the building, rattling glass and vibrating D-Day's guts. He guesses that they're using a five-hundred-pound incendiary bomb. In all likelihood, it's filled with a jellied petroleum containing white phosphorus. The explosive fuel is similar to napalm, but the fire it produces is harder to put out. D-Day is encouraged that the military is coming in with the drones. It tells him that they're trying to clear a path for the ground forces to come in, and it also tells him they're not ready to start leveling entire cities to halt the spread of the infection, whatever it is.

The drones fly west, turn in a tight loop and come back along the same path, this time from the opposite direction. Another wall of fire erupts, and another shock wave passes over D-Day. One thing he's certain of, whatever was in the path of those drones isn't there anymore. There's nothing there right now but a quarter mile of fire devouring everything it touches. *Fry, you bastards!* he thinks to himself.

Through the binoculars, he sees dozens of the reanimated dead staggering in the fire. A few walk out of the conflagration engulfed in flames but do not seem to notice their flesh burning away from their bodies. They walk until the muscles of their legs burn away, and they collapse. Eventually, they are just piles of smoldering black *stuff*. A few walk into store fronts, catching the displays on fire where the windows or doors have been broken. One building, in particular, begins pouring thick, black smoke from the ground floor.

The drones do another several-mile-wide loop around the Denver metro area, and then soar upward, gaining altitude and banking away from the downtown area. D-Day watches as they head south. *Maybe they're going to do the same thing in Colorado Springs,* he thinks. He wonders about Martha Cowher and whether or not she made it through the night. He pushes the thought from his mind and pulls the empty cart back on the maintenance path toward the elevator building.

Before he gets to the elevator, he hears the staccato sound of gunfire. He leaves the cart in the shelter of the maintenance building and walks on another of the defined paths to the south edge of the building. The numbers of the undead in the streets below D-Day's building have been in the hundreds—maybe in the thousands—but after the firebombing at the opposite end of downtown the dead are moving like moths to a literal flame. They're running, limping, or crawling toward the flames. Like lemmings, as some of the undead turn and begin moving toward the conflagration, others follow. Soon vast numbers are heading toward the inferno, leaving only a few dozen in the immediate area.

Now, from the east, multiple mine-resistant ambush-protected, or MRAP, vehicles are heading into the neighborhood. D-Day is well familiar with the vehicles, but he's used to seeing them in desert-sand color, not the flat black of the Department of Homeland Security vehicles he sees now. Through his binoculars, he watches as the vehicles work in groups of four. Each vehicle is manned by a driver, a man in the turret with a belt-fed rifle that D-Day is sure is an M249 light machine gun and a five-man fire team. The four trucks and teams move in a diamond formation, keeping fire on all points of the compass. Each five-man team has four people shooting and one functioning as the reloader, providing full magazines to the other three once the magazines they carry in their vests have been emptied. A sixth man emerges from the MRAP and replaces the reloader when his supplies run low, and the reloader steps into rear-facing firing position. The men rotate positions toward the vehicle, with the man closest to the MRAP jumping in the back and getting a rest. The man in the turret fires only when there's an immediate threat to the team that they haven't been able to deal with.

Surrounding these fire teams, the bodies of the undead are piling up.

D-Day thinks about all the conspiracy stories he's read about the "militarization" of DHS and the American police forces, with different departments buying the military vehicles like those on the streets below, and the massive quantities of ammunition DHS has supposedly been buying. D-Day's Facebook feed has been thick with these stories. As he watches this ballet of action below him play out, he can't help but think that the theories weren't the stuff of conspiracies. Either the government got lucky—if you can call this luck—and an event came along to justify their stockpile of equipment they were getting ready "just in case," or they knew something like this was coming. If this event was the reason behind a big so-secret-it's-not-secret domestic military build-up, that also means that DHS and the larger Department of Defense organization had to have advance knowledge that this was coming. That's a troubling thought for D-Day.

The diamond formation works well for a while. D-Day watches as the group of four MRAPs, and their teams advance down the street. He can see at least three other teams advancing down the next three streets to the east. With the firebombs having drawn the majority of the zombies in the vicinity to the south, the persistent firing, while effective, begins to draw a significant number of the undead from the north, west, and east.

The group of DHS operatives in front of D-Day's

building has advanced three hundred feet down the road toward downtown Denver. The strategy seems to be effective; the gunfire is constant now, and there are hundreds of dispatched zombie bodies lining the street and sidewalks on either side of the procession, with more coming from all directions now.

Things start going sideways when the glass on the second floor of the apartment building across the street shatters. A few zombies fall out, and then a few more, and then a steady stream of undead erupt from the building, falling to the ground or on top of other zombies. The first few are hurt in the fall, breaking legs and sustaining other injuries, but increasingly the remainder of them land on the pile, get up, and sprint after the black-clad DHS teams.

Faced with more than a hundred zombies tightly grouped, in addition to the existing hordes descending from the rear and sides, the team on the right side, closest to the building, quickly realizes they're about to be overrun. They start firing with less control, missing the headshots and simply wasting ammo. With the right side collapsing, the other teams are going to get overrun in short order.

The unit's commander must have called for retreat because all the teams return to the MRAPs while the men in the turrets using the automatic rifles provide cover fire. Once safely inside the MRAPs, the teams begin firing through the gun ports on the sides of the vehicles. D-Day looks around and sees the undead now coming in rivers from the areas behind and to the sides of the apartment building.

When he turns his attention back to the MRAPs, something else catches his eye. Flickering shadows are coming at the formation of vehicles from the south. He trains his binoculars on the distant movement and sees that the masses of undead that were drawn by the fire are returning. They're leading a new army—charred, smoldering undead follow in droves. This group of revenants is moving much slower than the others, owing to the damage the bodies' muscles have sustained from the fires.

The powerful MRAPs should have no problem muscling over a few, or even a few dozen, undead bodies. But the several thousand bearing down on them from all directions pose a problem. The MRAP is not an easy vehicle to maneuver in a tight, urban street. With four of them so close together, it's going to take some skilful driving to get out of there.

The MRAP in the rear begins to back up, knocking aside dozens of the hungry dead and running over many more. Crippled, broken creatures reach with mangled arms and hands in vain for the big black truck. The driver spins the wheel and gets the beast turned partially around. He turns the wheel the opposite direction and shifts it into gear to complete the turn. As it begins to accelerate away from the other MRAPs, the tires kick up a spray of the oily, black fluid that oozes from the corpses.

The MRAP on the right side of the diamond is

backing up as the spray of zombie juice hits the side of it, including the gun ports. It does the same Y-turn as the first MRAP and begins heading back to the east, now going upstream against a steady tide of undead bodies. The driver goes slow but doesn't try to avoid any of the zombies, not that he could if he tried.

The third MRAP, from the left side of the diamond, is completing its Y-turn as the smoldering horde reaches the lead MRAP. At the intersection, the second MRAP swerves and hits a parked car, spinning it halfway around and sending it up onto the sidewalk. The turret opens, and one of the DHS operatives scrambles out and onto the roof. He shoves the barrel of his rifle into the opening and fires several rounds back inside the armored vehicle. *Someone inside must have gotten infected,* D-Day thinks. *How? That spray of fluid that hit the gun ports? Is this THAT contagious?* The big vehicle hits another car, then veers onto the sidewalk and clips the corner of the check cashing place at the three-way confluence of Park Avenue, Twentieth Avenue, and Washington Street.

The DHS operative is thrown from the top of the MRAP. He lands awkwardly, and several undead are on him before he's able to bring his rifle to bear. D-Day can see him through the binoculars, and as blood is flowing from the wounds being ripped open, he's screaming loud enough that even at this distance, D-Day can hear him, his screams just out of sync with the image in the binoculars. The screams die down, and D-Day sees him hold out a small object and start laughing. He takes his eyes away from the binoculars and looks at the street corner with unaided eyes. He recognized the apple-sized object immediately, and when the grenade goes off, D-Day doesn't want to see it up close. There's a few seconds' pause, and then the explosion is large enough that D-Day feels the pulse of a shockwave from one hundred and fifty yards away.

He pulls the binoculars up and scans the corner again. Nothing there but bloody tissue and black zombie juice. Scattered away from the center of the blast, body parts are mixed together. An intact torso, arms, and head are trying to crawl into the street. A few arms and legs are jumbled. A severed head lies on its side, the eyes darting back and forth, the mouth opening and closing.

D-Day has seen enough. The MRAP has stopped a few hundred feet away in the middle of Twentieth Avenue. Through the binoculars, D-Day can see it move from side to side as something inside the armored box moves around. The rest of the big vehicles are driving away, headed east, back the way they came, so they've written off the occupants of the marooned MRAP. As they head east, D-Day only counts ten of the big vehicles, when there were sixteen to start. He wonders if the other five met a similar fate. If so, there's a potential bounty of ammo inside them. He files that bit of information away for later. After a minute, the sound of the vehicles fades and the streets once again belong to the teeming dead.

D-Day returns to the cart and pulls it into the

elevator. He pushes the button to the twelfth floor and holds his breath—again—while the car makes its descent. The power holds for another ride, and he stashes the cart down the hall by the east stairwell near the twelfth-floor maintenance closet, and then he heads to the common area that serves as the building's recreation room. Residents can reserve it for parties and meetings, and the building management hosts big shin-digs here for things like the Super Bowl or title fights.

Carmen is in the room, separating food. She's lining up canned foods into similar piles; canned corn in one stack, green beans in another, soups in another. She looks up at D-Day as he walks in.

"I saw all that from here," she says. "It didn't go well, did it?"

D-Day walks over to the windows and looks out. He sees piles of dead—actually dead—bodies on the ground. It's impossible to count them. Maybe a thousand? Twenty-eight men, five minutes. Five minutes to kill thirty-five undead each. Five minutes for a force of twenty-eight men in four light armored vehicles to become overwhelmed and lose a quarter of the armor and maybe as much of their manpower.

"No, it didn't go well," he says.

"Do you think they'll rescue us? Eventually, I mean."

He looks at her for a second before answering. "My take? Not unless they have a lot more men and a lot of ammo. If this was a probe, just their way of testing the way these ... creatures, you know, engage them in battle, then they learned a huge lesson. Maybe we'll see greater numbers of them later. If this was their main assault, we're not going anywhere anytime soon. You should note, though, that these were Department of Homeland Security and Army. That will make a difference."

"But what about those planes? Won't they come back?" she says, sounding hopeful.

"There's not much they can do for us. I think they hit Speer Boulevard because it's nice and wide open and had a big concentration of those things on it. I don't think they're looking to destroy big chunks of the city yet. That's good—it means that they still have hope they can get this under control. On the other hand, this is a big country with a lot of cities bigger than this one," he says. "They'll have higher priority than we do, I'm afraid."

Carmen looks crestfallen. "So why did they come here then?"

"I don't know. Maybe they had some ordinance left over after hitting Cheyenne, or Colorado Springs. Maybe they're based locally and it makes most sense to use them here. Look, I'm not one to paint a rosy picture just to make someone feel good. I'm sorry if that's what you're looking for, but false hope isn't productive. We can make it, but we're going to have to be tough. We have to control 110 other people in this building who we don't really know, and we have to be thinking a few steps ahead. The fact that DHS is still operating is a good sign. They might have a plan to get control. It just means we have to rely on ourselves for a while until they figure this thing out. But we have to have a plan B. If we put all our faith in the government to rescue us, we're as good as lost."

"I just want this to be a nightmare, you know? Something I can wake up from and everything will be okay," she says. "We can go back to watching bad TV shows and bitching about the price of gas. Normal stuff. Not ... people being eaten by freaking zombies."

"I'm still in shock over this too. I never in my life thought something like this could really happen. I was looking forward to a nice relaxing weekend riding my bike up to Central City and back," D-Day says.

Her eyes brighten a little. "What do you ride?" she asks.

"A Victory—

2012 Vegas 8-Ball."

"Nice!" she says. "I have ..." She pauses as she thinks of the motorcycle that she crashed into the west side of the building. "Had a two-thousand Soft Tail. I panicked out there, thought they were closer than they were, and I just lost it."

"Well, it's not exactly a situation you train for," D-Day says.

"Still, I have enough time in the saddle I should have handled that better. And now ... Bill is dead because of me," she says.

D-Day isn't sure what to say, so he lets that comment linger.

"We were through, you know, Bill and I," she continues. "We just didn't have the heart to break it to my folks yet. My dad had heart surgery last November and the time just never seemed right. Now I guess ... well, it's over anyway."

"I'm sorry. I didn't know. I could have ..." D-Day starts, debating whether or not he should tell her that her parents already know, but Carmen cuts him off.

"No no, I had to do it. I wasn't in love with him anymore, but I didn't hate him either. We just ... grew apart. I'm glad the last thing he heard was my voice. I'm glad that he didn't die at the hands of a stranger. No offense," she says.

"None taken," D-Day says, just as someone comes in wearing a backpack and carrying a duffel bag, both of them stuffed full of food.

"More supplies!" she calls out. "This apartment was loaded! Serious Costco shoppers, too! A lot of bulk stuff. From the pictures, looked like a nice family. Where ever they are, I hope they're okay. But their pantry is going to help us a lot!"

Carmen smiles at D-Day. "Back to work," she says.

He leaves her with the new girl and heads to the stairwell. He's been up for close to forty hours now, and he needs to get some rest. In his deployments to the warzones, he learned to catch a few winks any chance he got, and since he doesn't know when the next chance will be, he's going to take advantage of it.

HE'S BEEN asleep for ninety minutes when someone starts pounding on his door. He's upright, rifle ready before he realizes it.

"D-Day!" a woman's voice shouts. "We need you right away! Someone's been killed!"

CHAPTER 16

On the table, Toni cries out in pain. Danny turns to Elaine. "Get my kit from the Jeep."

Elaine heads for the front door while Danny gets his multi-tool out and cuts Toni's shirt off of her. He looks under the dressing that Ben's put in place. As soon as he does, fresh blood begins flowing from the wounds.

"Kyle," Danny says, "I'm going to take care of this as best as I can, and then Elaine and I are going to our place in the mountains. You guys are welcome to come, but the window is closing quick. You won't have much time before everything falls apart." He lowers his voice so only Kyle can hear him. "You may have to decide between saving her or saving all of you. You're all welcome to come with us, but she's not going to be able to travel where we're going, not in her condition."

Kyle looks over at his son, who is wracked with emotion as he strokes Toni's hair. Naomi stands behind Ben, rubbing a hand over his shoulders to comfort him. The boy who helped Ben bring Toni inside talks with two girls in sign language. Keith tells his dad about their night, going on about how awesome Stephenie is. Danielle sits on the couch and glares at the deaf blonde girl, and Andy and Natalie stand to the side, watching Toni with worry and exhaustion all over their faces.

Elaine comes back in with a medical kit, and Kyle says, "Okay guys, listen up. We have a couple of things to decide, and we need to do so quickly. Danny's going to do his best to patch Toni up, but she's not going to be able to make it to Danny's place in the mountains until she's healed a bit. I don't see any reason we all need to stay here with her ... and anyone who stays may never make it out of town."

"If she can't go, then I'm staying," Ben says.

"Ben, think about this ..." Naomi starts to say.

"Mom, I'm not leaving her. That's final," he replies.

"I'm staying too," Keith says. Danielle glares at him but says nothing.

Andy and Natalie say they're staying.

"We'll go with your man," Robert says. "No point in sticking around this place longer than we have to."

"I'm staying," Stephenie says out loud and signs at the same time.

Robert can't hide that he's upset with her. He signs, but does not say out loud, "What are you doing? We don't owe these people anything!"

"We'd have been overrun without them," she signs back, "and I can help them. They're going to need someone who can shoot."

"That's their problem. I won't let you risk your life for them," Robert signs.

"It's not up to you. Go if you want," Stephenie signs, then crosses her arms to signal she's done with the conversation.

Out loud Robert says, "Annie, will you try to talk some sense into her?"

"I think we're past that, Robert. She's made up her mind, and if she's staying, I'm staying," Annie says.

"Well, I guess I have no choice then. I guess I'm staying," Robert says.

"You have a choice. Don't hang this on us, Robert," Annie says.

Robert glances around the room at the people staring at him, conscious for the first time that they've been making a scene.

"We're sticking together, Annie. We're it—the three of us are all that's left," he says.

"Fine," Annie says. "But if you stay, it's YOUR choice. Don't try and blame us later if things don't go well."

"Fine," he says, and then turns and heads to the dining table and asks Danny if he can help with Toni.

BEN SITS NEXT TO TONI, who now rests in the

guest room on the queen-sized bed that was Ben's before he moved to Fort Collins. She is conscious, but groggy, after taking some narcotic pain pills Danny has in his medical kit.

Though he's already gone through this with Ben, Natalie, Andy, and Danielle, Danny recounts the ad-hoc surgery for the rest of the group.

"I removed a bullet and some fragments of bone from her shoulder. I'm pretty sure her shoulder blade is broken, but I don't know for sure, and I have no clue what to do about it other than keeping her from using it for a few weeks and hope it heals. I cleaned the wound and stitched it up to the best of my ability.

"I'm no doctor, but that's the wound that worries me the most. I also took several fragments of a bullet from her ribs and cleaned and stitched that wound up as well, but there seemed to be less damage. I think both bullets passed through the door of Ben's FJ, so it could have been a lot worse. I'm leaving a bottle of antibiotics for her, as she's got a huge risk of infection, and that's as likely to kill her as the gunshots. I'm at the limit of what I know how to do. It's in God's hands now."

Naomi comes out of the Pucketts' bedroom with a backpack over one shoulder and a carry-on sized suitcase being pulled by her other hand. Kyle goes over to her.

"We'll be after you guys as soon as we can," he says.

"I still don't like this, Kyle."

"Neither do I, but I'm not leaving the kids here by themselves, and I don't want you down here if things continue to get worse. You'll be safe up at Danny's Fortress of Solitude," Kyle says.

"I know I will, but you guys aren't going to be safe here. Please don't take any risks, and come up as soon as you can. Promise me," Naomi pleads.

"I promise, as soon as Toni can travel we'll be on our way," Kyle assures her.

Naomi sets her bag by the door and goes to guest room to talk to Een.

Danny comes over to Kyle again.

"Kyle, I want you guys to hole up at my place," he says.

"Danny, no, I ..." Kyle starts, but Danny holds up a hand and cuts him short.

"Look, I wouldn't ordinarily offer, but your house isn't secure. My house is. I WAY customized it. It cost me a fortune, but no one will know you're there if you don't want them to. And, there are some nifty toys in there," Danny says. He hands Kyle a large manila envelope. "Instructions, how to get in, set the alarm, and lock the place down. Grab as much of your food as you can and get over there. Carry Toni if you have to, but get down there as soon as you can."

Danny turns and looks down the hallway.

"Naomi," he calls. "Time to go."

Naomi comes out of the bedroom with tears on her cheeks. She kisses Kyle and says, "You promised. As soon as you can."

"I know, honey, I promise. You promise, too—be careful up there. Don't shoot yourself by accident or do anything crazy trying to keep up with them," Kyle says, nodding at Danny and Elaine.

"As if," Elaine snorts. "We'll make sure she's trained for anything we need her to do."

"Yeah, brother," Danny says. "I'll watch her like she's my sister."

"You *hate* your sister," Naomi says.

"Just because I hate her doesn't mean I'd let anything happen to her," he says, and then points at Kyle. "Seriously, get this gang over to my place ASAFP and get it locked down."

Danny cracks the door and looks around in front of the house.

"It's clear," he says. "Ladies, time to go."

The trio sprints out of the house and to Danny's Jeep. Naomi climbs in the back, and Elaine hands her bags back to her then climbs in the front seat. Danny fires up the engine, and as he puts it in gear, Elaine grabs her AR15 and gets it ready in case they meet trouble.

Kyle watches the black off-road vehicle drive down the street and disappear around the corner. His wife is gone, and he has no idea when he'll see her again.

He pushes the thought out of his head and goes back inside. He finds Stephenie, Annie, and Keith cleaning the blood off of the dining table with some bleach-based cleaning spray and paper towels.

"I hope it's okay we're using this stuff on your table,

Mr. Puckett," Annie says. "It does the best job with blood."

"Yeah, fine," he replies. "There's more paper towels in the laundry room if you need them. On top of the cabinets. And just call me Kyle, please."

Robert is going through the Sims' bags, reorganizing the gear they brought and loading magazines for their rifles.

The rest of the group is still in the guest room with Toni, so Kyle takes a minute and opens the folder Danny gave him.

He's only been in Danny's house a couple of times. He has a workshop in the garage, with an immaculate work bench, pristine toolboxes, well-maintained mountain bikes, golf clubs and, of course, a fifty-two-inch flat screen and a keg fridge with his home-brewed beer on tap. The garage was built with an extra ten feet of space, shortening the driveway, but allowing room for the fridge and TV. Part of that extra ten feet is walled off, though Kyle doesn't know what's behind it.

The house is appointed well, with most items upgraded from the builder's standard stock. It's a ranch, with three bedrooms and a study. Now that he's thinking about it, Kyle never saw stairs for a basement, and every other house in the neighborhood has one.

Looking at the contents of the folder, now he knows why. The homes in the neighborhood are semi-custom, meaning they start from a base set of plans, but each homeowner can make significant modifications if they have the money to do so. Danny, it's now obvious, had the money. Other than the model homes, his was the first house in the neighborhood, so Kyle doubts that anyone currently living in the Fox Run subdivision knows what was done when Danny's house was put together. He's included a scaled-down set of floor plans with numbers in locations that correspond to instructions.

1. *Unlock the door. The lock is electronic; lift the cover and enter the eight-digit code 53962568.*
2. *Pressing 'lock' on the inside keypad locks the door, and 'unlock' (of course) unlocks it. Entering the same code as above and pressing 'lock' will lock it AND set the alarm You have to enter the code and press 'unlock' to turn the alarm off.*
3. *Go to the basement. Open the closet door next to the guest bath. Inside you'll find another keypad. Enter 96984585. This will release a panel in the floor; lift it, and proceed down the stairs.*
4. *Same code entered into the keypad at the bottom of the stairs seals the access panel.*

IT GOES on with other instructions, but Kyle is admiring the layout of the basement. Based on plans he's included in the file folder, Danny had the basement built larger than the main floor. It extends an extra fifteen feet in the front and twenty in the rear, but that extra space must be covered by the front and back yards. This gives him enough square footage for two bathrooms, a home gym, two bedrooms, a media room, a kitchen, laundry room, and a workshop where he does his gunsmithing.

There's plenty of space—counting the extensions Danny had built, the finished space totals more than 2600 square feet—but with eleven people in the same subterranean area for an extended time, Kyle can see this underground palace becoming claustrophobic. But, given the alternative of the undead breaking into his house and killing all of them, he'll take close quarters over sunshine. He decides to get everyone moving.

"Okay, everyone, gather around!" he calls out.

The group, minus Toni, circles the island in the kitchen. Kyle looks around at them all, takes a breath and gets started.

"All right, we all know what's out there. We know they're deadly, and they're multiplying. We've all chosen to stay here until Toni can travel; then we head to the mountains to link up with Danny, Elaine, and Naomi.

"Until that time, we're going to go from here to Danny's place, two doors north. He's got his house set up like a fortress, and it is WAY more secure than this place. But we should move fast. We have a hundred and fifty feet to go, and if those things are out there, that might as well be a mile.

"Marc, you and Keith head next door to your place and get as much food and other crucial supplies as you can carry and bring it over. Someone should help you—any volunteers?"

"I'll go," Stephenie says, raising her hand.

"Oh, hell no," Danielle says. "I'll go with him."

Kyle frowns at the tension between the two girls. "I don't know what's going on here," he says, pointing a finger and wagging it between the two girls. "But put it on hold. This is life and death, girls, so act like adults, please. Danielle, you go with Keith."

Robert says something in sign language that, based on her expression, Stephenie doesn't like. Kyle ignores the exchange between them.

"The rest of you help loot this place," Kyle continues. "Food, toilet paper, toothpaste—anything you find that you think we'll need for an extended stay. Sims—you three grab your gear and the stuff the kids brought from Fort Collins and ferry it over. I'll help you with that. Ben, you get Toni over there. Carry her if you have to. Be sure to get the meds that Danny left. Any questions?"

"How long do you think we'll be here?" Natalie asks.

"I have no idea, Natalie," Kyle says. "Toni has two gunshot wounds and a broken shoulder blade. I have no clue how long it will be before she can travel. I'd say at least four weeks, but that's a complete guess."

There are several groans from the group when he says this.

"Guys, this is the reality of the situation," Kyle says. "Four weeks might not be it. It may be longer. I just don't know. If you want to go somewhere else, I won't stop you. But if you're staying, we need to get started on this move now."

"Let's go, Dad, we're wasting time," Keith says and starts for the front door.

That sparks everyone into motion. Danielle and Marc follow Keith. Natalie and Andy start pulling canned foods from the cabinets. Annie stays to help them while Robert and Stephenie shoulder their bags and grab their rifles. Kyle grabs his .22 rifle from the gun safe in his closet, checks the safety, inserts a magazine, racks the slide, grabs his go-bag and heads back out to the kitchen. He grabs the manila folder and turns to Robert and Stephenie.

"Let's go," he says.

CHAPTER 17

The first undead didn't show up at the Nelsons' farmhouse until well after sunrise. With no coroner or funeral home available to collect their dead, Virginia wants to get their people in the ground before they start to rot, though she doesn't quite put it that way to the rest of the family. She worked on a farm long enough to know what happens to dead things in even the mild heat of late May.

She recruits her son Tim and son-in-law, Steve, to help her clean the bodies and wrap them in linens, then in plastic. It's emotional work; she works on Steve's brother, so he doesn't have to. Steve works on her husband, Dale, and third son, Roger, while Tim works on their foreman, Hector.

DJ drives the big tractor with the front loader and backhoe attachments to the small family cemetery and trenches out four holes a couple of feet deep. He wants to get them buried deep enough no animals can get to them, but not so deep they can't get them out in case they need to be examined later for evidence. Hector's people might want his body too, and DJ doesn't want to be digging six feet deep to extricate any of them.

Steve and Tim load the cleaned, wrapped bodies on a cart, which they hook to one of the farm's many Ranger APVs, and they head to the graves.

DJ helps them place the bodies in the graves. They haven't had time to build proper coffins, but DJ managed to get some planks from the barn that are about eighteen inches wide and six feet long. He places these on top of each of the bodies as further protection against wildlife and to make it easier to dig them up, if needed, and not tear the bodies apart with shovels.

Vanessa, Roger's wife, can't stop crying. The Nelson children are more subdued. Tears streak their faces, but they don't sob or weep openly. Their stoic father raised them to keep their composure.

"This isn't how I pictured laying any of you to rest," Virginia says to the four dead men. "Not that I pictured having to do this at all, but hopefully you understand. We're in a strange time now, with bad things happening all around, and we have to do something for you, so this is the service you get. It doesn't mean that we don't love and respect you, it just ... it's just the way it is. I love you all. May God keep you safe at his side until we see you again."

She turns to the others. "Anyone else want to say some words?" she asks.

DJ clears his throat and removes his hat as he faces the open graves.

"Life ain't going to be the same without you here," he says. "But if you guys are listening; we're going to avenge you! You can take that to the bank!"

"DJ!" Vanessa exclaims. "That's not appropriate right now. My husband is dead because you had to go out there guns blazing, and the first thing you want to do is start digging more holes. Well, dig one for yourself!"

She turns on her heel and storms away, a fresh round of sobbing pouring out of her.

"I hope you're happy, DJ," Virginia says. "You have all the tact of a tornado." She lets out a heavy sigh. "I guess we're done here. Fill these holes in and put the backhoe away when you're done. Then you're going to apologize to Vanessa. You understand me?"

DJ stands, seething, without saying anything.

"Am I understood?" Virginia repeats.

"Yes," he says through gritted teeth.

"Good," she says and starts walking after Vanessa. The others all file after her. Tim stops next to DJ, his mouth opening slightly in anticipation of saying something.

"Don't, Tim," DJ says. "Not now. Just go, please. You'll just piss me off, and I don't want to say or do something I'll regret."

Tim closes his mouth, nods, and starts walking.

You mean something ELSE you'll regret, his inner voice says to him. As long as he can remember, he's had a little Jiminy Cricket voice that carries on an inner monologue with him. As he so often does, he tells this inner voice to shut the hell up. He climbs into the backhoe and shuts the door. Before he turns it on, he notices the thick, black cloud of smoke coming from the southeast, from Longview. He scans the horizon from left to right, east to west. The air is thick, and the tendrils of smoke from several fires contribute to the overall haziness of the vista.

No fire department, the voice says. *That means there's no police. No medical services. No government. No order. This got bad, fast.*

He nods in agreement and starts the diesel engine.

As he turns the arm and manipulates the scoop to pull dirt back into the holes, he thinks briefly about his lone stint away from the farm, working for the richest man in Longview, Karl Platte. Karl owned most of the south end of town, has several streets in town named after him, and had his own landscaping company to tend the commercial properties he owned and leased to businesses.

There was one man, Eugene, who drove all the equipment—front loaders, Bobcats, backhoes—you name it, he drove it. And he called them all the same thing: a machine. Eugene was driving a front loader one day and was called to the main office by Mr. Platte. Not wanting to stop the work and have a crew of high school kids and college dropouts standing idle, he called DJ over.

"You're the brightest kid in this crew," he said. "And by that, I mean least likely to fuck up. Climb up here and I'll show you how to run this machine."

He gave young DJ a ten-minute tutorial, which was all he needed for the basic tasks he would be doing. They had several truckloads of fill dirt brought in to make berm that would separate two of the buildings. A lot of that dirt had spilled into the parking lot, and they were instructed not to use the machinery to scoop it up to avoid damaging the pavement. So, DJ would be following the kids while they shoveled this wayward dirt into the front loader's bucket. Once they'd filled it up, he'd take the dirt and dump it at the end of the berm.

"Repeat as necessary," Eugene said. "You do good while I'm gone, and I'll teach you how to run the other machines. Running the machines is a good gig, kid. You get to sit in the comfort of the cab—some of them, like this one, have AC and a radio!—while these shmucks break their backs with a shovel and sweat themselves to death in the heat. Don't fuck this up."

DJ did well, and over the rest of that summer, Eugene taught him how to operate all of the company's heavy equipment.

He's the only one who ever thought you were worth anything, the voice says.

Eugene died that year, at the ripe age of forty-nine. He was a four-pack-a-day smoker, drank most of a fifth of Jack each night, and ate a diet consisting mostly of steak, bacon, sausage, and butter. Everyone who knew him outside of work said it was amazing he made it to forty-nine. DJ cried more at his funeral than he did at his own grandfather's.

After that, DJ became THE guy running the machines for the company. He enjoyed it, but like all endeavors, he liked to do things his way, and he was fired after he got into an argument with Karl Platte himself, which ended with DJ punching him. Today he doesn't even remember what he and Platte had disagreed about. After that, it was back to the farm, where he's been ever since.

He shakes the memories from his mind in time to see a trio of bloodied men coming toward the backhoe.

Something's not right, the voice says.

"No shit," DJ says out loud.

CHAPTER 18

D-Day opens his door to find Carmen's mother, Elizabeth, on the other side.

"D-Day, thank God!" she says. "People are freaking out. One of the people has been killed."

D-day is still shaking the cobwebs of sleep out of his mind. "What people? And what do you mean killed? In an accident, or was he murdered?"

"She. And she's from one of the floors below us, but she was found outside of the meeting area with a knife in her back."

"The rec room on twelve?" he asks, and Elizabeth nods. "Give me a minute," he says, and goes to get his gear.

D-Day puts on his tactical vest, checks that his guns are loaded, checks the spare magazines in the pockets of the vest, and says with a sigh, "All right, let's go."

Elizabeth walks down the hall to the east stairwell

and climbs from the tenth floor to the twelfth. A blanket covers a body by the community recreation room. Thirty people mill around, some upset, holding their hands over their mouths, their eyes watering. D-Day has seen the look from what they called FNGs in Iraq and Afghanistan. The glazed eyes and shocked faces of people who suffer from sleep deprivation and are scared from their first taste of battle isn't easy to forget, and these folks have it in spades.

Carmen sees D-Day approach before anyone else does and runs up to him.

"D-Day, thank God Mom found you! We don't know what to do here. These people need someone to calm them down," she says in a hushed, hurried sentence.

"Okay, got it. Tell me what happened," he replies as they approach the sheet-covered body. Before Carmen can tell him anything, people start peppering him with questions.

"Hey, what have you gotten us into?" demands a short, stocky man with blonde hair and a blonde mustache. "You had us all move higher in the building, and now people are getting killed! No one knew I was in my apartment—I would have been totally safe. Now we have a killer on the loose, and we're all at risk!"

A dark-haired woman jumps into the argument. "Yeah, you've had us moving bodies and breaking into apartments and have done nothing to ensure our safety. And it's not like we can call the police, right? No one is going to come collect evidence or dust for prints! How do you plan on catching the killer?"

Others in the crowd murmur their agreement with these two most vocal people, nodding heads and glaring at D-Day with their arms crossed and brows furrowed.

"Okay, listen up!" D-Day snaps. "I don't even know what happened yet. You all need to understand that we're under siege here. We have no place to go, and in desperate times, people do desperate things. Do not lose your heads and do not do anything rash. Now, who found the body?"

A middle-aged woman with short, curly black hair raises her hand. She reminds D-Day of Rhea Perlman. He points at her and says, "Come with me and tell me what happened. The rest of you," he points and waves his hand across the group, "either go to your apartments or sit down in the rec room; I don't care which. But don't get in my way."

The dark-haired woman won't let it go. "We have a right to know what's happening and what you plan to do about it."

"What's your name?" D-Day asks.

"Melissa."

"Melissa, if this were a police investigation you would get nowhere near it; they wouldn't let you. We're in the middle of what could be the end of days here, and I don't care what you want right now. Go home or go. Sit. Down. Now." D-Day glowers at her and she backs down. A few of the people leave for the stairs to go to their apartments, but the rest stick around the big room in hopes of hearing what D-Day will do about the situation.

D-Day turns to the woman who reminds him of Rhea Perlman. "What's your name?"

"Agnes. You can call me Aggie."

"Okay, Aggie," he says. "Let's go out into the hall-way. Tell me what happened."

"Um, okay ..." she starts. "Well, I had just brought two big bags of food up here from the third floor." She nods at Carmen, then at the body wrapped under the sheet. "She and Cheryl were organizing the big stack that was already here. So I set the bags down and started unloading them. Carmen was saying how tired she was, so I said I'd stay and help organize, and she could get some sleep. She told us what apartment she's in, just in case we need anything. So she introduced me to Cheryl, and then went to her place. Cheryl and I kept sorting through the canned food, putting the perishables in the fridge or the freezer. It was packed pretty full, you know, so since I'm just down the hall here on twelve, we decided to fill up my fridge and freezer, and if we filled that up, we'd fill up Cheryl's down on nine." She stops her recounting of events to take a breath.

"So anyway, I took a few backpacks full of deli meat, cheese, and fruits and veggies down to my place. We had just about got everything sorted, and I had one more backpack full of stuff to put in my fridge. After the earlier trips, it was just about full, so I had to take a few minutes and reorganize some of the stuff. When I came back, she was ... Cheryl was ... there. Like that." Aggie's voice cracks as she points at the body. "She had a knife sticking out of her back, and there was blood all underneath her. I think I started screaming because soon a bunch of people were here, and someone went and got Carmen, and then they got you."

"How long were you gone?" D-Day asks.

"Maybe ten minutes. I guess long enough for ..." she trails off as she looks at the shrouded body on the floor. After an awkward moment, Carmen speaks.

"We just didn't know what to do. You're the only authority figure here. They came to me because they think I'm tight with you, and I didn't know what else to do. Everyone else is worried about themselves, and you've been looking out for all of us," she says.

D-Day looks at Carmen. He's tired and knows she is too, but she looks good to him. He's only known her for a short time, and everyone is assuming they're "tight," whatever she meant by that, and he doesn't object to the notion. He shakes his head to clear the thoughts away and refocus on the situation at hand.

"First things first; let me check out her body," he says. "We'll see what it tells us and then we'll go from there." D-Day sees Aggie turn even whiter than she already was. "You don't have to be there for this part, Aggie," he says. She nods and heads into the rec room.

Carmen and D-Day approach the body. "You sure you want to help with this?" he asks her.

She gulps audibly. "If you want me here, then I'm here."

"I could use a second set of eyes," he says. "It's not like I know what I'm looking for."

He reaches down and pulls back the sheet. D-Day recognizes the woman who came into the rec room with the bags of food from the third floor right as he left little more than an hour ago. There's a pool of blood under her, soaking into the carpet. It doesn't make sense to him that a knife in the back would produce so much blood.

He rolls her away from him, exposing more of her face and neck. There are at least three punctures in her neck, and any of them could have pierced a major blood vessel and made the blood pool underneath her. D-Day takes a flashlight from his vest and shines it on the carpet leading away from Cheryl's body, and he catches a stream of blood drops, including some on the wall nearby. One of the punctures must have hit an artery.

"I'm no forensic scientist," he says, "but whoever did this most likely got blood all over them."

"So as long as we catch them with bloody clothes then we've got our killer," Carmen says. "Unless of course he changed his clothes like any person with half a brain would."

"What makes you say it's a he?" D-Day asks.

"I just assumed."

"Well, it so happens that women are more likely to kill by stabbing," D-Day says. "Something about women like to be more up close and personal while men are more likely to shoot or strangle."

Carmen rolls her eyes. 'Where'd you hear this? CSI?"

D-Day looks at her, trying to remember the source of that information, but draws a blank. "Maybe," he says.

"Well, I'm sure CBS would never lead you astray. What else does TV have to say about this one?" The sarcasm is heavy in Carmen's voice.

"Never rule out the obvious," he says, pointing at the knife. Carmen looks at it and sees that it's not a knife at all. It looks like a letter opener, and it's monogrammed.

"Do you know anyone with the initials 'MTU'?" she asks.

"Yeah, there's a lawyer, I saw his name on the building roster. Mike Upham. He caused some trouble earlier with your dad."

"Oh yeah, the guy who made a bunch of people move his stuff from the fifth floor to the ninth, right?"

"That's the one. I'll double-check, but he's the only one I can think of with a last name that starts with 'U'," D-Day says. He takes a folded set of papers from a pocket on his vest and flips through the pages, then folds them up again and puts them back in the pocket. "No other last names starting with U."

D-Day grabs the handle of the letter opener and pulls, meeting resistance for a moment, and then all at once the improvised weapon pulls free, almost sending him sprawling to the floor, but he catches his balance.

"So what have you found? Do you know who did it?" Melissa has wandered back over near D-Day.

D-Day turns toward her with the letter opener in his hand, blood dripping from it. She blanches at the sight of the blood. "Make yourself useful and help us roll her up in this blanket," he says.

Melissa tries to give D-Day a withering look, but it has no effect on him. She relents and walks over, helping roll the body to one side, spreading the blanket underneath it, and rolling the dead woman like a morbid burrito.

"Ugh, I need Purell!" Melissa says.

"There're a few bottles of it in there," Carmen says and nods her head toward the cache of supplies in the rec room. She turns to D-Day as nosy Melissa walks away to get some hand sanitizer. "She's a real pill."

"Yeah, a real warm, inviting personality, that one," D-Day says, then turns back to the business at hand. "So we have a monogrammed letter opener used to kill someone. Seems an odd choice of weapon. Whoever did this attacked and killed Cheryl in less than ten minutes with no one noticing what was happening until after the fact. And, they likely got blood all over them. Based on the monogram, our lead suspect is Mike Upham. So I guess our search starts there."

"Are you going there now?" Carmen asks.

"I should, yes. Otherwise, we'll have a lynching to

deal with too," D-Day replies, eyeing the group of people who still occupy the rec room.

"Do you want some company?"

"If you're up for it. I don't want to put you in harm's way, though. If he did this, I can't imagine it was planned. He has to be panicked right now, and panicky people are dangerous and unpredictable," D-Day says.

"All the more reason for you to take someone with you. But if I go, I want a gun," Carmen says.

"Do you want me to deputize you too?" D-Day asks.

Carmen smiles. "Sure thing, Sheriff. Get me a Bible and swear me in."

D-Day smiles back. It's a tired smile, but genuine. He likes her toughness in spite of what she's been through. That kind of resilience is a good quality in his eyes. And speaking of eyes, she's pretty easy on those too.

"All right," he says, kicking his mind into action. "We'll stop by my place and get you set up with a gun. Let's tell these people what's going on before they have multiple aneurysms, then we'll go catch a killer."

"That's a phrase that a day ago would have seemed completely unreal," Carmen says. "But now it's like, I won't be surprised if anything happens."

As if to punctuate her statement, Melissa begins screaming.

CHAPTER 19

Kyle Puckett stands on Danny Harris's porch, looking at the instructions Danny left for him. He lifts the cover on the keypad next to the door and punches in the eight-digit code. He's rewarded with the sound of a motor humming and steel bolts retracting. He turns the knob, opens the door, and steps inside, followed by Robert and Stephenie.

"Will one of you stay here and get the door if anyone comes with supplies?" he asks.

"I'll do it," Stephenie says.

"Be careful," Robert signs to her.

"Duh," she says in response. Robert gives her a look she refers to as "the stink-eye," but he doesn't say anything. He takes Stephenie's pack from her and follows Kyle.

Kyle takes a quick look around the main floor. Even with all their packing and hurried exit this morning, the house is spotless, well organized and everything appears to be in its place. He turns his attention back to the folder.

The next line of instructions reads, *"Go to the basement. Open the closet door next to the guest bath."* He goes to the guest bath, finds the closet next to it and opens the door. *"Inside you'll find another keypad. Enter 96984585."*

Kyle does as instructed. He hears another motor humming, followed by the sound of steel bars locking in place. The floor at the front edge of the closet lifts six inches into the air.

"This will release a panel in the floor; lift it, and proceed down the stairs.

He grabs the handle that is now exposed and lifts the panel. He's aided by a pair of large hydraulic pistons, one on each side, similar to what you would see on an SUV's lift gate, only much bigger. The panel extends nine feet to the back of the closet. Underneath the panel, a set of stairs descends into the basement. He looks at Robert, gives him a small shrug, and descends the stairs with Robert a couple of steps behind him. Kyle notices that the stairway is a couple of steps longer than his, meaning the basement is about eighteen inches deeper in the ground than his own basement two doors away. *That's how he got it covered by the landscaping. He went down deeper,* he thinks to himself. Danny is much more clever than Kyle ever gave him credit for.

The room at the foot of the stairs is impressive. It's an open floorplan, with the main living area all technically one room. A large semi-circular sectional sofa surrounds a round coffee table. A massive flat-screen TV dominates the wall in front of the sofa. To the left is the doorway to the basement's master bedroom, with its own bathroom and huge walk-in closet. To the right are the kitchen and dining area. Kyle turns and heads that direction. Just before the kitchen is a hallway to the left that leads to under-stairs storage, the home gym, the second bedroom, and the main bathroom.

The open kitchen is L-shaped, with the refrigerator, cabinets, a microwave, and toaster sharing the wall with the bathroom. The sink, dishwasher, and a small cooktop/oven combo are on the outside wall. Just off of the kitchen is a round dining table with seats for six people, though you could probably crowd eight around it in a pinch.

Beyond the dining area is a storage room. The basement would normally end there, but Danny's modification has a door leading down three steps into his workshop.

"This place is incredible," Robert says. "What did you say this guy does?"

"Gunsmith," Kyle says.

"Jesus. He must be phenomenal at it."

"He says he's not the best, but he's very good. He does a lot of custom stuff; people come to him with special orders, stuff like that," Kyle says, hoping that is enough information because, other than that high-level pitch, he can't begin to describe what Danny does.

Voices catch their attention. Marc, Keith, and

Danielle come down the stairs with backpacks, boxes and a laundry basket full of food, clothing and various sundries.

"We're just gonna set this stuff down and go back for more," Marc says. "We can sort it later."

"Yeah, good idea," Kyle says. "I'll come help." He turns to Robert. "You and Stephenie direct traffic over here, okay? I'll be back soon."

"You got it, Mr. Puckett," Robert says

"Kyle, please. I can't take that Mr. Puckett stuff."

"You got it, Kyle."

On their way out, Kyle, Marc, and the crew pass Natalie, Andy, and Annie with a similar load of goods.

"Where's Ben and Toni?" Kyle asks them.

"He's getting her up, but she's really groggy," Natalie says. "And we have more boxes ready to go if anyone has time to grab them. Otherwise, we can come back for them."

Kyle and Danielle divert to the Puckett house to get the last few boxes, and Kyle takes the opportunity to check on Ben. Marc and Keith continue to their house.

"Ben?" Kyle says as he walks in. "You need help?"

He goes down the short hallway to the guest room and finds Ben standing in front of Toni, who is sitting on the edge of the bed. After performing her impromptu surgery, Danny has torn a sheet into long strips of cloth and used them to wrap around her wrist and arm and secure it to her chest so she can't move her right shoulder. She looks uncomfortable with her arm secured to her body this way, but it's important to let her injuries heal.

"Hey Dad," Ben says. "I think we're about to get moving. She's having a hard time waking up, but she's getting there."

"Okay. Clock's ticking, though, son. If you aren't headed over by the time we're done taking all our stuff over, we'll need to carry her."

"Got it, Dad. I'll ask for help if we need it."

Kyle does a quick once-over of the kitchen and decides they have grabbed the most important stuff. He goes to the bedroom, grabs a backpack from his closet, and fills it with boxer shorts and socks. He heads back to the kitchen, where he and Danielle grab the boxes that the other kids left behind, and head back to Danny's house. On the way out the door, he sees Ben and Toni moving down the hallway from the guest room.

"We're right behind you, Dad," Ben says. The boy's father nods and leaves the door open for them.

"You're sure you can do this?" Ben asks Toni. "We can get a chair or something for you to sit on and a couple of us can carry you."

"I want to walk," she says. He helps her step down from the doorway, pulling the door shut behind him and verifying he locked it. It's only one hundred and fifty feet down the sidewalk to Danny's walkway, but for the injured girl it's a more complicated journey.

She's more unsteady than she thought she would be. They're making slow progress and what should take no more than a minute at a normal walking pace has taken two, and they're only half way there.

A screech from the end of the block startles them. Ben looks to the right to see a bloodied woman running with a limp, headed straight for them.

"Toni, pick up the pace. We have to move," Ben says.

The groggy girl steps faster for a couple of strides but stumbles and almost falls. Ben catches her by her left arm and keeps her upright, but it must have hurt her as she yelps, and she's back to her slower pace. The undead woman is closing the distance faster than they're making progress to the house. Ben looks back at his dad's house and estimates that it's just as far back there as it is to the Harris place.

"Come on, Toni, this is serious. We have to move faster," he says.

She again quickens her pace, but Ben can tell it's not going to be fast enough.

They're almost to the walkway that leads to Danny's front door. Ben turns Toni toward the house.

"Get inside!" he shouts. Behind him, the undead woman screams again. Ben bends down and grabs a soft-ball-sized rock from the bed that borders the grass of the front lawn. He turns and throws it as hard as he can. He misses his mark, but not by much; he had aimed for her head, but the missile strikes the woman in the throat. It's enough to knock her off balance, and she tumbles to the street a few feet from the sidewalk. Ben starts to sprint for the house, but the zombie is on her feet before he can make his move. She screams again, but this time, the sound is more of a gurgle muffled by a mouthful of the oily black fluid they'd seen at the scene of the accident earlier.

Ben grabs another rock and hurls it. On this throw his aim is better; he hits her in the head, and she falls to the street. She gets up again, but she's not moving as quickly as before. Ben makes his move for the door with the battered undead woman a few paces behind. Ahead of him, Toni has reached the entrance to the house.

Stephenie Sims opens the door and sees the zombie trailing behind the pair.

"Holy shit!" she exclaims. She steps around Toni, onto the porch, and raises her rifle. "Down!!" she yells at Ben.

The younger Puckett drops to the concrete, and Stephenie fires the gun twice, the reports echoing around the neighborhood. The zombie goes down, this time for good. In the seconds that follow, more undead screams can be heard from farther away.

Ben gets to his feet and hustles through the door, and Stephenie slams it behind him. Robert comes up the stairs with the page from the folder with the instructions on it and enters the code that locks the door and sets the alarm. Ben is helping Toni down the stairs, where everyone else is already gathered. Kyle consults a notepad he took from his go-bag. He writes on it for a minute, then does a roll call.

"Everyone, please answer when I call your name," he says. "Ben."

"I'm right here, Dad. So is Toni."

Kyle puts a check mark by each of the names.

"Keith?" Kyle says.

"Present and accounted for," the younger Wallace says.

Kyle goes through the rest of the names, each person acknowledging their presence. Counting himself, there are eleven people in the basement.

"Does anyone have anything else they need to get?" he asks.

"Well, you know how it is. We'll say no but in five minutes someone will realize they've forgotten something important," Keith says.

"Well, then, let's double-check," Kyle says.

They do a quick accounting of their personal effects, and the consensus is that they have everything they believe to be critical. Kyle takes the page of instructions from Robert and enters the code in the touchpad at the bottom of the stairs. A motor whirs, and the access panel that camouflaged the stairway pulls itself shut. Another motor whirs and steel bolts, two inches in diameter and a foot long, are guided in place. There are two on each side of the panel and two at the end at the top of the stairs. The strongest pry bar will never break that panel loose.

Kyle turns to face the group.

"Well, we're locked in," he says. "More importantly, those things are locked out. Let's take stock of our supplies and see what information we can get from the news."

"Mr. Puck, er, Kyle?" Robert says.

"Yes, Robert?"

"Your friend Danny has a DVD in here with a sticky note that says 'play me'."

Kyle finds the remote that rests on the round coffee table, studies it for a second, and then presses the button labeled "all on."

The TV lights up, with the manufacturer's logo spinning in the center of the screen. The logo disappears, and a message in the upper right of the screen says "Ch. 31 TBS" but the screen is just black. Kyle searches for the mode button that says "DVD" and presses it. The screen changes over to the DVD player's menu. It's a smart player, Internet connected, that streams different online services, but the highlighted option reads "Blu-Ray/DVD." He takes the disc from Robert, finds the eject button, drops the disc on the tray, and presses play. The tray retracts and Kyle can hear the disc spinning inside the machine.

The screen goes black, and then flashes white, and Danny's face appears.

"Well, hello. I'm going to assume I'm talking to Kyle or Marc since you're the only two people I'd give this to. Welcome to the headquarters of Harris Tactical, LLC. If you've followed my instructions, you're sealed in the basement, but that also means that all hell has broken loose."

On-screen, Danny takes a sip of a drink—some whiskey by the looks of it—and continues.

"There are two beds down here, one king and one queen, one in each of the bedrooms. If there are more than three or four of you, there are cots under the beds and in the storage room. There are enough for ten people, plus additional room on the couches.

"In the folder you'll find instructions on how to access my workshop. This will give you additional space and is also a fallback room, a panic room, if you will. The basement is secure, but in the event of a breach it would take artillery to get into the workshop once you've sealed yourself inside."

"You'll be able to hide out down here for a long time, provided you have enough food. You DID bring enough food, didn't you? I hope so."

He takes another drink, then continues. The DVD plays on for about twenty minutes, going over the details of the fortress that Danny has created; the solar power, the UPS, the air exchanger, the water storage, and filtration system. He's even had the window wells sealed and covered so you cannot see them from the outside. He's installed concrete bunkers outside each window, with sealed doors that open to tunnels that come up under the neighbors' window wells. Using these tunnels, they can access the houses on either side without having to go outside to do so. Danny has set the place up to be completely self-sufficient for sixty days regarding food and water—for him and Elaine. For the eleven people holed up there now, Kyle does some fast math and figures they have fifteen or sixteen days' worth, including the food they've brought with them; more if they ration it from the start. On-screen, Danny is wrapping up his video message.

"So that's it, friends. You know most of the secrets of my lair, both legally installed and extra-legal, if you will. I don't know what's brought us to this point, but it must be serious if I gave you 'the package.' Keep your heads down, don't get stir crazy, and keep your wits about you. Unless we've been nuked by the Ruskies or zombies have taken over the world, whatever this is should be over soon. Sit tight and be ready for anything. Good luck!"

Danny reaches for the camera, his hand disappearing to the side of the lens, and a second later the screen goes black.

CHAPTER 20

DJ turns the shovel of the backhoe toward the oncoming trio of bloodied men. The first one, the fastest, is only a dozen yards away. It slows down, and it seems like it's not sure where to go next. It must not see DJ sitting in the external seat at the controls of the backhoe. It's clear to DJ, though, that this rotting fellow should not be vertical. The ripped neck, the torn abdomen with the liver peeking out are telltale signs. This guy is obviously one of the undead the newscasts have been talking about. DJ raises the arm on the backhoe, folds the shovel underneath it, and as the creature watches the movement with great interest, DJ brings it down like a hammer, driving the zombie into the ground.

The other two are approaching along the same route as the first one. DJ extends the arm and scoop, and like a grade school kid flicking a paper football, the backhoe flicks the closest creature backward into the lagging one, and they collapse, one on top of the other. He brings the arm straight down, the teeth on the shovel tearing both of the undead men in half. He lifts the shovel and pivots the arm away from them so he can get a good look at the terrible trio.

The first one, the nail, is smashed flat. DJ's stomach turns when he sees the mass of sludge, meat, and bone where he pancaked poor Thing 1. Things 2 and 3 are still "alive," if you can call it that. The lower bodies lie where he separated them from their torsos, but the upper halves are pulling themselves toward the backhoe. He brings the arm around again, tucks the shovel, and splats the farthest one, but the other is too close to reach with the shovel. DJ peers over the edge of the control deck and doesn't see Thing 3, so he jumps down from the backhoe control seat and runs to the cab of the tractor. He misses the arm that swipes at his foot as he steps up into the cab.

He lifts the stabilizer arms and drives the tractor away from the creatures, turning in a wide circle and pointing the nose back at the gory scene. No Thing 3 in sight. He keeps advancing at a crawl, thinking he must not see it in the weeds, or it's in a rut made by the massive wheels. But still, he sees nothing. He makes a wide arc again, searching the ground for signs of road-kill zombie, but after a second pass, he sees nothing.

He removes his hat and scratches the top of his head, puzzled at where this half-zom has gone. He goes to put his hat back on, but it's caught on something. He tugs a little harder and hears a growl. Then he smells death.

He lets go of the hat and jumps in the seat, turning to see what he already knows; the zombie is right behind him. It's apparent from the crushed torso and the pattern left by the tractor tire that the tractor ran the thing over. It must have clung to the tire and rode to the top, like a grim kind of Ferris Wheel. Then it got tossed onto the back of the cab and pulled itself in through the open rear window. It has DJ's hat clutched in its teeth, gnashing at the orange fabric, staining it brown and black with the slime secreting from its mouth.

"Gross!" DJ says. The creature spits out the hat and reaches for DJ, who backs against the door to the cab, fumbling for the latch. He finds it and spills out, falling five feet and landing flat on his back. He grunts, the air leaving his body against his will. His diaphragm convulses, out of sync with his lungs for a moment. Above him, the zombie has pulled itself to the edge of the doorway. It gives a final pull and is airborne, falling toward DJ.

He fumbles around him, still trying to catch his breath when his hand grasps a stick the diameter of a broom handle. It's only eighteen inches long, but he thrusts it out in front of him and catches the falling harbinger of death in the mouth. The weight of the creature drives the stick into its brain, pausing for a millisecond when it meets the skull; then the stick punches out the back of the head. Black fluid runs down the stick onto DJs work gloves. He pushes the thing to the side, letting it flop on the ground.

After a minute, he sits up and takes a deep breath, his first normal one since the fall from the tractor. He hears a noise and sees two more undead coming toward him from the road. He scrambles back into the cab of the tractor, closes the rear window, throws his hat and gloves outside, closes the door, and gets the tractor moving back to the farmhouse.

DJ has it going about twenty miles per hour on the dirt utility road. It's part of the same road that Ben and the others drove over last night, but for the first time since the battle, he's not thinking about that. He's focused on the zombies that are keeping pace with the tractor. He speeds up to thirty miles per hour, making the ride much bumpier, and finally, the horrible-looking former people start dropping back. With the backhoe attachment on the tractor, DJ can't get it going faster. He curses himself for not bringing his rifle with him and makes a mental note not ever to leave it behind again.

He sees his parents' house and the big barn as he comes over a rise in the road. He glances back and doesn't see the undead.

Maybe they gave up, the voice in his head says.

"I don't think that's how it works," he says out loud.

He heads for the big barn, which is, in reality, a three-hundred-foot-long building with a thirty-foot-wide, twenty-foot-tall door that pivots up like an old-fashioned one-piece garage door. He presses the button on the garage door opener remote control and holds it for a count of five before he sees the door start to rise. He glances back again and sees the two zombies coming down the rise behind him, the lead one only a couple hundred yards back.

He has to slow the tractor down as he enters the barn so he doesn't crash into any of the other equipment, which allows the lead zombie to catch up by a few yards. Once he crosses the threshold, he can't start lowering the door until the tractor is all the way inside —backhoe arm and all—because of the electric eye safety sensors that have to be installed for the commercial-grade garage door opener to work. This costs precious seconds that allow the zombie to gain even more ground.

DJ vaults from the cab of the tractor and sees the creature approaching the barn. The door is not going to make it down before it gets there. He climbs back into the cab of the tractor and grabs the opener's remote control, and hops back down. The edge of the door is about six feet from the ground as the zombie collides with it. Its feet come off of the ground like it's been clotheslined by a linebacker, and it lands with a thud, kicking up a puff of dust. DJ is looking around for anything he can use as a weapon.

The zombie's momentum carried past the bottom of the door, so when it hit the ground it tripped the sensor, and the door begins to rise back up. So does the zombie.

It gets up, oblivious to the broken collarbone it suffered in its collision with the door or the way the left arm hangs slack as a result and advances into the barn. DJ presses the button again, sending the door back on its downward march, hopefully closing all the way before the second zombie gets there.

DJ has grabbed a pitchfork for his weapon. The zombie sees him, and just as it had no care about the closing barn door, it doesn't register the five-tined farm tool as a threat. It just rushes full speed at DJ, who thrusts the business end of the pitchfork at the zombie's head. He misses, sending two of the tines through the neck just under the jaw. Momentum carries the zombie forward, striking DJ and taking him down to the ground. The handle of the pitchfork keeps the snapping jaws from making contact with DJ's flesh, but the one good arm scratches and claws at him. He fights with the surprisingly strong creature, finally getting hold of the pitchfork's handle and using it to lever the horrible thing off of him. As he does so, the pitchfork twists under the zombie's weight and DJ hears a crack. The body of the creature goes limp. DJ gets to his feet, still holding the pitchfork. He looks down at the foul-smelling beast and see the eyes still moving, trying to focus on him, the jaws still working up and down hoping for a meal.

"Yeah!" he shouts. "You aren't so tough with your neck busted, are you?!"

He pulls the pitchfork from the neck and jams it in the creature's head. All movement stops. A shuffling sound to his left makes DJ pivot, the pitchfork held in front of him. The second zombie is about to strike him, and he shoves the pitchfork forward and side-steps the assault. This time, the tines go through the head, and the sack of meat goes down in a heap. The arms and legs are still twitching, but not in a coordinated fashion. DJ pulls the pitchfork out of the head and rams it home again.

Other than his heart pounding in his ears and his breath coming in gasps, he hears nothing else in the barn.

He looks appreciatively at the pitchfork.

"You're coming with me," he says to the tool. He walks to the side door and cracks it open. He doesn't see any of the undead nearby, so he sprints for the main house.

Zombies: o. *DJ:* 5 the voice says.

"Damn straight," he answers it.

CHAPTER 21

Denver Colorado

Melissa's scream still hangs in the air. D-Day and Carmen spin around to see that the dead body of the woman named Cheryl is sitting up, still wrapped in the sheet that they had cocooned her in moments before.

"What the fuck ..." Carmen says, her words trailing off as the body begins to thrash and fight against the fabric constraints. Beneath the blanket they can see the jaw working, biting at the cloth as though it were an animal and not a couple of layers of cloth. Snarling, guttural noises come from the creature. It loses its balance and topples over, thrashing now on the floor, the blanket starting to loosen. Fresh screams pierce the air.

D-Day takes a few long strides over to the reanimated corpse, drawing his suppressed pistol as he does so. He puts a boot on the thing's neck, takes aim and fires a shot into the side of its head. It convulses once more, then settles down, only its legs showing any sign of movement. D-Day fires a second shot and, this time, all movement stops.

He takes a deep breath before turning around and addressing the crowd of terrified faces. Of course, Melissa speaks first, her face frozen in a terrified grin.

"How could that happen? How can she come back after she was killed? She wasn't bitten by one of those things; she was stabbed!"

"We don't know that she wasn't bitten. Maybe it was just a scratch; maybe she came in contact with infected material. I don't know, but there are a lot of possibilities," D-Day says. "The important thing is that everyone stays alert. It's obvious that there's a lot about this disease, or whatever it is, about how it spreads, that we don't know."

"That's just great," Melissa says. "The blind leading the blind."

"I want a gun," the blonde man says. "You have extras, right? I want one."

Several people begin to murmur, and D-Day sees several heads nodding.

"Stop it, right now!" he exclaims. "I'm not giving any guns to any of you! I don't run an armory. If you don't have your own weapons, it's not my job to provide them to you. And you," he turns to Melissa. "If you're not happy with how I'm doing things, you can do whatever the hell you want to do. If you want to be the mayor of Shit Towne, be my guest! But when you do something stupid, which I'm sure you will, and you put my life at risk, or someone else I care about, I'll drop you in a second and won't think twice about it."

For a few tense and awkward seconds that feel like an eternity, no one speaks. Melissa just stares at D-Day, seething, saying nothing.

"Well then, if we're done with the bullshit, I'm going to try to find out who killed ..." D-Day trails off, trying to remember the dead woman's name.

"Cheryl," Aggie says.

D-Day looks at the Rhea Perlman doppelganger. "Thank you. Cheryl. I suggest that you all go back to your apartments, but if you stay out, I strongly recommend that you don't go alone. And if you have anything—a gun," he pauses and looks at the blond man, "or a baseball bat or whatever weapon you can find, I suggest you bring it wherever you go. We need to rely on each other to get through this, so please, everyone, keep your heads on straight and don't give in to panic. Panic will kill you before the zombies do. Any questions?"

A petite red-haired woman speaks up.

"The president is on TV," she says.

Everyone rushes to find a spot in front of the large flat-panel screen.

"Turn it up!" the blonde man says. The red head

points the remote at the screen and presses the volume button.

NELSON FARMS, **North of Longview, Colorado**

DJ makes it to the house without encountering any additional zombies. He finds the family sitting around the dining table. Vanessa has stopped crying and is drinking coffee. Virginia looks up at DJ, startled by his appearance.

"What the hell happened to you?" she asks, getting up. She approaches him but recoils and wrinkles her nose. "Jesus, boy, you stink!"

"Yeah," he says, still breathing hard. "It's zombie blood. After you all had left, a few of them showed up."

Tim jumps up from the table.

"What? How many? Are you okay?" he asks questions rapid-fire.

"There was five total. They're all dead, now, again, but these things are fast, and they are *strong*," he says, emphasizing their strength. He still has a hold of the pitchfork, and he gestures with it. "And it's like the news said, you have to get the head to kill them. I cut one in half with the backhoe and ran it over with the tractor, and it *still* came after me."

A drop of black zombie blood drips from the pitchfork onto the beige carpet, staining the spot like ink.

"DJ, get that thing out of the dining room, please," Virginia says.

"I don't think any of us should go anywhere without a weapon," he says. "If you encounter one of these things without a way to defend yourself, you're done for. I had the tractor going all out, and I still could not outrun one of them."

"Fine, DJ, then clean those tines off. I don't want that goop all over the house. It stinks."

DJ's youngest brother, Bill, calls out from the family room.

"Hey guys," he shouts. "The president is on TV."

They all file into the family room, where Bill lies on the couch, his wounded leg elevated on a pile of pillows. On the screen, President Obama sits at a desk, a blue background behind him, the American flag to the left and the flag bearing the Presidential Seal on the right.

"Turn it up," Tim says.

DANNY HARRIS'S BASEMENT, **Longview, Colorado**

Danny's instructional video has just ended, so Kyle turns the knob back to "TV" and scans through the channels until he finds one that still has a signal. He's about to say something when Natalie speaks up.

"Look, it's the President!" she exclaims.

Kyle points the remote and turns the volume up a few notches. President Obama begins to speak.

"Good timing!" Keith says.

"Shhh!" Danielle admonishes him.

"MY FELLOW AMERICANS, and all people who can receive this broadcast, I never thought I would be delivering a speech like this. No leader can be prepared for what has happened over the last eighteen hours. I can't believe that we're fighting an actual zombie plague, but when the evidence rules out all other options, you're left with the truth, and there's no benefit to denying it or trying to wish it away. If you're receiving this, I pray for your continued safety and implore you to stay sheltered. It's not an exaggeration to say that your life depends on it.

The events overnight and this morning are extraordinary. What has happened isn't an American problem, or a Christian problem, or a Muslim problem; it's a human problem. Riots have occurred in every nation, impacting people of every race, creed, and religion. We've all seen the most gruesome images imaginable, and many of you have had to do awful things just to survive.

The damage to our infrastructure has been severe. The loss of life has been astounding. The horrors of these attacks continue today, and each one is unspeakably tragic for those involved. It's important that no one assign blame to one group or another. Now is not a time for the familiar politics of hate, for drawing lines in the sand or turning inward as a nation. Now is not a time for division. We're facing an unprecedented moment in history. For the first time, we are united as a species against a common problem, a common cause. We can't afford not to work together.

So, I am in touch with the leaders of other nations. We're developing strategies to fight back against the hordes of the infected, which threaten the lives and safety of the citizens of the world. I want to assure you that help is coming. The military is preparing for counter-assaults and will begin re-taking our cities. One by one, we will take back our cities, our nations, our world.

But make no mistake. It will not happen overnight. It will not be easy. And it will not be without sacrifice. To help protect those who have survived the night, I will remind you that I have declared martial law. A strict curfew is in effect for the whole of the United States. We've had reports of looting, stealing, even murder of our citizens as they have been fighting for survival. This behavior is not acceptable and will be dealt with swiftly and severely. I urge everyone within the reach of my voice to remain calm and if you've found a safe place, stay there. Help is coming. I repeat that—Help. Is. Coming. Together, we will persevere.

God bless you and keep you safe, God bless the United States of America, and God bless all people around the world.

DENVER, **Colorado**

"I am so glad he's our President," the red-haired woman says. "We're going to be rescued!"

"I hope so," D-Day says. "But it's not going to happen right away. Like he said, we have to work together, and we have to help each other."

"Just tell us what to do, and we're ready," Carmen says. Heads nod around the room, even the blonde man who has been complaining.

D-Day looks over the crowd of twenty people. The President's speech seems to have galvanized them, at least for the moment. As he gets ready to lay out his plan, he doesn't notice that Melissa, the biggest complainer of the lot, has slipped out of the room.

"All right, folks," he says. "We've got a good start, but we still have work to do."

NELSON FARMS, **North of Longview**

"Well, that was a waste of time," DJ says.

"Here we go," says Vanessa. "Why can't you just shut up for five minutes."

"Because I'm a realist. We're on our own out here. Longview is burning. I counted at least a dozen fires earlier, or at least a dozen plumes of smoke, so maybe there's more. There's no fire department to put them out. No police. No communication. How long do you think we're going to have power? Water? Those things take people to keep running, and I doubt there're many folks heading to work today."

"But he said the Army is coming," Vanessa counters.

"This country spans four time zones and has—had—three hundred million people. There's what—a million people in the military? And a ton of them are deployed overseas. Who knows if they'll make it back here. We need to be ready to fend for ourselves for a long time."

"He's right," Virginia says.

"Mom, I—what?" DJ stammers.

"What?" Tim says.

"He's right," she repeats. "We need to be prepared to weather this storm for a while. Assuming the military can fight this thing, we'd be fools to think they're going to start here. They'll start in DC, New York, LA—the biggest, most important cities. They may get here eventually, but we need to last until they do."

Everyone is silent for a few seconds, Virginia's comments sinking in.

"Okay," she says. "We have work to do."

DANNY HARRIS'S BASEMENT, **Longview, Colorado**

"What did all of that mean?" Natalie asks.

"Where was he? Isn't Washington overrun too?" Annie says.

"He's in Area 51," Keith says. "Safe in the desert with the aliens. Maybe that's what started all this: aliens!"

"You're an idiot," Danielle says without a hint of humor.

"Okay, enough," Kyle says. "He's probably in NORAD, under Cheyenne Mountain, or still on Air Force One. I think they can keep that thing in the air for weeks. Anyway, that's not important. Natalie, you asked what that meant. The way I see it, it didn't mean anything. We were prepared to hole up here for a few weeks until Toni's healed and can travel, and that just reinforces that's what we need to do."

"Agreed," Marc says. "We've got food enough to last a while, we're safe and secure here, and I've brought some of my equipment so as long as the Internet stays intact, I can get us information about what's happening in the world. In fact, I can get information for a while after the 'net' goes down." He pantomimes typing to underscore his point.

"Okay. So we need to get the perishable food put away, sort out living arrangements, job duties, et cetera," Kyle says. "And we wait out those things out there. The zombies or whatever they are."

"Zeds," Ben says.

"What?" Andy asks.

"Zeds. It's Canadian for 'Z'. Zed is easier to say than zombie."

Kyle considers this for a second.

"I like it," he says. "Let's get to it, kids. It's Zed's World now. We just live in it, and we have work to do."

ALSO BY RICH BAKER

Please take a moment and sample the first chapter of

Zed's World Book Three: No Way Out

PART ONE

D-DAY

Denver, Colorado Saturday May 18, 2013: Z-Day Plus 1

President Obama has just finished a speech urging people to stay where they are and shelter in place; the military is working on a plan to retake the country from the dead.

"I am so glad he's our president," a red-haired woman says. "We're going to be rescued!"

D-Day looks at her. She's tired, dirty, and based on the reddish-black stains on her clothes and the smell coming from her, she's been helping dispose of the bodies of the undead. Still, after a speech promising the government is coming to the rescue, she's wearing a smile. He doesn't want to blow out that flicker of hope but feels he needs to set appropriate expectations.

"I hope so," he says. "But it's not going to happen right away. Like he said, we have to work together, and we have to help each other." He makes eye contact with the blonde man who has been complaining about D-Day's handling of security and wanting one of D-Day's weapons. "All of us."

"Just tell us what to do, and we're ready, willing and able. We're going to survive this thing!" the woman replies. Heads nod around the room, even Blondie's.

D-Day looks over the crowd of twenty people. The president's speech seems to have galvanized them, and at least for the moment, they have forgotten about the murdered woman who lies wrapped in a blanket just outside the common room. As he gets ready to lay out his plan, he doesn't notice that Melissa, the biggest complainer of the lot, has slipped away from the group and disappeared.

"All right, folks," he says. "Here's the deal. This building has a bank of solar panels on the roof and a UPS setup to run the critical things like the power locks in the event of a power outage."

"What is a UPS?" a woman asks with her hand raised.

"UPS. Uninterruptible Power Supply. It's a bank of batteries that the solar panels keep charged. But these batteries will not power the whole building once the grid goes down, so we have to conserve energy."

Another hand goes up. "Why will the grid go down? Isn't that stuff all automated?"

"Not really. Most of our power locally comes from coal-fired plants, which need a lot of human attention, and humans seem to be in short supply now. Even if there are people at the plants, they require fuel, and that means trains are bringing coal and pipelines pushing natural gas. Those supplies will run out pretty quick without people running them. And even then, if we have fuel, the grids are interconnected and when plants in other parts of the country go down, it will put an increasing strain on any that are still operational until eventually, the grid goes down anyway. The big concern here is when the power goes, so does our fresh water supply."

"This isn't sounding good for our long-term survival," Blondie says.

"You're sure about all of this, like, you really know what you're talking about?" a young man with coke-bottle glasses asks. He reminds D-Day of that episode of The Twilight Zone with Burgess Meredith, where his character loves to read, but after the apocalypse, he breaks his glasses. Poor bastard.

"Yeah, I'm sure. Look – we can do a few things to buy ourselves some time. Water is the biggest concern, so we need to fill any container we can find with water while we still have pressure in the pipes. That's our top priority."

"I can help with that," Blondie says.

"You should fill sinks and bathtubs in each apartment you search," Carmen says. "I started doing that last night before...all the excitement."

"Good idea," D-Day says.

"Can we shower?" the red-haired woman asks.

"Yes, you should do that before the power goes out. It could be the last one for a while."

Coke-bottles speaks up. "What else should we do?"

"After water, food is the next important thing. We need to collect the perishable food from all the apartments. Where's Aggie?" D-Day looks around until he spots the Rhea Perlman doppelganger raising her hand. "Aggie can tell you which apartments people have been to already, and you can work your way out from there. Is everyone on board with this?"

Heads nod around the room and people start talking amongst themselves. D-Day interrupts them.

"A couple more things, folks. Please." They stop talking and turn their attention back to him. "When the power does go out, everyone needs to open refrigerators as seldom as possible. Every time you open one, the food is going spoil that much faster. Also, weapons," he looks at Blondie, "will be on the finders-keepers policy. I just ask that you talk to me, so I can ensure you know how to use them. Ok?"

Again, they all nod.

"Last thing," he continues, and points toward the doorway, toward the dead body that lies just out of sight in the hallway. "We still have a murderer in the building. I don't think anyone's in grave danger, but if you're going anywhere in the building, you need to pair up. Don't go anywhere alone. Everyone on board with that?"

They all nod their assent, and then Blondie speaks

up again. "Are you still going to investigate the murder?"

"Yes, I am. I need to examine the body and see if there are any clues that can help identify the killer, or what made her turn into a zombie like she did, and I'll go on from there. I'll keep you all informed if I find anything. I'm no policeman, so that's the best I can give you right now. Fair enough?"

"Yeah," Blondie says. "And I'm sorry about before. I was just.."

D-Day cuts him off.

"Save it. I appreciate the apology, but I recognize that we're all in uncharted territory here. No one could be prepared for this. Everyone just keep a level head and focus on the task at hand, and we'll be fine. Anything else?"

Everyone looks around the room at the others present but say nothing.

"Good," D-Day concludes. "Let's get to it!"

That is good enough for the group, and people begin to pair off and set out to gather supplies. D-Day turns to Carmen.

"You're sure you want to go after a murderer with me? It could be dangerous," he says, walking toward the doorway to the common room.

She points at the dead body as they round the corner. "So is collecting food. That's all she was doing and look at what happened to her."

"Good point. Do you know if your mom is done updating the building roster, and mapping where everyone has moved?" he asks. After they stopped the initial wave of the undead and secured the building, people have, for the most part, moved to the empty apartments on the higher floors, rendering the existing building map from the main office useless.

"Not done, but I think she's gotten through the 10th floor," she replies.

"Okay. Will you go get it and meet me at my apartment when you're ready to go?"

"You bet," she says. "Where are you going?"

"I'm going to get rid of her," he nods at the body, "but first I need to look her over and see what we're missing. She wasn't bitten, at least not that we know of, so we need to know how she turned gray. Here, take this," he says, and hands her the electronic key to his door. "In case you get there before me."

"That's trusting," she says through a smile.

"Right now, you're the only one I do trust."

"I'll tell my parents you said that," she says with a sarcastic lilt to her voice, "They'll be bursting with pride that you trust me and hurt that they didn't make the shortlist. Way to win them over." Before he can respond, she walks away, flashing a grin to let him know she's kidding. He realizes that he's smiling back. He likes this woman; even in the middle of the zombie apocalypse, she's flirty and has him grinning like an idiot.

Carmen disappears behind the stairwell door, leaving D-Day alone with his thoughts and a dead body.

ABOUT THE AUTHOR

Rich Baker traces his love of zombies back to the Dan O'Bannon movie *Return of the Living Dead*, which was his first introduction to the genre. He was hooked, devouring any movies or books he could get his hands on. Reality and a well-paying day job kept his passion for writing at bay until he met and spoke with a few guys who were writing apocalyptic zombie fiction, and he put pen to paper (or fingers to keyboard, as it were).

Rich would like to thank WJ Lundy for showing faith in Zed's World and bringing Rich to the rest of the crew at Phalanx, Brian Parker for demonstrating that writing and an all-consuming job and family life can mutually exist, and Joe for all the jokes. The examples provided by these fine gentlemen (term used loosely) has been inspirational.

Zed's World Book Three is available now in paperback, Kindle e-book and Audible!

twitter.com/rbakerbooks
http://www.rbakerbooks.com/

BOOKS UNDER THE SHIELD OF
PHALANX PRESS

FIVE ROADS TO TEXAS

| LUNDY | PARKER | BAKER | HANSEN | GAMBOA |

From the best story tellers of Phalanx Press comes a frightening tale of Armageddon.

It spread fast- no time to understand it- let alone learn
how to fight it.
Once it reached you, it was too late. All you could do
is run.
Rumored safe zones and potential for a cure drifted
across the populace, forcing tough decisions to
be made.
They say only the strong survive. Well they forgot
about the smart, the inventive and the lucky.

*Follow five different groups from across the U.S.A. as
they make their way to what could be America's last
stand in the Lone Star State.*

AFTER THE ROADS

BRIAN PARKER

The infected rule the world beyond the protective walls of the Texas Safe Zone.

Fort Bliss, Texas is home to four million refugees, trapped behind the hastily-erected walls of the Army base--too many people and not enough food.

In a desperate gamble, the soldiers responsible for securing the walls begin searching for pre-outbreak food storage locations. Not everyone will make it home.

For Sidney Bannister, the Safe Zone's refugee camps have become a nightmare that she can no longer endure. She must find a way to leave before her baby is born, or risk never experiencing freedom again.

Follow Sidney's story from the Phalanx Press collaborative novel Five Roads to Texas.

FOR WHICH WE STAND

JOSEPH HANSEN

El Paso wasn't the Promised Land that Ian and his crew had hoped for but it wasn't a total bust either. The concept of a safe haven in today's world was a fool's errand at best. This was the consensus of their tiny band and to keep moving, their only salvation. While others waited in their pens the four from the private security company moved on taking on as many they could help, in hopes that they too would join the fight. Their journey was long and arduous but it was worth it... they hope.

El Paso is where the final evidence that this is more than a simple lab experiment gone wrong. It was too focused with too many players who knew too much too early in the game causing assumptions to be made. Assumptions that gained strength with every step they took until the small troop was convinced that this was not just a simple virus of natural origins, America was under attack.

For Which We Stand is a post-apocalyptic thriller that lends credence to the fears that many share. Is it possible? No one can say, Five Roads to Texas is but one of hundreds end of the world scenarios. We all know it's coming, how and when is the only question.

SIXTH CYCLE

CARL SINCLAIR & DARREN WEARMOUTH

Nuclear war has destroyed human civilization.

Captain Jake Phillips wakes into a dangerous new world, where he finds the remaining fragments of the population living in a series of strongholds, connected across the country. Uneasy alliances have maintained their safety, but things are about to change. --

Discovery **leads to danger.** -- Skye Reed, a tracker from the Omega stronghold, uncovers a threat that could spell the end for their fragile society. With friends and enemies revealing truths about the past, she will need to decide who to trust.

Available on Amazon.

DEAD ISLAND: OPERATION ZULU

ALLEN GAMBOA

Ten years after the world was nearly brought to its knees by a zombie Armageddon, there is a race for the antidote! On a remote Caribbean island, surrounded by a horde of hungry living dead, a team of American and Australian commandos must rescue the Antidotes' scientist. Filled with zombies, guns, Russian bad guys, shady government types, serial killers and elevator muzak. Dead Island is an action packed blood soaked horror adventure.

TORMENT (THE SOLDIER BOOK ONE)

W.J LUNDY

From the War on Terror a world crippling Bio-Weapon is released. The United States scrambles teams of scientists from the Centers For Disease Control. America's top field agent are tasked with collecting samples and developing a cure.

Thus, begins the greatest outbreak in the history of human kind. In the wake of the fast spreading pandemic, state and local governments, desperate for answers, rush to provide relief to the devastated and overwhelmed communities. Experts in Bio-Medical Research are desperately summoned to Atlanta and military facilities across the country.

On a cold morning, the men of India Company, Second Platoon, are alerted and rapid-deployed to Virginia. Their mission: to recover and escort experts in bio-medicine, specifically in the development and production of vaccines. With faulty intelligence and half-truths, Second Platoon moves forward. What they find is worse than anyone could have predicted. What was a rescue mission, turns into a struggle for their own survival.

DONOVAN'S WAR

W.J. LUNDY

With everything around him gone. Tommy Donovan must return to the war he has been hiding from. When his sister is taken, the Government fails to act. Tommy Donovan will take the law into his own hands. But, this time he isn't a soldier, and there will be no laws to protect evil. This time it's personal and he is making the rules.

A PATH OF ASHES

BRIAN PARKER

Evil doesn't become extinct, it evolves. Our world is a violent place. Murder, terrorism, racism and social inequality, these are some of the forces that attempt to destroy our society while the State is forced to increase its response to these actions. Our own annihilation is barely held at bay by the belief that we've somehow evolved beyond our ancestors' base desires.

From this cesspool of emotions emerges a madman, intent on leading the world into anarchy. When his group of computer hackers infiltrate the Department of Defense network, they initiate a nuclear war that will irrevocably alter our world.

Aeric Gaines and his roommate, Tyler, survive the devastation of the war, only to find that the politically correct world where they'd been raised was a lie. All humans have basic needs such as food, water and shelter...but we will fight for what we *desire*.

A Path of Ashes is a three-book series about life in post-apocalyptic America, a nation devoid of leadership, electricity and human rights. The world as we know it may have burned, but humanity found a way to survive and this is their story.

HUMAN ELEMENT

AJ POWERS

The Neuroweb began as the greatest invention since written language. A simple brain implant that allowed the user to access information, entertainment, and even pain relief. The Neuroweb was the beginning of a golden age for mankind...

Until it was compromised.

Everyone with the implant lost their most important commodity: their free will. The collective human consciousness was hacked, and now directed by artificial intelligence. Only those without the Neuroweb have a chance of resisting...If they dare. Aaran has legitimate reason to believe he's the last free-thinking human alive. After his family was killed in the purge, he fled for his life. Now, he aimlessly wanders through the suburbs of Cincinnati alone, desperate to find a reason to live.

When he meets a girl like him - another free thinker -

they search together for a cause worth fighting for.
Worth dying for.

AS THE ASH FELL

AJ POWERS

Life in the frozen wastelands of Texas is anything but easy, but for Clay Whitaker there is always more at stake than mere survival.

It's been seven years since the ash billowed into the atmosphere, triggering some of the harshest winters in recorded history. Populations are thinning. Food is scarce. Despair overwhelming. With no way to sustain order, societies collapsed, leaving people to fend for themselves.

Clay and his sister Megan have taken a handful of orphaned children into their home--a home soaring sixteen stories into the sky. With roughly six short months a year to gather enough food and supplies to last the long, brutal winter, Clay must spend most of his time away from his family to scavenge, hunt, and barter.

When Clay rescues a young woman named Kelsey

from a group of Screamers, his life is catapulted into a new direction, forcing him to make decisions he never thought he would have to make.

Now, with winter rolling in earlier than ever, Clay's divided attention is putting him, and his family, at risk.

INVASION OF THE DEAD SERIES

OWEN BAILLIE

This is the first book in a series of nine, about an ordinary bunch of friends, and their plight to survive an apocalypse in Australia. -- Deep beneath defense headquarters in the Australian Capital Territory, the last ranking Army chief and a brilliant scientist struggle with answers to the collapse of the world, and the aftermath of an unprecedented virus. Is it a natural mutation, or does the infection contain -- more sinister roots? -- One hundred and fifty miles away, five friends returning from a month-long camping trip slowly discover that death has swept through the country. What greets them in a gradual revelation is an enemy beyond compare. -- Armed with dwindling ammunition, the friends must overcome their disagreements, utilize their individual skills, and face unimaginable horrors as they battle to reach their hometown...

THIS BOOK WAS FORMATTED BY

CARLSINCLAIR.NET

www.ingramcontent.com/pod-product-compliance
Lightning Source LLC
Chambersburg PA
CBHW062019170626
46813CB00001B/221